CITRON
PRESS

BRUCE **DURIE**

Bruce Durie has been a science journalist, Senior Lecturer in Life Sciences and subsequently Head of External Affairs at Kingston University, Director of the Edinburgh Science Festival, a regular contributor to New Scientist and other periodicals, broadcaster, radio panel games host and maker of medical videos. His book "Medicine" was short-listed for the COPUS Prize and his parody of Sherlock Holmes, "The Mystery of the Pneumonic Numismatis", was performed nationwide by Simon Williams and William Simons. He performed his one-man play "MacPherson's Rant" at the 1992 Edinburgh Fringe. He currently works for Fife College, Kirkcaldy, Scotland. His wife and son are far more interesting.

CITRON PRESS

Fresh ideas from

NEW AUTHORS
CO-OPERATIVE

Published by Citron Press
Connors Corp. Ltd., Suite 155, Business Design Centre,
52 Upper Street, Islington Green, London N1 0QH, Great Britain
www.citronpress.co.uk

This Book is a Work of Fiction. Names Characters, Places and Incidents are either products of the author's imagination or are used fictitiously. Any resemblance to actual events or locales or persons, living or dead, is entirely coincidental.

ISBN 0754400034

Printed and bound in Great Britain by Esparto Digital Ltd, Slack Lane, Derby.

A copy of this book is held at the British Library.

THE HIGH HISTORY OF THE HOLY QUAIL

BRUCE **DURIE**

VOLUME THE FIRST IN THE END OF ALL MAGICK SAGA

CHAPTER THE FIRST

In which Slouch, catamite-in-training, gets frightened witless by an apparition and learns something of his destiny as wizard's apprentice.

CHAPTER THE SECOND

In which Slouch becomes apprenticed to Vizagriz, most puissant wizard, learns something of the value of himself in relation to Gold Thalers, and falls hopelessly in love with a Handmaiden to the Fiery Swan, Vesta, poor bugger.

CHAPTER THE THIRD

In which Great Events are set in motion and Vizagriz gains a new enemy. As if one more would make any difference.

CHAPTER THE FOURTH

In which Slouch learns more of Magick and even more of the nature of Vizagriz. There are sundry dark conjurations, unfortunately.

CHAPTER THE FIFTH

In which there is much camping out, of divers kinds, and Slouch comes to realise that a Quest is not all frolics and bunting.

CHAPTER THE SIXTH

In which, after a rainstorm, Slouch and his companions meet with the Faerie-folk and learn of Webs.

CHAPTER THE SEVENTH

In which Slouch meets two heroes, discovers that the World is flat, just like life, and learns something of the true nature of Magick.

CHAPTER THE EIGHTH

In which Slouch learns more of the nature of Magick, and of oxcart drivers. He also learns about beer, tavern-owners' daughters and fights in hostelries.

CHAPTER THE NINTH
In which Slouch takes part in a circus, gleans more of the nature of heroes and meets a Web Weaver.

CHAPTER THE TENTH
In which Slouch and the Questers learn more of Webs and Weavers and hear something to their advantage, mostly that they are not on the menu.

CHAPTER THE ELEVENTH
In which Slouch and his companions on the Quest enter the Tomb of the Unknown Lunch and confront their worst nightmare. Again. Why does it have to be snakes?

CHAPTER THE TWELFTH
In which Slouch and the Questers find the Holy Quail and discover something of its properties, such as they are.

CHAPTER THE THIRTEENTH
In which Slouch plays his part in the Quest and a baking dæmon comes to a suitable end, not without some troubles beforehand.

CHAPTER THE FOURTEENTH
In which there is much explanation, many surprises, a homecoming - but not for all of the Questers - and an end to all Magick.

CHAPTER THE FIFTEENTH
In which much has changed but everything is the same. For some people, anyway.

CHAPTER THE SIXTEENTH
In which Slouch gets a bit maudlin towards the end but you can skip that bit.

CHAPTER THE FIRST

In which Slouch, catamite-in-training, gets frightened witless by an apparition and learns something of his destiny as wizard's apprentice.

It was a dark and stormy Knight. In fact, it was an eight-foot tall dark and stormy Knight, and the Knight was standing in front of me, obsidian armour somehow shining in the blackness of the star-black, Bibble-black fastness of the Watching Hour. I was simply walking back to the SamBernardo Catamite Training Agency having delivered a parcel on behalf of Brer Dryberg. The last thing I expected was to bump into a huge, jet-dark warrior, armoured totally in shiny blackness, leaning on his sword. And humming. I confess that my bowels turned to water, more effectively than the last time I had had a Jacana Kurrmah with extra lime-frog pickle. I suppose I must have stood there fully five minutes – or it could have been five seconds. Hard to tell, really.

I was rooted to the very paving stones, mouthing strangled inanities like a cageful of mute eunuchs on dope. The Knight drew himself up to his full height, already the size of a wardrobe, and flexed his arms. There was a creaking that sounded uncomfortably like the gates of hell opening. That broke the spell and I was conscious again of the huge fulgent shape in front of me in the small alley. He appeared to fill it in all directions, and I was just working out whether to try and dodge past him, turn around and bolt, or simply sink down and gibber like a demented panda, when the vast form before me made the sound I least expected.

He cleared his throat.

Actually, it sounded more like hot iron being dragged over an anvil, and I was assuming he had a throat. Somewhere deep within me – round about the position of my last meal, which was halfway up my gorge by that time – I found the words to say, 'Err, can I help you?' Pathetic, I know, but it's all I could come up with at the time.

The helmet swung towards me and I looked into the visor, which appeared to contain an infinity of nothing. The motion of the helmet continued onwards to – I hoped, considering I had no idea what might be within – look at me.

'Sorry?' a deep-dark-resonant-pulsating-mechanical voice said. 'Where am I?'

Politeness being the better part of valour, or so I judged at the time, I thought it wise to answer him. 'This is Pally Alley. In the Porter Quarter.'

'Ahhh,' said the Dark Thing. 'But which city? Hmmm?'

'Well, it's Al Faq'Ahl. Chief city of the Province of Ditton.'

'Ahhh. Bang on target for once. Good!'

I had as much clue what was going on as you do, so I thought I'd try to be as helpful as possible – always a good idea when you're right in it up to the neck. 'Were you looking for someone?'

'Be you Slouch?'

This stunned me so much, I nearly dropped the copper dinar Master Mindador had given me for delivering Brer Dryberg's parcel. I was not so much amazed that a mysterious creature dressed entirely in what seemed to be the basic stuff of the night should know my name, as that anyone outside of SamBernardo's should know it at all.

'Err, if it please Your Lordship, yes. I am Slouch.' He said nothing. 'Can I help?' I added.

'That's the general idea. You are, just let me check, Slouch, apprentice to Vizagriz, wizard of this parish?'

That threw me. 'Errr, no. I think you must have the wrong apprentice.' I was relieved, not to say nearly fainting. If he wasn't looking for me in particular, as opposed to any random victim to skewer on what looked like a wicked sword, he might just move off elsewhere and frighten some other poor berk to death.

'I don't know Vizagriz, but I'm sure he lives around here somewhere. I could help you find him. If you like.'

'I seek Slouch. Are there more than one of you?'

'You mean catamites-in-training? Yes. Yes. SamBernardo's has the City concession on bum-boy supply. If you would like...'

'No, I specifically seek Slouch. Are you the only Slouch in this alley at this time?'

I looked around, hoping I'd find a namesake hiding in a doorway. No such luck. 'Well, I seem to be. Are you sure it's me you want?'

'Positive. But you aren't apprenticed to Vizagriz?'

'No. Never even met him, although I did once see him at the market square in the Fish Quarter, giving a stall-holder some stick for getting his thumb in the scales. Scales of the balance, that is. Not the scales of the fish. Turned him into a giant lizard, he did. The fishmonger, that is. For about three minutes. They said it was a record for an off-hand transformation, and...'

I stopped, because the warrior had raised his arm, and plunged it into the deepness of his armour. It went right through, and appeared again holding a book of some sort, which he started to thumb through, leaning his sword against his legs while he did so.

'Hang on, what day is this?'

'Well, Wodin's Day. Third week of the constellation of Rumpot.'

'Bugger!' the visor intoned, the head shaking back and forth. The Knight consulted a device strapped to its wrist. 'Far-Eastern rubbish! If I don't crack this one and get back on time, I'll never make it to the golf course. Rumpot, is it?'

'Yes,' I nodded, trying to be helpful. 'Last day of the Festival and Holy Day of the sacred Gettiz Endawey.'

The warrior was thumbing through the book again. 'But according to the PhilosoPhax, you shouldn't be here until next month. What's going on, I'd like to know?'

'Well, Brer Dryberg asked me to take a parcel to Master Mindador, the Thaumaturge, and I've just got back.'

'Aaaahhhhhh!' It sounded like a wind soughing through a dry cave. 'So a wizard's involved, then?'

'Well, yes. Master Mindador is a wizard. Of sorts. Struck off, I believe, but makes his living conjuring up minor illusions at drinks parties and the like. Was it him you wanted?'

'NO!! It is YOU I want,' he all but shouted, pointing at me in a disconcerting manner. 'But just my luck to hit the time-stream when some magician starts casting spells around your presence. Bloody wizards. Bane of my life. Well, you know what this means, don't you?'

Run me though with the huge black sword? I thought. Beat me senseless with that PhilosoPhax book? Or worse still report me to Brer Dryberg. And that would mean extra kitchen duty. On my day off too, probably. But he put me out of my misery.

'It means I've got to stick around this pathetic place until you DO become apprentice to Vizagriz. What a pain!'

'But I'm at the Agency. I can't be. I mean – me, an apprentice to a wizard? I doubt if Brer Dryberg...'

He held up his hand like a God bringing a world to its last judgement. I've seen pictures of it.

'Shut up! Let me think. The PhilosoPhax definitely says that by the next full moons you will be in this alley, carrying an important message on behalf of the wizard. So what I suggest you do is this. Go back to wherever you are currently staying, and hand in your notice.'

'I can't. I'm indentured for life, or until someone buys me.'

'WILL YOU KEEP SCHTUMM? Thank you!' He flexed his armour, which sighed, like the death-wind of a volcano. 'Then, a month from now, be back here at this very time, and I will give you the message for Vizagriz.'

'Look, I don't mean to be rude, but if you want to get a message to Vizagriz, I can show you his cottage. I think it's in The Street of the Hanging Baskets. It's only a few blocks away. Past the Council cess pit and flagon bank, next to...'

He drew himself up even taller, if that were possible, and looked like he might explode. 'NO! It has to come from you. And within a month from now. So I'll tell you what. You go to Vizagriz, ask him to take you on as his apprentice, and just make sure you get back here a month from tonight, at this time. No later! If I miss my golf game, the whole fabric of existence could be threatened even more than it is at the moment. Can you remember all that?'

'Yes, but, I mean, I can't just become a wizard's apprentice. He'd have to ask for me. And he may not want an apprentice. Might have one or two already. There's probably an entrance exam. Or something. Apart from that, he'd have to buy me from the Agency, and they might not let me go! Brer Dryberg says he's got plans for me at the next Saturnalia.'

'Ah! I see. Vizagriz won't be able to take you on unless he buys you from the. Agency, eh? Well, that's easily solved. How much are you worth?'

'I've no idea,' I said, genuinely confused. 'A fully-trained catamite costs about five Gold Thalers, but I'm not at that stage yet, and then there's the reimbursement of the rest of my indenture, and the tuck shop bill, and...'

The warrior was fumbling about inside his chest again, which I found strangely discomfiting. He threw me a pouch, which I managed to catch, despite all my tremblings. 'Well, take this. It should cover the costs. Give it to Vizagriz, tell him that we met, explain that you have to be back here to get a message for him in a month's time, and remember, I'll be waiting. Now off you go!'

I was dumbfounded. Again. As I set off down the Pally Alley, I heard a sound like a dinner gong going off.

'SLOUCH!'

I stopped dead. 'Yes?' I muttered in a small voice.

'Don't make me come looking for you!'

'Errghlllhhfx,' I garbled, then bolted.

The rest of the journey back to the Agency was a blur to me, and I probably did it in record time. I went straight to my cot and crouched under the covers running the events of the past half hour through my mind. What had it all been about? Was I really to be apprenticed to a wizard? Should I give the pouch to Vizagriz? The pouch! I let it go for the first time. Undrawing the strings around it, I peered into the neck and nearly died of fright again. There must be ten, no, twenty-odd Gold Thalers in here; more than even a master craftsman makes in a year! Two years!

This gave me a real quandary. I could buy myself out. But where would I go? The only place I knew was Al Faq'Ahl; I could set up in business, but what as? All I knew was being a kitchen drudge and pot-boy; I could...

But all this was fantasy. Whatever I did, the large Knight would surely find me, and I would be meted some horrible death for disobeying a direct command from someone – something – more powerful, more knowledgeable and, above all, bigger than I was.

Apart from that, how would I explain my sudden acquisition of wealth? I had no family to speak of. All I knew about myself was that I was to all intents an orphan. I had gathered hints from Brer Dryberg and Brer Roger that I might well be the by-blow of a chance meeting between a Royal Princess and an errant adventurer, probably also Royal or at least Awfully Well Connected but in some way disgraced, and sent out into the world to atone for his sins. So much atoning had he done that I was the result, and I had been left on the doorstep of the Catamite Training Agency in the hope that I might learn a trade and be of some use.

At least, I liked to believe this, but there was scant evidence for it. I had not even been able to nurture the hope that one day I might be able to meet my mother or father and be re-enfolded into whatever gentle life they might be leading. I had no likeness of either of them, no lingering memories, not even a lock of hair. All the romances I had read dealing with this topic always included some physical evidence, at the very least a strawberry birth mark on the left thigh or a picture in a locket. But I was unblemished, unremembered, and unhappy.

No, my only way out of this was to actually brave the wizard Vizagriz, and confront him with the story about the dark and stormy Knight, in the hope that he would take me seriously and not turn me into a frog or some such for my audacity.

I resolved that the next day I would approach the great mage and offer myself, and my Gold Thalers, to his service. And with that I fell into a fitful sleep, dreaming of infinite blackness, roiling star-births, and the deep, mournful despair of the oxterworld, where dæmons live.

Not, as they say, a pretty sight.

The next day I awoke as the sun peeked over the parapet of SamBernardo's, and for a blissful moment or so, I lay basking in that glorious limpid state between wake and sleepy-bye-byes, recalling the flavour of my last dream, which was about The Knight.

AARRGGH! The Knight! I woke with a sudden, horrible crunch that dragged me upright and sweating. Was it a dream? I fervently hoped so, and praying to whatever Gods look after foundling catamites-in-training, felt around for the bag of gold. It wasn't here! Oh no! Yes it was! I had a clammy feeling all over as I realised I had no option to go through with it and seek out Vizagriz.

I opened the bag and emptied the coins into my hand. There were twenty-four of them, round and dull-shiny with the last Dikkeadh but two's head on one side and a Gribbin, symbol of Al Faq'Ahl on the other. I put all but one back into the pouch and gazed at it, stupefied, horrified, terrified and mystified.

Just then, our Bunkmaster, Nark, came in. He was the senior lad in the dormitories, and responsible for good order, getting everyone up, and most particularly, making life a sheer bloody misery for anyone of lower standing or size. Especially me. He didn't like me much, and the feeling was more than mutual.

'RIGHT!! Hands on socks! Sun's up and so should you be! Out of those stink-pits and about your duty!'

His gaze fastened on me, as it usually did. 'Especially you, Slug! You're on Breakfast Duty today.'

I was so dumbfounded by my inner thoughts that I continued staring into the middle distance, until my entire field of vision was filled by the appalling sight of Nark's face, about half an inch from mine.

'DID YOU HEAR ME, SLUG??!' he shouted, as if I couldn't. There was a fine career for this chap, either in the militia, or better still as an usher at one of the entertainment palaces in the Fish Quarter. I said nothing, although I hated being called Slug. Should have been used to it by then, of course.

'I said - DID YOU HEAR ME???!!!' he repeated, obviously for my benefit.

'Er, yes. Sorry Nark. Miles away.'

'Miles away? MILES AWAY??!! Well, get yourself here, sonny-boy. And in three seconds flat you better be there, dishing up eggs and porridge like your life depended on it. WHICH IT DOES!!'

If you get the impression from this that Nark was a self-important bully and a bit thick at that, you'd be right, but you didn't hear it from me, OK? I was pulling on my breeches and boots hurriedly. 'Er, sorry Nark' I stuttered, 'but I can't today. I've got to...'

'You WHAT!!!!!' I've never met anyone who used so many exclamation marks in common parlance. One of Nature's sergeants, was Nark. 'You CAN'T???!! And why not, might I ask? Or is it because you've got something more important to do?'

'Well, yes, actually, I've got to...'

'You what? Oh, I see. I get it. Got to go and see our mum the Princess have we? Or swan up to the Palace to have a private audience with the Dikkeadh himself? Or perhaps go and slay a couple of dragons, eh?'

'Well, no, it's just that, well, I've got to go and be a wizard's apprentice.'

This set the other boys in the dormitory tittering. They had all been listening, in the sure and certain knowledge that this was different from the normal morning's sport Nark generally had with me. Nark picked this one up gleefully.

'Oh, we've got to go and be a wizard's apprentice! Oh, well, that's all right then. I understand. Can't stay here if we've got to be a wizard's apprentice, can we? Dear me no. Well, off you go then, eh?'

I got up off my bed and started for the door, when Nark grabbed me by my collar. 'In a pig's eye, sunny Jim. I've had enough of you and your fantasies.'

I was surprised Nark knew a word like "fantasies" since his normal vocabulary contained about ten words each of half as many letters. But I admit I was distracted that morning, and hadn't spotted the irony in his sandpaper-like voice.

'Now, you get yourself down to that kitchen, and after brekkie is finished, you'll scrub every floor in the pantry until shines so bright it'll dazzle a blind blubber-worm.' He gave me a shove towards the door.

'But really, Nark. I met this, this, and anyway, he gave me a bag of gold and told me to go and apprentice myself to Vizagriz and if I didn't come back in a month...' I admit, it even sounded lame to me.

'Oh, bag of gold, is it? And where is this bag of gold, then? Buried it at the end of a rainbow, did we?'

'No,' I said defiantly. 'It's here.' I held the bag up with my left hand. My right was clutching the single Thaler like a vice.

A strange look crossed Nark's piggy eyes. 'Let me see that,' he said, and snatched the bag before I could pull it away. 'Marbles, probably.' He looked in the neck of the bag, and his expression changed. He looked about at the rest of the lads, still waiting for the resolution to this unaccustomed but welcome interruption to their daily drudgery. 'And what are you lot staring at? GET WEAVING!!! Jart! You do breakfast duty. Slug here will be a while.'

When the lads had stampeded out of the dormitory, knowing what was good for them, Nark turned on me again. 'OK, Slug, where'd you get this, eh? Knicked, is it?'

'No, I said – this Knight I met in Pally Alley gave it to me. I have to give it to Vizagriz the wizard.'

Nark was obviously thinking, and thinking was obviously painful, but he had a glimmering of a scheme in what passed for his brain. 'Well, I think it's knicked! So, I tell you what. I'll take it down to the militia, who'll find it's rightful owner, and just because I like you,' he grabbed a handful of my shirt and a handful of my skin with it, 'I won't even report it as a theft or tell Brer Dryberg, IF,' he paused for emphasis, 'IF you never - never - ever - say - anything - about - it! Right?' Each word was punctuated by a headbutt in the face.

I sat in the middle of the dormitory floor, tears of rage, outrage, inrage and lack of courage welling up inside of me. I tried to appeal to his reason, a sad mistake. 'But Nark, I HAVE to! The Knight said he'd come looking for me, and it's important. I don't know why. Just give me it back, will you? I really have to go and see Vizagriz.' I trailed off into blubbing.

He was tossing the bag from hand to hand, grinning like a Southlands ape. 'Sod off, Slug. If you know what's good for you, you'll keep quiet about this. Like I say, I'll look after it.'

He swaggered out of the dormitory, casting me a backwards, leering glance as he chuckled his way downstairs, doubtless delighted at his marvellous acquisition of a bag of gold Thalers and my terrible discomfiture. Only six o'clock and already I'd made his day twice.

I had no idea what to do next, and spent the next hour on my bed, sobbing my eyes out. When I calmed down, I realised my right fist had instinctively clenched itself round the Thaler I had been examining. Nark had missed on!. This cheered me up somewhat and since it was obvious that I wasn't being missed from my duties, I decided the only thing to do was to see Vizagriz and explain the situation to him. After all, wizards were reasonable people, weren't they? Well, weren't they?

Picture the scene. Through a cobwebby window there is a dark, smoke-filled room, eerily lit by the flickering of six candles, each one held in a severed hand placed at the point of a hexagon drawn in goat's blood. In a corner, within another, smaller hexagon whose vertices are the heads of various animals impaled on a silver knife stuck into a notch in the floor, a small, dark man is hunched over a bubbling pot, chuckling to himself. In the lambent light you see a lectern supporting a large black book open at a page covered in weird, distressingly familiar yet indecipherable symbols and unknowable words in an ancient script with annotations scribbled around. At the bottom of the page there is a drawing of a being so horrible to look upon the artist must have lost his sanity in depicting it.

A cat yowls then is silent. A hiss and a splutter are greeted with even more chuckling.

Then a high, reedy voice starts an incantation, keening and ululating until you think you might go mad from the listening. Then stops. And in its place, a strangulated voice that is hardly a voice says "Seek the place where webs are woven " and your peering gaze tells what your mind knows is impossible - on one of the knife blades the head of a monkey is mouthing these words. It falls silent, and next to it a chicken's head seems to say "Find the weaver and ask the question", before falling lifeless, which it surely is. A lizard next hisses "There is a jewel without equal". A rat's head squeaks "A man must read the words". The head of a large dog, voiced low and growling, snaps is jaws from which comes, "It is far, but near. It is inside, but without. It is high, but deep".

And just as you think you can listen no more to this foul chorus of the surely-dead, the last head in the ghastly hexagon gives forth with the voice a cat might have, saying "Once found, it must once again be lost, or all is lost".

The candles go out, to the sound of more cackling. Both moons emerge from behind clouds, as if they had been hiding. A malign calm settles on the hovel and a greasy odour slowly disperses into the night air.

CHAPTER THE SECOND

In which Slouch becomes apprenticed to Vizagriz, most puissant wizard, learns something of the value of himself in relation to Gold Thalers, and falls hopelessly in love with a Handmaiden to the Fiery Swan, Vesta, poor bugger.

I confess I was in something of a daze as I crept out of SamBernardo's Catamite Training Agency later that morning. I was half-convinced my meeting with the Dark and Stormy Knight was just a dream, and had no bag of gold Thalers to prove otherwise. I was humiliated by my treatment at the hands of Nark; and I had no idea what would happen next. But one thing was clear to me – I had had a basinful of SamBernardo's, Brer Dryberg, Nark, and being called "Slug".

The way was clear, then. I would go to Vizagriz, explain the situation, become his apprentice and... well, see what happened next. Not much of a plan, I'll grant you, but there didn't seem to be many options right there and then.

I turned deosil from the Agency and wandered into Market Square in the Porter Quarter. Like most cities in the province of Ditton, Al Faq'Ahl was divided into quarters. Unlike any other, however, it had five of them. This was at the whim of a previous Dikkeadh, as the quasi-elected dynastic chief administrator was known, and had been that way for over three Gyrations. Recognising that all cities had to have a commercial sector, a docks or lading area, a slum district and a place for the middle classes to live, most of the cities in the province had early on decided to quarter themselves according to geo-topography and taste into these four areas. In most of the other cities like Glesca, Caerculdea, Cowcaddens and Lumphinnans there was no problem with that. But Al Faq'Ahl, being the capital, had to be different.

Having an entire tier of administration centred on one city means there are scores if not hundreds of councillors, functionaries, grimaldis and managerialists, not to mention the thousands of tortiflexers, estates agents and figurers, and they all have to live somewhere.

They couldn't live in the Head Quarter – that was reserved for Palace staff and High Lords, and was expensive anyway. Not that anyone actually lived there, dear me no! Got a place in the country, only use this town house for the odd visit, see a bit of theatre, that sort of thing, dontcha know. Funny it was always busy, then.

They couldn't live in the Porter Quarter, since it was commercial, not residential, and you wouldn't get a licence to have a house there. Every building had to be a place of business, and ground rates were charged accordingly. For the money it would cost to have a house in the Porter Quarter and not run it as a profit-making enterprise, you could afford to live in the Head Quarter and the country.

Likewise, they wouldn't be seen dead in the Fish Quarter, which was too near the harbour, too far to commute and too smelly for words. (Although to be fair, there was a recent plan to renovate some of the warehouses as accommodation for the merchant classes, but it probably wouldn't come to anything, since who in their right mind would pay as much for a box inside a derelict storage building overlooking the docks as for a small farm in the country with free fresh air thrown in?)

And no-one who didn't have to would live anywhere near the Farter Quarter, which combined all the bad points of the others and was rough to boot.

The two basic qualifications for going into the Farter Quarter were that either you had brain damage, or were willing to acquire it, probably at the wrong end of a blunt instrument wielded by one of the obliging locals. They're good that way. Not any other way, mind.

Hence, the Garden Suburb Quarter was born. That was where those who worked (if that's the word) in administrative and other non-productive jobs had their houses. Each one was identical in every respect except wallpaper, curtains and colour of front door to all the others. This was what they called individualism. In every case there was a patch of lawn at the front, bearing a plaster statute of what appeared to be a talisman to ward off attacks by gnomes, and at the back there was a sort of garden whose sole purpose was to provide food for the large variety of seed-eating birds, which in turn were the main source of nourishment for the many seed-eating-bird-eating cats which prowled the Quarter.

The cats themselves were interesting, since there were a lot fewer of them than anyone imagined, only it didn't seem that way, especially on their choir practice nights. The truth of the matter is that every family in the Garden Suburb Quarter would admit to owning a cat, but there were only a third as many cats as you would predict on the basis of that fact alone.

It has been posited by those with a taste for researching this and like questions of universal import, that perhaps families shared cats, or in some way cats imagined they lived at more than one house. Most people of sound mind find that unlikely, on the basis that you would either know whether a cat was yours or whether it wasn't, right? There must be some more mystical explanation, but for the life of me I can't figure one out.

There is no question that the cats are happy with arrangement. This is a testament to their intelligence, which is certainly greater than that of dogs. You don't get cats working for the Militia, do you?

Anyway, of all the five Quarters, the Garden Suburb Quarter was by far the most pleasant and by a long chalk the least interesting. There were dark mutterings about strange rites performed with packs of cards and rubbers of some sort, and it was not unknown for a streetful of residents to cram into one house and show each other drawings of where they had been last Equinox for their holidays. It has been said that there are even occasions where a number of them get together and enthuse over items of kitchenware, but this has never been proven and let's face it, who would admit to that?

I was pondering all this and more when I noticed I was at Hanging Basket Street. I could tell. The Hanging Baskets are a bit of a giveaway.

Hanging Basket Street was at the node where all five quarters met. Well, not so much met, but stood in the same queue trying to ignore each other. Much is made of the felicitous position of Hanging Basket Street. (As it says in the guidebook – "Al Faq'Ahl, City of a Thousand Pleasures" – one of which, I might say, is not reading that guidebook, which contains such useful information as the translation into all of the likely languages encountered such handy phrases as "Help, we have been set upon by bandits and they have stolen our cutlery" and "Can you tell me where I can hire an orchid, two bridles and a gold lamé cushion for the weekend", but let it pass.) The fact is that its name derives, not from rows of pleasant, suspended flower arrangements as any sane mortal might expect, but from the unsavoury habit, not long abandoned, of hanging thieves, malfeasants and scoundrels in a sort of basket-cage affair until they repented, died of thirst or, more likely – and this is where the wizards come in – were carted off in order that unspeakable practices could be performed on or with the aid of bits of their bodies. The baskets still hung there, more as a trade sign than out of any functional capacity, but they served to underline the grimness of the place.

One or two wizards had set up shop near a handy supply of their basic materials – dead man's eyes, hand of a thief, left foot from a heretic, that sort of thing – and based on the principle that the best place to have a shoe shop is next to another shoe shop, in no time at all there were wizards all over the place. It wasn't so much a moving-in as a race migration, by all accounts. It will come a surprise to no-one that these wizards managed to get the properties at a fairly advantageous price, though whether this was due to a local recognition that the neighbourhood had finally gone, or (more probably) to the sure and certain knowledge of what would happen to anyone who chose not to sell to an interested wizard, is anyone's guess. All I can say is – I wish I'd been there when the Poll Tax collectors came round once a year, not that they did any more.

All I had to do now was find Vizagriz. I assumed, silly me, that he would have a sign on his door saying something like: Vizagriz – Mage and Haruspex. Appointments only. Closed Tyr's Day And New Moons. Or something. In fact, there was no indication from any of the doors who or what might be inside. After a fruitless wander up and down the street a couple of times, I espied an apprentice slopping out from one of the houses further along the street. So I hailed him.

'Hail,' I hailed.

He looked up in a manner that indicated he wasn't much bothered whether he saw me or not, but I happened to be in his field of vision and I caught his eye. Since he only had one, that was no great trick. The apprentice was a hunch-backed, lame-legged, one-eyed, (I said that, didn't I?) knock-kneed runt of a lad, and I couldn't help feeling sorry for him.

'Wot?' he slobbered. Not put off, I continued.

'I wonder if you can help me, good apprentice. I seek the Mighty wizard...'

'Flub!' he dribbled.

'Pardon?'

'Flub. Me name's Flub!'

'Ah. Right. Well, be so kind as to tell me good, er, Flub, where I might find the lodgings or placement of the Most Puissant Mage, Vizagriz.' Say what you like about SamBernardo's, they do teach you manners.

'Here,' he drooled.

'What, you mean this is his house. And you are his apprentice?'

'No. I mean it's here. This isn't his house. and I'm not his apprentice. Hasn't got one. But it's here.'

I was confused, I admit it. 'So, if I take you aright – and stop me if I am in any way mistaken on this – you are saying, kindly, that this isn't his house, but that it is here. Yes?'

'Sright.'

'Okay. Well pardon my confusion then, but if this isn't the house of Vizagriz, that Most Sage and Wise, er, Magician, but it is here, then where is it? Pray?'

'Told you. It's here!'

'Ah. Right. I see. You mean it IS in this street.'

''Sright.'

'And where, do tell, in this street is it?' I felt I was getting somewhere.

'It's here.'

I was wrong. 'No, sorry, you're going to have to take me through this again. Just once. The house is, er, here. But this isn't it.'

'Yip!'

'So, is it the one next door?'

He looked around and sniffed the air. 'Hard to tell. Don't think so. Not just at the moment.'

I could cheerfully have throttled him. 'Sir, I vouchsafe you do not intentionally seek to riddle me, but I am still none the wiser. If, happenstance, you could point out exactly where I might find the house of that Most Potent and, er, Potent Mystic, the great Vizagriz...,' next time, I thought, I must bring a thesaurus, '...I would be forever in your debt.'

'Just think about it,' he slavered.

'I have thought about it. I have a sore head thinking about it. JUST TELL ME WILL YOU...er, be so good.'

'No. I mean, you just have to think about Vizagriz's house and it'll be here.'

I was taken aback by this, I admit it. 'What, you mean, it's not here, but if I think about it, it will be?'

'No, it's here all right. But wizards' houses don't have fixed positions. If you want to see one, you think about it and it's the door in front of you.'

Well, I thought, give it a try. I thought about Vizagriz, although I only had the sketchiest picture in my mind of what he looked like from the time I had seen him in the market. But for an instant my head swam, the air fogged, and there I was standing, well, in exactly the same place. That is, I was in the same place in Hanging Basket Street, about ten strides from the corner, but now the hunchback Flub was about eight doors away, and still slopping out. Somehow, the house had come to me and the street had sort of shuffled itself quietly, without telling anyone. I didn't think I'd ever get used to this. Must be murder for the postman, I thought, but on the other hand wizards probably didn't get much mail. No-one in their right senses was going to deluge them with offers of new windows, incitements to join the Grimoire of the Month Club or life insurance. Not unless they had some pretty spectacular life insurance themselves and a definite reservation in the oxterworld of their choice.

Nonetheless, there in front of me was a door, and on the door was a small gold plaque which said: Vizagriz - Mage and Haruspex. Appointments only. Closed Tyr's Day And New Moons. Bit of a coincidence, I thought.

I took a deep breath and plucked up my courage to knock. I was not ready for the sensation that reached my hand when it encountered not the hard, resounding feel of a door being tapped, but a soft, squelchiness that defied description and made me feel not a little queasy. 'Dew yew moind?' a faraway but disturbingly close whisper said.

I jumped back. 'There is a bleedin' doorbell, yew knaow!' There was indeed a doorbell, but I hesitated to pull the handle in case it squealed, or something. Then the thought of the Knight and what he'd do to me if I didn't go through with this came flooding back to me. I reached out and made to pull the doorbell chain, but it wriggled free of my grasp and another whisper said, 'All right, all right. I get the idea!' And somewhere in the middle distance there was the sound of a bell clanging.

I was just about getting over this when I heard approaching, heavily muffled footsteps and a dragging sound. I was starting to wonder if it was Flub coming down the street when the door flew open, thudded against the inner wall with a jelly-like spludge and a "Eaowch! Bleedin' 'ell!" and there standing before me was a tall, imposing figure with a long, white flowing beard, eyebrows you could impale flies with, a nose that would chop firewood and the two most piercing blue eyes I had ever seen. The aquiline face was topped by a pointed hat of excessive dimensions above a long, black robe studded with what I took to be astrological symbols.

The face peered down at me, drew back, opened its mouth and said, 'Not today thank you. Don't want any.' Before I could say anything at all the door was shut again with a stifled "Oooff" and I was back in the street, outside a completely different house. Like I say, they probably didn't get many brush salesmen down Hanging Basket Street.

What I really wanted most at that time was solitude and quiet repose, preferably elsewhere, but I knew I had to go through with it. So hey-ho, with a heavy heart and a trembling knee, let's try again, I thought. Once more I concentrated on Vizagriz and his frightening appearance, of which I now had a much better idea, and once again the universe shimmered and there I was outside the creepy door. I approached it and made to pull the doorbell chain again, but it said, 'I know, I know,' and set itself clanging.

There was the same shuffling and dragging as before and the door flew open even more forcibly, to the accompaniment of "Gawdstrufe" and there once again was Vizagriz.

'I thought I said already, but just so we're all clear on it: I've got some, I don't want any, and I won't join. Nor will I give donations or subscribe to Cyclopsopaedias. I already have double glazing, don't need my carpets cleaned and can't be bothered with surveys. Moreover, nor am I interested in religions of any sort and I haven't got any change so I can't buy a flag. What I can do, however, is promise to turn you into something so gruesome you won't find it in any bestiary this side of the oxterworld if you don't GO AWAY!'

Vizagriz made to slam the door, which visibly winced at the prospect, but at that minute my sweaty palm dropped the Thaler it had been holding and the gold rattled gently on the cobbles in hanging Basket Street. Not knowing what to do, I stood there quivering, until Vizagriz said, 'On the other hand, I haven't had a visitor for ages. Come in.'

Dazed, I scrabbled up the coin and followed the Mage into his cottage. Well, I say cottage, which is what it was from the outside, but inside it seemed to be much larger. Trick of the light, I thought, but then I noticed at least twice as many windows as there were from the street side and a staircase which by all rights ought to have gone nowhere but the roof, although it definitely led to at least two floors above.

I became aware that the wizard was peering at me in an amused way as if he understood my confusion. 'Don't worry about the house,' he said. 'It isn't really here. Only the outside is, and we're not there anymore. Now, what can I do for you?'

He was saying this to me, but I could see his eyes were more interested in the coin I was clutching like it held my very soul.

'I'm Slouch.'

'I know.'

'How do you know?'

'That's what wizards do.'

I found out later that what wizards do is make comments like that one just to keep everybody on their toes, but it was undeniably impressive at the time.

'Er, well, I've got to become your apprentice. He said so.'

'Indeed? And who said so? Your father, fed up with you hanging around the house eating all day? Your current prentice-master, who realises your true worth and therefore wants to shift you off on some dippy Mage who won't notice the difference? The cat's mother? Who?'

I was now shaking like a palace hairdresser's wrist. 'He, he, he gave me this. A bagful of them, in fact,' I stuttered and held up to him the Thaler which he disdained to take, moving back in his chair and lifting his hands away.

'Put it on the table, boy. I've been around too long to be taken in by that one. Unsolicited gold from unspecified sources? Probably with a binding spell or curse attached, I shouldn't but wonder. I should cocoa. Tchah!'

I put the coin on the table, and although Vizagriz wouldn't put his hands near it, neither did he take his eyes off it. I thought at the time he was warding off whatever enchantment might well be on it, but I realise now it was just sheer greed. 'So. From the beginning. Who are you, what do you want, and who is "He" who sent you here with the gold? In that order.'

I had recovered enough of my wits to remember my manners. 'May't please you, Great Mage, I am Slouch, as I, er, said, and presently a catamite-in-training at SamBernardo's, but originally a foundling, though they do say I was got on a Palace Lady by a visiting Knight who forswore to abandon his quest and therefore ne'er knew of the legacy he had left to the Princess who...'

'Yes, yes, yes, No doubt. Get on with it.'

'Anyway, I was in this area last night and He stopped me, said I was to be your apprentice, gave me the gold and told me to meet him there a month from tonight, which is last night, at this time, I mean at the same time, and not to miss it or the world's curtain material would be pulled apart...'

'"Fabric of existence disrupted" more likely?' offered Vizagriz, visibly amused.

'Er, yes, thank you, may't please Your Potency, fabric of existence, er, and that he'd miss golf, whatever that is, and He gave me these and told me to give them to you and, well, here I am. I think.'

'Interesting. Very interesting indeed. And who is "He", this mysterious benefactor of ours, I wonder?'

'I don't know, honest, but he was sort of tall, and dressed in armour that was as black as anything you could imagine, blacker even, and he looked like...'

'...A Dark and Stormy Knight?' Vizagriz ventured, now obviously shaken and not at all chuffed. 'Are you saying you met, actually met, the Dark and Stormy Knight?'

'Er, well, I suppose so.'

The change in Vizagriz was remarkable, if a bit startling. He shot up and started pacing the floor of the cottage. It may have been my imagination, but I could have sworn the walls moved back a bit to give him room. 'Then why the HELL didn't you come to me at once? Why wait a day when there's no time to lose? What did you think you were playing at? You meet the Herald of Great Events who tells you, quite specifically, am I right, to come to me, and you spend an entire night and a morning fannying about like he'd invited you to a fruitball match? Gahhh!'

At this, I am not ashamed to say, I burst into tears. I mean, large mystical beings in armour, bags of gold, a biffing from Nark, houses that moved about and couldn't be relied upon to stay the same size for five minutes, a door that took umbrage at being opened and now a wizard shouting at me, And all this on no breakfast – I mean, what would you have done? Right. So I did.

As I was sniffling and blubbing, Vizagriz calmed down a bit. 'All right, all right. Wipe your nose. I'm not really surprised. After all, you couldn't have known what the true importance of this was. Now, let me get it exactly clear what the Knight said to you.'

He sat down opposite me on a footstool that shimmied out of a dark corner and placed itself under what I took to be his backside, only in those robes you couldn't tell, and waited until my shoulders had stopped shaking a bit.

'Right. He met you here, or rather there, in Hanging Basket Street did he?'

'Y-yes, er n-no. In Pally Alley. It's just round the corner.'

'Yes, thank you I know where it is. It doesn't move around much, not like some places, eh?' He winked. It was horrible.

'And, and he asked if I was your apprentice. Knew my name and everything.'

'Knew your name? Now that's very interesting,' said Vizagriz, palpably disturbed by this. 'Then what?'

'Then I said I wasn't your app-app-app...'

'Apprentice,' he added, helpfully.

'Yes, and he said I had better be, and then he realised he was where he thought he was but it wasn't when he thought, but it would be next month and...'

'Hold on, you mean he thought he was here, in Al Faq'Ahl, but a month from now?'

'Uhuh. And he said I should meet him there at the time he thought it was, if you see what I mean, and that I wasn't to make him come looking for me.'

'No, well, I shouldn't if I were you. Got a nasty temper that one, if lacking any sense of timing.'

I was getting an inkling of what was going on here, I felt. 'You mean, Oh Great and Powerful Magician, that you know this Knight?'

'Know him? Oh yes, I know him all right. Never met him before, of course, but I know of him all right.'

'So who is he then, er, if I may be so bold as to enquire of Your Magnificence...'

'Look, will you stop all that verbal gold-lacquering? Fair sets my teeth on edge. It's fine for the Royal Palace, where you were no doubt destined by SamBernardo's, but it gets in the way a bit down here, don't you think?'

'Yes, thank you. But...'

'Who is he? He's only the Herald of Great Events, as I think I said. He turns up when something manifestly important is going to happen and more or less gets all the right people together at the right time to make it happen as it should, or at least might. Sort of an inter-temporal traffic policemen, really. Or celestial party-organiser.' He went back to musing a bit.

'But, if I can ask, what sort of great event will it be?'

'Buggered if I know,' said Vizagriz, 'but I'm damn sure I'd better find out and sharpish.'

'So that you can take your part in it?' I ventured.

'No fear!' he said, standing up. 'So I can be as far away from it as possible when it happens, and if you've any sense you'll do the same, young feller-me-lad.'

I admit I was downcast by this. In the past few minutes I had had the feeling that something momentous or at the very least interesting was about to happen and that I might well be at least around when it happened, if not actually a party to it. But Vizagriz's last pronouncement dashed my hopes a bit. 'Does that mean then, that I can't be..., that you won't be wanting me as..., that you don't need...'

'What? An apprentice?'

'Well, yes.'

Vizagriz stuck the end of his beard in his mouth and sucked it, a mannerism I then found quirky but in later years came to detest warmly. 'Oh, I don't know. We have got the gold, after all, so I could buy you out. And I suppose I do need an apprentice. Haven't had any help since the last one got himself turned into...er, left. And in any case, you've got to be around to meet the Knight again in a month so I might as well keep you here till then and try and find out what's so special about you.'

'Special?'

'Well, he picked you to come looking for, didn't he? You must have something to do with it, even if it's only taking a message to someone or the like. Can't be any harm in that. On the other hand...'

He strode towards a large bookcase I hadn't noticed before - could have sworn, in fact, wasn't there, and ran his hands along the upper shelf. 'Now let's see. Grimoires, Necronomicons, Clavicles, Pentagram templates, Ah yes, here it is.' A volume slid out from the bookcase and settled in his hand, then appeared to turn its own pages as if by, well, Magick I suppose. Vizagriz was muttering to himself. 'Where is it. Stooge, stooge, stooge, stooge...Ahah! Stooge Eternal!'

He brought the book back to the table and I noticed it's cover. 'If I can say...' I started.

'What? Hmmm?' the wizard muttered distractedly as he read. 'What?'

'I think, well, I think that's the book He had, and...'

Vizagriz's head shot up. 'What? He had a PhilosoPhax? This is worse than I thought if he's got his hands on a PhilosoPhax.'

'Sorry, what is it?'

'It's the PhilosoPhax. Don't you know what that is? Oh no, I suppose you wouldn't. Well, I guess your apprentice training starts here.' He settled back on his stool and tapped the book.

'This, me lad, is the single most important tome ever produced. It is the PhilosoPhax.'

'Yes, you said.'

'Don't come clever with me, sonny-Jim. This is crucial stuff. This book contains information on Great Events and the people in them, allows you to predict forward what will happen from any given date and also has instructions for dealing with almost any contingency. What is more, it is in loose-leaf format so that it can be updated, which happens regularly and automatically, as long as you pay the subscription.'

'What's the subscription?'

The wizard shuddered slightly. 'You really don't want to know. But it's part of the reason there aren't as many cats in the Garden Suburb Quarter as everyone thinks, right?'

I didn't want to pursue the thought.

'I haven't bothered and it's a second-hand copy anyway. Not up to date, really. But basically, it's a sort of, sort of, well Manager of Time and Place. Yes, a Time Manager and a Place Manager. Wouldn't be without one. But if the Knight has one, well, you can imagine!'

I couldn't and said so.

'It means he is starting to interfere directly in events rather than indirectly as he's supposed to, which means it's a lot worse that we thought.'

Than you thought, I said to myself. This is about as bad as I could ever have imagined already never mind getting any worse. But I didn't feel it was my place to say so.

'Anyway!' He slammed the PhilosoPhax shut and stood up. 'Anyway, what I suppose I should do is go up to SamBernardo's and buy you out, eh? How much did the Knight leave you, did you say?'

Vizagriz reached out to tap the Thaler and just too late, stopped his hand an inch from it. No use. A bolt of actinic blue light shot up from the bag and encircled his wrist briefly before flying out of the window. Vizagriz was not happy.

'Bugger! Bugger, bugger, BUGGER!!' He shouted. 'I knew it! Bloody Recognition spell! Now I'm really in it!'

'Are you hurt?' I asked, startled.

'No. No, not really. Just pissed off. I should have spotted that one, but I forgot. You know what this means?'

'Er, not really...'

'It means I'm bound to this gold and can only use it for the purpose it was intended, and I won't be released until either the task is over or the gold is properly spent. That's all.'

'Oh. So...'

'So the first thing to do is to buy you out, as I said. How much did the

Knight give you?'

'Twenty-four Thalers, counting this one.'

'Good Gribbin! Twenty-four Thalers!'

'Will that be enough?' I asked, innocently. He shot me what I believe is called an old-fashioned look.

'Oh, I should think so.'

'But I don't have them. They were taken from me by Nark, our Bunkmaster. He'll have given them to Brer Dryberg by now.'

'So, that's were we go. We'll see Brer Dryberg, get the money and buy you out.' Vizagriz held out his hand and a tall, wooden staff with a knobbly end just sort of settled itself into it. 'Let's go and do that then, shall we?'

I shrugged and headed for the door but Vizagriz put out his staff to stop me. 'No, not that way. Not yet, anyway. Never know where it'll lead to. Rather depends on what the last person to pass the door was thinking about. Once I ended up in a house of dubious reputation away over in Spank. Took days to get back. Not that I minded. Can you picture SamBernardo's in your mind, or what passes for it?'

I ignored the insult and said I could.

'Good, Kindly do so, then. Got it? Now open the door and step out.'

I conjured, if that's the word, a picture of the catamite training agency in my head, reached for the door handle (which wriggled out of my grasp and opened itself, in a barely concealed huff) and stepped out, followed by Vizagriz. To my utter amazement we were right outside the agency. I was gobsmacked, no other word for it! I looked back, but there was no sign of the cottage, any of it, not even the door.

'Where's it gone? The cottage?'

'Oh, it's back where it always was,' said Vizagriz.

'In Hanging Basket Street?' I tried, hoping he'd explain.

'Not really,' he explained. 'Come on! They might even give us elevenses.'

SamBernardo's is an impressive place. It had at one time been a castle, part of the defences of Al Faq'Ahl. It had a drawbridge going over a moat, which once had been the den of foul, ancient creatures, waiting to prey on hapless travellers who fell into the deep waters, but more often were hurled from the castle ramparts on account of some misdemeanour like wearing the wrong shoes on a Frig's Day. It was rumoured that there had been at one time (and perhaps still was) an underground tunnel or cave system joining the moat to the largest lake in the land, far to the North, and known haunt of mysterious denizens, remnants of a farther past when such giants bestrode the world amongst fiery skies and fierce, tropical heat.

Nowadays, anyone falling to the moat was more likely to bounce a couple of times then sink slowly to the depths, there to be granted a mercifully quick demise on account of poisoning, asphyxiation or corrosion from the appalling liquors and vapours that thirteen centuries of less than perfect sewerage had bestowed on the castle's first defence.

Either way, the moat was not pleasant to look at, smell or think about. The drawbridge - hardly ever raised now and probably rusted open, led to a portcullis-and-oaken-doors affair that was more decorative than functional. Entry was typically gained by a smaller hatch cut into the solid oak of the original portals and manned, if that's the word, by a eunuch of immense size and stentorian wheezing. He was called Lunch.

The castle itself towered above the city. It was perched atop a hill that had been formed from the lava outpourings of a long-dead volcano. The early building in Al Faq'Ahl had been almost exclusively on the spine and slopes of this crag-and-tail, leading to the architectural nonsense of houses that were four stories high on one side and a major cause of vertigo on the other. The populace of the city had arranged itself so that the merchants had their businesses on the ground floor frontages and lived above. One floor higher were their servants, staff, older children and slaves (all of which amounted to the same thing in most cases) and above those were dismal, light-deprived, freezing, draughty hovels inhabited by those known, in terms of social class if not altitude, as the Lower Orders. That was the front, facing the road leading to the castle. It was the habit of the inhabitants at the front of the building to dispose of their wastes by tipping them out of the windows to hurtle down and slide off the strategically-placed canopies and lean-tos over the shop fronts and into a guttering channel in the middle of the road where it sat, festering malevolently and waiting for a decent shower to wash it down to the Porter Quarter at the River Lethe. Not for nothing was this thoroughfare known as The High Street.

Citizens out walking or patronising the emporia and taverns would keep knowingly to the insides, under the canopies where possible and scuttling from one to the next where there were gaps. Visitors and newcomers would amble blithely up the outside, smirking at the natives who crowded onto the pavements and wondering why they did so until a bucket of slops down the neck enlightened them as to the reason. By convention, all waste was disposed of at a certain time of day and the city authorities obligingly fired a cannon to tell everyone it was time to put the products of their insides outside. Locals stood stock still when The Gun went off. Tourists looked up to see what the noise was and got a faceful, or several if it had been a productive weekend.

At the back of the buildings, where there were another five or six stories to play with, the less faceful arranged themselves in some sort of pecking order in a ramshackle way down the crags that fell away from the spine of The High Street. They tended to dispose of their foetid ordure either by hoying it into the many vennels and alleys that wound their way down to the low roads, hoping that gravity would finish the job, or else straight onto the rocks the houses were hewn from. It was often said that the Castle Rock had never been scaled by any invading army as they could not find a path to climb it. Too right they couldn't – it was far too slippery. And who'd want to, anyway?

Now, the castle had no function other than to house SamBernardo's – orphanage, refuge of the destitute and training academy for catamites-to-be. This had come about at a time when the city fathers were looking for an easy source of money. They had tried staging vast military parades in the castle's main square, figuring that the public would pay good money to see a bunch of overdressed soldiery flounce up and down trying to look fierce and playing hired instruments extremely badly. That didn't last long. For a time, everyone who attended was given a mark of indelible dye as proof of attendance and payment and it was made an offence punishable by purchase of a life subscription to be caught not sporting one of these decorations. It didn't take anyone very long to work out that cheaper versions could be forged by the many itinerant skin artists down in the Farter Quarter. They had to be renewed every year about the time the militia started checking, but that was a small price to pay, in both senses, for getting out of what became known, obviously, as The Annual Tattoo.

The next get-rich-slow scheme had been to mount a yearly Festival in the castle grounds and invite anyone who wanted to perform to do so, provided only they could afford to rent a space to do it in. Mummers, jongleurs, fire-eaters and body-piercers, players of lutes, acrobats and reciters of verse all flocked to Al Faq'Ahl to put on their particular entertainments for the edification of the good citizenry, who even went along with this farce for a good many years before realising that nine-tenths of what was on offer was rubbish and no substitute for a quiet night in torturing the skivvies or going down the tavern for a sing-song. Those who considered themselves the literati and cognoscenti of the city continued to attend, more to be seen doing so, or not to be seen not doing so, or some other tortured logic, and the more abstruse the performance they more they affected to love it. This decadence came to be known as The Cringe and it finally fell away like rotten fruit that has hung around too long and let the worms get at it.

The city continued to promote this event after its natural demise since it did bring in a fair proportion of the gullible from the surrounding and less sophisticated countryside. They appointed a Director of Festivities to organise it. This position had to be filled annually since, after the Festival was over and found by the city treasurers not to have made as much as they had poured into it, the incumbent was generally hauled to one of the rank city dungeons and never seen again. The upshot of this was that people of genuine talent never applied for the post and it went to comic singers of steadily less and less ability until it scarcely mattered who applied since they couldn't ever make it pay and were going to be bunged into an oubliette afterwards anyway. It is said, although there is no evidence to back it up, that the sad collection of forgotten wastrels whose number swells by one every year formed themselves into a Cringe Club and hold underground performances entirely for their own amusement and attended solely by them plus a few bored jailers who like to pelt them with fruit. Not that the fruit was unwelcome, since it makes a nice change from rats and straw porridge. Since it was also one of the few chances anyone got to stretch their legs, this was known as The Stand-Up. And pretty dire it was, in all probability.

Finally, giving in to the inevitable, the city fathers (so called because they begot more bastards than most, on account of the typical price exacted from young and not-so-young women who wanted a favour, licence or rent rebate) put the castle on the market. It nearly became a wax works. It nearly became a theme park. But finally it was turned into SamBernardo's and the last remaining soldiers were turned out.

SamBernardo himself was that not too rare specimen, the philanthropist who got rich on account of, rather than prior to, his philanthropy. He had been a moderately successful merchant who spotted a niche market in the homeless and destitute who thronged the streets of Al Faq'Ahl begging for dinars or scraps of food and attempting to wrestle something tuneful out of bone flutes and pigs bladders dressed in their old Militia uniforms. They had even created an especially horrid-sounding device for the purpose - a wheezing, parping, braying thing called the Bag O' Pipes on the basis that the worse the noise, the more quickly someone will pay to have it stop. Added to these were the hundreds of waifs and strays who were cast onto the streets by despairing families or who turned up from Deity knows where, probably thinking to find a job in entertainment - the Festival reputation of the city having lingered long after the reality had withered on the vine.

Such a rabble, opined SamBernardo, had a cost, even if only in what someone was paid to burn their bodies after the Death Squads had bumped them all off in one of its regular culls. But did they have a value? Ah yes, he told the city fathers, because they are a commodity. Isn't everything? They can be trained, re-educated, put to useful service and - more to the point - kept out of the way so as not to embarrass the more sensitive citizenry and its gentle ladyfolk.

The bottom line was various forms of slavery. The first flowerings of his imagination were a series of programmes such as the Youth Trading Scheme, where youngsters were taught the rudiments of a craft then indentured to an artisan who wasn't obliged to pay them anything just so long as he took them off the city's hands.

Then there was the programme for the blind who, SamBernardo thought, could be most usefully employed chained to mill wheel which they could push round all day. Cheaper than a donkey and more amenable to a tickle with the whip. Man Power Training, he called that one.

But best of all, and the scheme which came to occupy almost all his time, energy and accommodation, was the catamite business. There was an almost insatiable demand for young, unblemished boys to do various forms of intimate service to the more decadent and louche artistocrats, high priests and senior functionaries of which Al Faq'Ahl had a profusion. His motto, "Don't Sit On Your Backside – Rent It", got immediate approbation from the city's leaders. Not only did it fit with their political prejudices, the Dikkeadh himself was said to have muttered, in one of his rare moments of lucidity, that he could think of nothing better to do with the strays and orphans. Actually, what had happened was that some hapless official had once said in the hearing of His Magnificence: "What shall we do with these tiny mites?" "Sod 'em," came the answer. And in such ways is whim turned into law. It mattered not a whit that the official in question was actually referring, at the time, to a particularly tenacious infestation of lice current in the palace. Everyone heard him ask the question, everyone heard the Dikkeadh's answer, and no-one was left in any doubt as to what SamBernardo would do about it. All he needed, he said, was premises.

He petitioned the city council for, and was granted, a long-term lease on the castle, installed as the administrators an order of clerics well-known for its adherence to the discipline of the lash and the cold shower and established the basis of a highly profitable trade. Since he solved three of the city's problems at once – getting the rabble off the streets, taking the castle off its books and providing a steady supply of well-mannered, biddable youngsters for its elders – he was onto a winner from the start.

SamBernardo was gone – the life of debauchery he had led on the profits from his good works had finally taken its toll, but not for a surprisingly long time considering the girth he attained, not to mention the battering he gave his liver – and the undisputed head of SamBernardo's was the current Pryer of the Order of Penitent Martyrs of the Flesh, Brer Dryberg.

It was to the good Brer that Vizagriz and I were now heading – without an appointment. This had just occurred to me and I expressed my fears to the wizard.

'I think we should have sent a message that we coming, you know.'

'Oh? Why waste time and paper? We would have come anyway.'

'But he doesn't know we're coming.'

'Well he will when we turn up, won't he?'

'He may not see us.'

'Blind, is he?'

'No, I mean, if we don't have an appointment...' I tailed of hopelessly as Vizagriz was already pummelling at the oak door with the knobbly end of the obligatory wizard's staff.

There was a shuffling, wheezing, coughing noise. A tiny spy-hole opened in the door and it says something for the closeness of the eyes that peered through that both could be seen together.

'Ah. There you are. Should have heard you hiding. Vizagriz. Wizard. To see Brer Dryberg,' said Vizagriz the wizard.

'Do you have an appointment?'

'Told you so,' I opined.

'Shut up. I most certainly do have an appointment. I have several. I am Wizard-at-Large to the Court of Can the Ripe. I am Immediate Past President of the Sages of the Purple Ride. And I am the official transformer-into-frogs of anybody who doesn't do what they are bloody well told. Bit of respect here. Present my compliments to Brer Dryberg, tell him I've got one of his catamites and if he won't see me would he like a fist-fight in the cart park.'

I was aghast. I had never heard anyone speak to the Order like that, even its minor dogsbodies. Still, Lunch was obviously impressed. Nobody messed with wizards. In fact, just like physicians, everybody kept out of their way until they absolutely had to go and see them.

'I'll tell him you're without and, er, requesting an audience. What's it about?'

'I won't need an audience, since I'm not here to perform. And it's about elevenses time, so get a move on.'

'Did you say you want a catamite?'

'I don't, but I appear to have one. Believe he's one of yours. Brought him back, want to talk about it.'

'Lunch, it's me, Slouch,' I piped up, standing back so the doorman could see me.

'Ah. The runaway. You're in trouble, me lad.' And with that the spy-hole slapped shut, the door hatch creaked open and the fat eunuch wheezed to one side.

'About time,' muttered Vizagriz as he stepped inside.

'Nearly eleven, like you said,' answered Lunch, who was a bit deaf as well as a lot fat and a load stupid.

Still, he'd obviously had the wit to send someone to announce our arrival to Brer

Dryberg. I could see, scuttling across the castle yard, hands in sleeves, the hateful figure of Brer Harvey, Dean of Discipline and a mean over-arm with the lash and the leather strap. He was also Brer Dryberg's right-hand lick-spittle when it came to anything underhand or distasteful. But I had no doubt his mind was on exactly what he had in store for a runaway SamBernardo's trainee as soon as he got his hands on him.

He skidded to a halt in front of Vizagriz and bowed. 'Puissant wizard,' he hissed. 'Brer Dryberg's compliments and his gratitude for bringing back this runaway. He trusts you have not been discommoded and wonders if you would join him for a light repast by way of his gratitude. And you,' he turned on me to spit, 'you will go straight to my study and await my pleasure. Do not bother to wear the trousers.'

'The boy stays with me,' said Vizagriz.

'Really, Mage, there is no need to trouble yourself further with this insect. He will be dealt with as befits his unpleasant aspect and his worse behaviour.'

'He stays with me. Now let's see your Pryer. Repast sounds good, though I can't swear I'll go with the "light" part.'

'As you wish, Sage. Walk this way.'

If Vizagriz had a snappy retort to that one, he didn't bother to let it go. He was obviously on his best visiting behaviour.

Brer Harvey scuttled, Vizagriz strode and I cowered all the way up through the inner portals and into the main body of the castle. We approached that part which was known, partly in reference to its earlier, military uses and largely because of its present purpose, as The Battery, the main "education" centre of SamBernardo's and home to the administrative offices and the studies of the seniors of the Order. We ascended the stairs to a floor where I had never been and which most of the boys hope never to be called to. Brer Harvey knocked tentatively on the door, coughed discreetly and opened it.

'The Honoured Wizard, Vizagriz,' he intoned. I didn't even rate a mention but I was grateful for that. Inside the study were a seated Brer Dryberg and a standing-to-attention Nark, the hated Bunkmaster, staring straight at me with undiluted venom. On the table before Brer Dryberg was the bag of gold Thalers.

Brer Dryberg got up, just slowly enough so that no-one was in any doubt who was in charge here and that if he hadn't wanted to stand he wouldn't have bothered. 'An honour indeed, Vizagriz, to have such a renowned wizard visit us, and all to return a worthless miscreant who is barely worth the walk.'

'We didn't walk,' said Vizagriz and left it like that.

'Still, to take time out of your busy schedule. Come, take some wine and a platter and we'll let the Dean deal with the boy.'

'It's not just about the boy,' said Vizagriz, pointing to a golden pitcher of wine which obligingly filled a nearby goblet. 'There's the matter of some gold Thalers which, if I am not mistaken, are in that bag you have there.'

'Ah yes. Nark here brought them to me earlier. It would appear the boy has also been thieving. I doubt there's enough skin on his body to take the flaying he deserves. The Deity alone knows where he got such a purse. Doubtless we'll be getting a visit from some merchant with a sore head and a grievance before long.'

Vizagriz plucked the goblet out of the air and took a long pull at it, putting it down carefully on the table. 'He stole them from me, as it happens,' he said.

I was so astonished I let out a squeak and started to babble.

'Silence when you speak to Brer Dryberg,' shouted Nark and even he had the grace to go a bit pink at the ears when he realised what he had said. Still the point was well taken. I clamped my mouth shut.

'From you, wizard? And how did he come to do that?' Brer Dryberg asked, sitting himself down again and accepting a goblet of wine from Brer Harvey. He didn't exactly say that wizards weren't well know for the state of their finances, but the implication was there, right enough. Vizagriz let it pass, if he noticed it.

'I dare say the gold was found on the boy this morning. Which means he acquired it last night. And as one of your Brers will no doubt confirm, he was out near Hanging Basket Street last night on an errand.'

Brer Dryberg consulted a sheet of parchment that Brer Harvey handed him. 'Yes. An errand for me, delivering something to a respected colleague who happens to live in that area, certainly. But can we be sure the boy stole the purse from you? How could, after all, any small boy take gold from a powerful wizard, when everyone knows how much care wizards take to guard their gold?'

'How he got them is not the issue. Nor is the supposed miserliness of wizards. The fact is, the purse is mine. And I will have it back.'

'I fear,' said Brer Dryberg, 'that will not be possible. Even now one of my staff is informing the Militia of the theft. They will want to hold the coins as evidence, pending a thorough investigation, no doubt. Twenty Thalers is a lot of money.'

'Twenty-three. Isn't that right, Nark?' Vizagriz said, raising his magnificent eyebrows and pinning Nark to the wall with a glare.

Brer Dryberg cut across any exchange there might have been. 'I haven't counted them. We'll leave that to the Militia. If, as indeed will surely prove to be the case, they turn out to be yours, doubtless they will be restored to you. In the meantime we must again thank you for taking the trouble to return the stray to us. Rest assured his punishment will be... appropriate.'

'I will punish him. The loss was mine and I will take the responsibility for dealing with it. In any case, I intend to buy the boy and he will be mine to do with as I please, relieving you of the obligation.'

Brer Dryberg's eyes glittered briefly. 'Ah, well, if you seek to make a purchase, honoured Mage – though I am not sure you will find this one ready yet. He is early in his training and...'

'...And he'll be cheap then. What's the going rate for them at this size?' Vizagriz said, the majority of his attention being focused on a platter he was heaping with cold meats and cheeses.

'Well, normally SamBernardo's would charge fi-se-eight Thalers for a fully-trained catamite, all guarantees and warranties etc etc. But a half-schooled one we could let go for four. No indemnities against his behaviour or performance, mind.'

'Four it is, then,' munched Vizagriz around a mouthful of ham. 'I'll just take the change. Nineteen Thalers, I believe. Correct me if my arithmetic fails me.'

'Ah. No. I fear we must ask for separate payment. As I explained, this bag of gold must go to the Militia. You understand.'

'I understand that anyone who touches that gold is in for a nasty shock, is what I understand,' Vizagriz crumbed, reaching for bread.

'I beg your pardon? A threat? Surely not.' Brer Dryberg drew his brows together and reached out to draw the pouch closer, fearing its imminent disappearance. He wasn't fooling anyone with the "Militia" story, but he had to keep it up.

'Oh no,' replied Vizagriz. 'At least, not from me. This gold is ensourceled, that's all.'

Brer Dryberg's hand shot back like a lizard's tongue. 'Ensourceled? In what way? By whom?'

'That I have yet to determine. But what I do know is that the gold was intended for specific purposes, one of which was to acquire this lad. Try to use it for anything else and it won't work. Worse than that, in fact.'

'In what way "worse"?' As far as Brer Dryberg was concerned, and as far as gold was concerned, there was nothing worse than not having his hot hands on it. But I must confess I didn't like the way this was headed. I was grateful, however, that the attention was off me for the moment. It wasn't to last, though. Nark saw to that.

'Beggin' yer pardon, Pryer, but if the gold is cursed, how could the boy handle it and not come to harm?'

'Oh, that's a good one,' said Vizagriz putting down his now-empty platter. 'Good one, that. You're not as dim as you look, are you, Nark. Or maybe you're just having a good day. In the first place, how do you know he hasn't been cursed? Perhaps the curse is to be sold to me. I can be very testy when roused. In the second place, what if he's bound up with the charm? Maybe he has some part to play in whatever the gold is supposed to do. And in the third place, it's none of your business in the first place. I'll ask Brer Dryberg if he couldn't kindly contain you from displaying your ignorance of matters mystical.' He licked his fingers and, before anyone could get a word in, continued. 'But don't take my word for it. Try to use the gold for something else. Send one of your Order down to the market to buy something with one of these coins. But make sure he's dispensable. Hate you to lose a good one. Send Nark, for instance.'

Nark started to splutter but Brer Dryberg's upraised hand halted him. 'I accept what you say, wizard. You are, after all, the master of all things thaumaturgical and know better than we poor divines what transpires in the darker corners of the Deity's domain. But you must see – there is no actual...', he made a vague circling motion with his hand, '...proof of what you say.'

'Proof?' Vizagriz replied and twirled his hand in exactly the same manner as Brer Dryberg had, but with a different effect. The bag spilled its contents. 'Touch a coin. No?' Brer Dryberg, Nark and Brer Harvey all managed the nicest piece of formation shrinking-back it has ever been my pleasure to witness. 'Now watch,' Vizagriz said and reached out to the small heap of gold discs. A spark leaped from them, wrapped itself around his wrist and shot out of the study window.

'Now that,' said the wizard, 'is what we in the trade call a Recognition. The gold knows I'm here, knows I'm something to do with it and has reported that fact back to somewhere. Now you touch it. It won't hurt you. But it will be reported back. And if you're not right for it, someone – something – will come and tell you so. Not soon, necessarily. But one day. And telling you could take a long time. Eternity, for instance.'

The two Brers and Nark were still stretching themselves as far away from the gold as possible. Vizagriz picked up five of the coins and threw them on the table before Brer Dryberg who tried to push himself through the back of his chair just a bit more.

'On the other hand, if I use the gold for one of its intended purposes, that's all right. It's just gold, then. So I buy Slouch with it. You get the gold, it is no longer ensourceled, it's job being done. Call it five shall we? Don't bother to wrap him.'

Vizagriz rose to his feet, picked up a peach, bit into it and slurped, somewhat ruining the effect he had just built up. Just at that moment, however, the door opened to show, framed in its arch, a small, stunted, dark-looking man ushering in the most beautiful girl I had ever seen. The dwarfish man had not seen us and started to introduce the girl. He got no further than 'Forgive this intrusion Brer Dryberg, but I have brought...', when a shaft of electric blue shot from the remaining coins, darted across the room and spun around him and the girl before whizzing down the stairs right past a servant who dropped his tray, his bowel contents and his dignity all in a split second.

It was Brer Dryberg who broke the startled silence. 'Well, Master Mindador. It seems that whatever geas this wizard has had placed upon him, you are bound up in it too. Perhaps he will explain it to you. Vizagriz?'

To his credit, Vizagriz kept up an air of amused insouciance through all this. 'Mindador. Indeed. And what did you say the lovely lady's name was?'

'Er, forgive me, this is Winolene, recently chosen as Handmaiden to the Fiery Swan, Vesta. But, but, but what was that?'

'That, Mindador, was a summons of a kind. You seem to be with us in whatever will happen next. As is the boy here.'

Winolene looked at me for the first time and... well, I hoped she would smile and a burst of radiance would spill from her like sunshine through a stained-glass window. In fact, she sniffed. And in that sound was the shattering of my heart. I was snapped back into reality by Vizagriz saying, 'Come on, lad. You're bought and paid for and we have work to do. Brer Dryberg has visitors and this room's a bit cramped for eight. I give you good day Brer Dryberg, Brer Harvey. Mindador, I'll be in touch. Don't leave town, there's no point. I'll be back to you within a month, all right? My Lady, excuse us. Now, Brer Dryberg, if you'll instruct what's his name at the gate to let us pass it would save a little time and a lot of mess.'

Brer Dryberg recovered his composure when he realised we were leaving and that at least some of the gold had stuck to his fingers, without any sorcerous implications. 'Ah, yes. Our unfortunate doorman. He's not all there, you know.'

'That tends to be the case with eunuchs.'

Word of our meeting with Brer Dryberg had obviously reached the front door before we did. As Vizagriz and I approached Lunch he waddled about trying to be useful at opening the door, look respectful towards the wizard and get invisible all at the same time. He managed none of them very well and Vizagriz stood sighing and tapping his foot while the eunuch fiddled ineptly with bolts and handles, finally stepping through the open-at-last hatch. I followed.

As we strode down The High Street, Vizagriz said to me, 'So why is he called "Lunch"? Daft name.'

'Apparently he was once a kitchen slave whose main duty was to provide lunch and whenever anyone shouted "Lunch" he would appear. So it sort of stuck. When he got too fat and wheezy the Order moved him to lighter duties.'

'Daft name,' Vizagriz repeated. 'I don't know who's thicker, him or his door.'

And that's how I became apprenticed to a wizard.

CHAPTER THE THIRD

In which Great Events are set in motion and Vizagriz gains a new enemy. As if one more would make any difference.

Master Mindador was more than a little miffed. SamBernardo's is not an impressive place, when you come to think about it. It's just a big, old pile where a bunch of fat monks give unwanted boys a rudimentary education that equips them to be no better than slaves who can read and write a bit and maybe play the flute. Mindador was sick to death of being at the beck and call of Brer Dryberg. Ever since he had been struck off – no, ever since he had forsworn the confining halter of orthodox Magick to tread the lonely path of sole enlightenment, yes that's more like it – ever since then, he had put up with the insults and slights heaped upon him by the Pryer and carried out the minor commission he got from the Order, all the while continuing his lonely, wee-small-hours search for a portway that would lead him to realms of power and riches. And he was very nearly there!

The package he had received from Brer Dryberg the previous night had been a missing item from his catalogue of requirements that would allow him to communicate with... Best not to even think the name until safe at home and behind his protective hexagrams. An unguarded thought could bring forth entities of dreadful power and bad tempers which it would take some foul sacrifice to return whence they came. But with the Relic of Um he could now finish his spells and call upon one such, binding it with a cantrip so strong it would eagerly do his bidding and return willingly to its dark pit in the oxterworld, and at no risk to Master Mindador, that was the main thing.

It was over a year since Brer Dryberg had asked him – and none too politely – to find the artefact of his desire. The Order wanted it, and the Order should have it, but they needed a thaumaturge and necromancer to help. No point going through the established channels, Brer Dryberg had explained to Mindador on their first meeting. They are all so hidebound by convention, they wouldn't see the point. And anyway, they gossiped like fishwives whereas this task required a certain, well, delicacy of approach and not to be shouted from the rooftops. Might as well nail a declaration to the palace door as ask a wizard to do something on the quiet, he had said. So would Master Mindador help, in capacity as a potent Mage of less structured affiliations?

Mind you, one thing being in an established sect of Magick did, it brought you work. There were always referrals from other wizards, second opinions sought from alchemists, a bit of contract work that got spread around and occasionally a big, multidisciplinary job that required a team of specialists. The Death Wars had been one of these. There was no war as such and very few deaths, but it had been a hard one. It had happened, a few gyrations ago, that Yule Day – the only day in the calendar which didn't fall into any of the 13 constellations – was also a time of spectacular and fell conjunctions. Many a portway was wearing very thin indeed and there was evidence of seepage from the oxterworld all over the place. Almost every wizard, thaumaturge, mage, sage, sorcerer, witch, warlock, conjuror and necromancer who could hold a wand and say an incantation without dribbling was called in to mount a vast, day-long defence that would keep out whatever felt it would be a good idea to jump through and have a look, and to stop things and people from the normal realm getting sucked away elsewhere and elsewhen. Most practitioners of Magick were involved in some way, the majority in the consortium that put up the defensive barriers and a few from the darker Sects who were doing their damnedest to open the portways and have a shufti. A few of these were doing so on the instructions of dæmons who had some dread purpose in crossing the planes. Others were curious. And the rest were just keen to cause a bit of mayhem in the expectation that there would be lot more work about when somebody had to clean it all up and get things back to hexagon one.

It had worked, too. The defences were so strong and the Magick-wielders so vigilant that very little escaped from wherever and very little of this realm got mixed in with the rest. There was the odd apparition, the desecration of a temple or two and some pretty spectacular sky effects to go with the obligatory ground-shaking and darkness-at-noon. The atmospherics were no bad thing – in fact, the wizards had let quite a lot of that happen, on the basis that it didn't do any real harm and looked dead spooky to the public, who would be even more grateful when everything calmed down. It also allowed the settling of certain old scores. It was no coincidence that the temples which did get ravening dæmons manifested into them to cause a fairish amount of damage before a wizard turned up to obliterate the offending entity were those whose priests had been the least sympathetic towards Magick or had outright criticised the Sects.

Minor potentates who were not as respectful of the local Magick Circle as they might have been got a rude awakening as to the possibilities inherent in the wizards taking their stuffed crocodiles elsewhere.

The Dikkeadh himself received a nasty shock when his favourite teddy bear developed fangs and glowing eyes until the palace Mage-in-Residence blasted it to sawdust and felt. Having performed this valuable service didn't stop the wizard in question getting himself eviscerated for his trouble, an event known long afterwards as "Bo-Bo's Revenge" and rendered more philosophically as "You work your guts out and what do you get? You get your guts out".

However, in the main, people were grateful. Truth to tell, there had been little risk and very few accidents. But everyone was a teensy bit more careful round wizards from then on and their rates went up by twice inflation without a murmur from the populace. It was the crowning triumph of this public relations exercise to call it The Death Wars and to hint darkly, as most wizards subsequently did, that "You didn't know the half of it" and "You only got the fireworks - I was four hours between the planes, struggling with Shoggothh himself who was making a bee-line for Vesta's temple" and similar war stories.

Master Mindador, at that time a minor mage with the Reformed Orthodox and reading for a postgraduate diploma in Hands of Glory, had been a sort of project manager in the Death Wars. Not experienced enough to be trusted with incanting as such he had been put in charge of a large squad of apprentices and acolytes whose job was to keep the cauldrons boiling and make sure no-one ran out of Grok fire or essence of eyesquint at a crucial moment. He had, in fact, been quite good at this - running around with a clipboard checking schedules and moving people from one task to another just before the demand changed, ordering more jars from the pottery warehouse and keeping the carters busy bring fresh supplies from the apothecaries stores, which had been granted a late licence for the occasion and were coining it selling a frightened public charms and nostrums, plus small, overpriced bottles of smelling salts and poppy juice for diarrhoea.

It had been this experience that had persuaded Mindador his future was not in Magick as such, but in the management of Magick. What could magicians not achieve if they were properly organised? If they conformed to certain practices and rites rather than going their own ways? If they all had to use the same forms? Sadly, his insights had not been welcomed. His dissertation on the subject had been turned down flat by the College of Knowledge and his short-term contract regretfully not renewed by the Reformed Orthodox. Forced to go it alone, he hung up his shingle as a thaumaturge with a sideline in doing the books for a couple of alchemists and seethed at his untoward treatment.

It was a short step from there to getting into the less savoury end of contract Magick where a magician was hired to do one small part of an overall spell, on piece work. No single practitioner ever new what the end result was and few cared to ask. However, this exercise had gone spectacularly wrong and resulted in turning a small city into a vast raspberry jelly that promptly melted - not the effect intended, but a predictable result of using soft fruit instead of hard-to-get carnivorous plant life from then other side of the world. The mistake, which was on the part of one lazy herbalist, had gone unnoticed by everyone else, each of whom had no control over the other processes going on before, alongside or after theirs.

However, anyone associated with the project got canned, Mindador amongst them. The administrators of the city in question - who only wanted their roofs turned to silver, not an outrageous request - got a good ticking off and had to revise their direct labour procedures.

Struck off, Mindador found it even harder to make a living. Brer Dryberg's commission came as a Deitysend, therefore. It wasn't particularly good money, but it was on a rolling contract and Mindador felt he could stretch it for a good year or more with monthly retainers plus a bonus on results.

And now he had the Relic of Um. The order had had to call in a few favours to get it and results were expected pronto - Brer Dryberg had left him in no doubts about that. And better still, he had managed to find a virgin of noble blood and one who was dedicated to Vesta, moreover. Nothing could go wrong. Brer Dryberg had approved of Winolene. Winolene had no idea what was going on. And Mindador had received a gold Thaler on account.

The only potential fly in the ointment was the Recognition he had received from the coins, but that fitted too. There would have to be a Quest and it looked like Vizagriz was in for it. The coins had Recognised that he, Mindador, was involved, so he was clearly on the right track. Much as he hated having another wizard tied up in this, he dismissed the thought - after all, Vizagriz and that snivelling brat he had with him would be out of his hair in, what, a month? That left him plenty of time to find out what he needed to know.

He scurried back to his rented hovel in Pally Alley, thinking, 'This is the big one. This is it. I'll make my name, get rich, move out of that shack and set up right on one of the six corners of Hanging Basket Street with a branch office just outside the Palace. Then they'll see. They'll see.'

Cackling like a inexpertly-drawn chicken, he had sped off to prepare for the night's work.

He would divine the whereabouts of The Holy Quail.

'How are you feeling, my dear – oh, do have another turquoise delight, they are rather good, aren't they? Hard to come by, this particular flavour but worth the trouble, I always think. I shall have a box sent round to your priestess.'

Brer Dryberg was at his most unctuous and Winolene was quite enjoying it. She didn't always get treated like a grown-up. And she was nearly sixteen! At home her father had still considered her a baby and her mother was a bitch – never letting her do anything, go anywhere. Complaining if she came home late. And those farm boys – Oh! It made her skin creep just to think of them with their big teeth and unwashed hair. But now she was in the city, life would be different. Chosen as a Handmaiden to The Fiery Swan, Vesta. What more could a girl ask? Five years away in Al Faq'Al with other girls her own age, a dress allowance and music lessons. Frequent attendances at palace function and no end of young militia officers and the sons of artistocrats turning up at Vesta's ceremonies to see the Handmaidens dance. What a life! And if there were boring parts – like tuition from Brer Dryberg and a bunch of other smelly old men, well, that wasn't so bad, she could put up with it. He was still talking. Winolene took another turquoise delight and bit into it, delicately and making sure none of the powdered sugar got down her chin.

'Are you still faint? Quite a shock, I know. But nothing to worry about.'

Winolene had been quite shocked when the flash of blue had spun around her and even more so when the wizard – what a strange old man with his beard and funny hat – had said that Mindador was "bound up" in something or other. But Brer Dryberg had explained that it was just a Recognition spell placed on the coins that indicated they were intended for some high purpose and that, no doubt, there was some sacred purpose of the Goddess's to fulfil. Nothing more than that. And Mindador? Of course he was Recognised. Was he not a powerful mage and involved in matters of great moment? No, doubtless one of the Thalers was destined for the offertory in Vesta's temple and she, Winolene, should have the honour to carry it there and give it up to Vesta, for which she would receive much glory.

She had rallied after this farrago of loose logic, and Brer Dryberg had actually poured her a minute thimbleful of wine. Wine! If only they could see her at home, now that she was so free and sophisticated.

'But you came here to discuss your tuition, I know. It is typically the case that the Order provides a tutor in Religious Instruction for Vesta's Handmaidens. I fear, however, that it will not be possible on this occasion, all of our more senior Brers being fully occupied on other matters. That was why I asked Master Mindador to escort you here from the temple – he, I feel, is a worthy instructor for one of the Chosen.'

Winolene furtively wiped her sugary fingers on the couch and coughed slightly to cover the movement and the sound. 'Brer Dryberg, I am grateful to you for making these arrangements. Will my tuition be here? Or at the temple?'

'Oh, it is never at the temple. Our Order maintains a certain, um, distance when it comes to young ladies, especially those charming enough to be Chosen of Vesta. That is why only the more senior Brers, whose vows and piety are more securely founded, usually take tutorials, but always, always here at SamBernardo's. However...' he trailed off and reached for the box of sweetmeats.

'Yes?' Winolene prompted.

'Oh, I was just thinking. You have been put to considerable discomfort by today's events and by the rearrangements we have, reluctantly, been forced to make for your instruction, so might I suggest that as Master Mindador's, er, chambers are closer to your temple than SamBernardo's, it might be more convenient for you to take instruction there. Yes?'

'If the priestess allows it, Brer Dryberg. She is not favourably disposed to the... to that part of the city.'

'Yes, it is true, wizards do tend to congregate in the less sophisticated areas of our great capital. It is due, I am told, to their desire for quiet contemplation away from the distractions of more colourful districts. Some even live in caves, would you believe. But I feel sure your priestess will acquiesce when she knows whose tutee you are to be. Mindador is held in high regard by the Sisters. Now, you must have other things you wish to do on such a beautiful morning rather than listen to an old man. Enjoy your walk back to the temple, and remember to stay under the canopies.'

Winolene had taken her leave, curtsied in the approved manner and made suitably genteel comments about the soft furnishings in the Pryer's study. What a lot she had learned in her short weeks at the temple. As she sauntered back to the temple, enjoying the opportunity to look in the merchants' windows and haughtily dismiss the goods offered to her by street hawkers, she mused on how different her life would be when she left the temple, met a nice young palace guard officer or a rising tortiflexer and settled down. One thing was sure – she was never leaving Al Faq'Al and she was certainly never going back to the country, not until she could afford a cottage somewhere.

The city was in the fag end of a gay mood after the end of the recent Festival. Coloured banners were still on display and gaudy handbills promoting this or that entertainment were still stuck up on walls and tavern doors. Across the street a babbling, weeping Festival director was being dragged to the dungeons. Such a refined city, Winolene thought. And one month from tonight she would start her tuition in Religious Instruction with Mindador. He was old and a bit creepy, but it was only 13 times a year and perhaps he had a handsome apprentice.

Picture the scene. Through a cobwebby window there is a dark, smoke-filled room, eerily lit by the flickering of six candles, each one held in a severed hand placed at the point of a hexagon drawn in goat's blood. It's the same picture as before.

The last thing this picture needs is a four-armed dæmon appearing out of nowhere into a column of smoke swirling within the larger hexagon.

You got it.

Mindador turned a raised his scrawny arms at the huge, blue figure. Whatever it had below its waist was lost to view in the roiling mists. Each of its arms was folded across a massive chest above which were massive jowls from which protruded tusks, up and down, and two eyes of coal-ember red. Atop the head and surmounting the pointed ears was a chef's hat.

'O great dæmon. Attend to thy conjuror, the mighty one, who hast summoned thee here to answer three questions. I require of thee and command thee, give thy answers truly and without dissembling, ere thou art cast back into that nether-realm from which thou hast lately arisen and taken this form. And tell unto me, great one, the answers to my speirs, by Bal, by Bok and by Kendle.'

The dæmon raised his great head until it nearly touched the roof of Mindador's shack and opened its maw, the tusks glistening in the candle light. 'What's the recipe today, Jim?'

Mindador now looked directly at the dæmon. 'I abjure thee and conjure thee, by all the instruments of mine Art, thou knowest what it is I seek, now tell me where I might find it.'

'First, the Missing Ingredient, sorcerer.'

Mindador reached into his sleeve and drew out a rag roll which he proceeded to unwrap. 'Here is the last Relic of Um, which I will offer unto thee, great dæmon, in return for they answers. Speak, and await thy reward.'

'What was it you wanted to know?'

'Who will find that which I seek?'

'Three times three times three nights from tonight, take one wizard. Spin until giddy. Raise to a high dudgeon. And put to one side.'

'How will he find it?'

'Place all the mixture in a cart lined with straw and set it off at a steady pace, until done.'

'Where will he quest?'

'Empty onto a flat surface, then leave to cool overnight. Next day, put in a high place. Now, my missing ingredient!'

Mindador unwrapped the Relic and threw it to the dæmon, who caught it with three of his hands. It was a foot. 'Tasty,' he boomed.

Mindador threw a handful of sulphurous powder into the dæmon's smoke. 'One last boon, O mighty spirit. Tell what it is that thou shalt do with the Last Relic of Um.'

'Nice shortcrust pastry and some onion gravy, I think,' and with that the dæmon licked its lips with two tongues simultaneously and disappeared with a noise that sounded like a huge oven door shutting, which is exactly what is was. The smoke cleared and as the first fingers of dawn crept over the sill of the grimy window, the candles blew out.

No sign of a handsome apprentice, you'll notice.

CHAPTER THE FOURTH

In which Slouch learns more of Magick and even more of the nature of Vizagriz. There are sundry dark conjurations, unfortunately.

When I got back from the big Tyr's Day shopping to Vizagriz's cottage in Hanging Basket Street he was happily boiling up his cauldron, humming to himself.

'Get everything?' he shot across his shoulder at me.

I hesitated. This wasn't going to be pretty. 'Not really. The apothecary's all out of Wort and can't get Lizard Gizzard. Not your brand, anyway.'

Vizagriz spun around. 'Can't get Gizzard? Rubbish!'

'Says his supplier let him down. Didn't have Newt eyes either. Just toad, and you don't like toad.'

'Why not? Why no Newt Eyes? Newts being born blind all of a sudden?'

'Gets a delivery on Mondays, but this week being a holiday, the cart didn't come.'

'Oh dear. What about the Mandrake roots?'

'Normally he says yes, today there's none left.'

'And the Unicorn Hoof?'

'There's... been a run on it.' Even I winced.

'The Viper Venom? Any Viper Venom?'

'Well, he sort of sucked through his teeth and said "Arm and a leg job, sunshine". Apparently he'll order it special if you leave a deposit but he can't keep a big stock, prices being what they are just now.'

Vizagriz slumped down in a chair, resignedly. Equally resignedly, the chair slumped up to meet him. 'The green bile of dragon? He MUST have green bile of dragon!'

'Seems I'm the fourth apprentice he's told today, there's no call for it.'

'Oh. come on! Everybody uses green bile of dragon.'

'Not round here, apparently. They've all moved on to Gryphon Essence.'

'Gryphon Essence? That synthetic rubbish?'

'Yes, but he gets it on keg, and there's no wastage.'

'Good grief. So what DID he have?'

'He said he could do you a favour on some nearly-new almost-out-of-sell-by-date Snark Bladder. If you wanted it bulk."

'I'll bet he could. I'll just bet he could. Nobody's used Snark since the Death Wars. He probably thought he could get clever and corner the market and now he's stuck with a ton of the stuff. Well he's not offloading it on me, that's for sure! So what DID you manage to get?'

'I got pigsease and shaved batfur.'

'Better than nowt, I suppose. Not better than newt, though. How much was the pigsease?'

'Er, a quarter-Thaler the firkin...'

'A WHOLE QUARTER???' He really did put a row of question marks after it, or at least it sounded like he did. 'But you can get it for eight dinars a can down the road at Unsafe Way!'

'Ah. Well. He explained that to me. Seems they can buy cans in bulk, what with them having the shelf space, but he has to have tankerfuls and it's more expensive. Something about the purchasing power of big multiples, but I didn't really catch it.'

Vizagriz harrumphed a bit, and went back to his cauldron, which was stirring itself doggedly in the absence of his guiding hand.

'Oh,' I said, in an attempt to brighten him up, although I shouldn't have bothered really. 'I got powdered stinkhorn mustard and rancid Yak butter.'

'Tremendous,' said Vizagriz sourly. 'So if the Dark One comes round we can always slap a poultice on him. Never mind, though,' he sighed, 'I've probably got enough of the necessary for this spell at least. What we'll do if there's a sudden call for exorcisms is anybody's guess. Did you get down the necromancers' chandler? Or isn't anyone planning to die in the near future?'

Sarcasm. Always a bad sign. 'Yes, I did. I got most of it.'

'Such as...?'

'Well, I thought you wouldn't want the gunpowder he got in a fire sale.' Vizagriz closed his eyes and inhaled slowly. 'So I stocked up on Babywax candles, Blind Eyes and Dead Man's Hands. We were almost out of them.'

'OK. Not to worry. Not your fault. Where's the change?' He held out a claw-like hand. Old skinflint.

'Er...,' I shuffled.

'There IS change, isn't there?'

'Well, not as such.'

Vizagriz fixed me with a steely glare. 'You haven't been down that "What The Scryer Saw" parlour, have you?'

'No.'

'Or bought any of them "Magick Beans" again? I told you about Magick Beans. Damn near had the roof off last time!'

'No, but there isn't any change. The Dead Man's Hands were expensive. A Florin each.'

I thought he'd explode. 'A FLORIN?! They were three sesterts last month!'

'Seems that was a limited offer while stocks lasted. They come dearer now. Not so much thieving going on these days, so his supply's cut off, as it were. And the Grinch talon flake is out of season so it has to come from the Howling Desert.'

'Yes there bloody well is thieving going on, and it's all down at those shops! Oooo, that Apothecary. Just 'cause he's got a captive market. The sooner one of the big SuperPotion places opens up, the better. He won't know what's hit him, grasping little sod. I've a good mind to pop down there and turn all his Spanish Fly into itching powder. "Howling desert" indeed! He grows it all down his mum's allotment in the Garden Suburb Quarter, cheeky beggar.'

Vizagriz kicked the table leg, and didn't even flinch when he did more damage to himself than to the furniture, which simply hitched up its coverlet, moved a few inches away and settled down again with a rustling noise that indicated no more than mild irritation.

'Anyway. Better get to bed. Busy day tomorrow,' Vizagriz said. He looked somewhat distracted.

'Tomorrow? Wodin's Day? What's happening on Wodin's Day?' I was genuinely puzzled.

'What week is it?'

'Third Week. Constellation of Cuckoo.'

'Right. And what happened a month ago yesterday?'

'I was – Oh my Deity!'

'That's right. Tomorrow night is a month from when you met The Dark and Stormy Knight. And he said...'

'He said, "Be back here to get a message for Vizagriz in a month's time", or something like that.'

'Right. And what else did he say? Hmm?'

'He said, "Don't make me come looking for you." I remember that bit very clearly, now you mention it.'

'It's good advice,' said Vizagriz. 'And I don't want him coming round here, either. There's enough trouble with evil entities trying to get in from the oxterworld without bringing mystical messengers along as well. I'm still annoyed that Recognition went off from here when I touched the gold Thaler. They've got my address now.'

'Is that a problem?' I asked, genuinely interested and genuinely worried. Vizagriz looked worried, too.

'Not as such. But once they know where you are they tend to keep coming to ask you to do things. I'll get no peace. Old friend of mine, Greyshanks, got noticed by some Higher Plane and they were never off his back. "Go on this quest" and "Recover these precious jewels" and "Seek that hidden temple". Never let up. Poor old sod's life was a misery. Never at home, business fell to bits. Wasn't good for his health, either.'

'Where is he now?'

'Most of him is in a basket chair at his sister's. Bits of him are in various nether-realms. Still, he can always look at the pile of treasure he got on his various adventures. Only trouble is, he can't spend it.'

'Why not?'

'There's nothing he could buy that would make sense to any part of him that still works, and he can't even walk to the shops any more. That, plus the drooling – well, it wasn't much of a pension plan, was it. That's the trouble with treasure – it looks nice and sounds like a great idea, but you rarely get the chance to enjoy it. Ever wondered why wizards aren't rich?'

'I always thought you had eschewed the petty and venal in the quest for higher enlightenment.'

Vizagriz chuckled. 'Oh, dear. Dear, dear, dear. That's a good one. There's nothing any of us would like more than a pile of gold, jewels and valuable statuary lying about the house. Not worth the trouble, though.'

'Why not?'

'Well, first, it tends to belong to something else, who generally regards it as a bit of a cheek that a wizard took it and is prepared to spend a considerable portion of eternity getting it back. Second, why do people go looking for treasure?'

'Because they want it?' I ventured.

'Correct. And if I had some, a lot of people would want to get their hands on that, wouldn't they? There'd be no end of heroes, adventurers, renegade sorcerers and the like turning up trying to get it off me. And third, with every gain, there's a loss. With every acquisition, there's a price to pay. In Greyshanks' case it was his mind and a few useful bits of his anatomy. Not worth it.'

'I see,' I said.

'You don't,' he declared. 'You think you do, but you don't. The fact is, there's only a certain amount of treasure and precious stuff in existence and all it does is get recycled every so often. We're all chasing a bit of a finite amount. Stands to reason there's more wanted than can go around, so there's an everlasting round of moving it about. That's what makes adventures. And that's what makes heroes.'

I had heard of heroes. Who hadn't? Strong, tall, brave, good with a sword, handy with the distressed maidens, firm of purpose and hardy of resolve. There were even illustrated stories which went about among the younger catamites-in-training at SamBernardo's that told of the exploits of such valiant heroes as Rupert of Henzo and Fierce Harold. I said as much.

Vizagriz snorted. 'Well, you haven't met one yet, is all I can say. Mostly they're just a bunch of lads who were good at sports and not much else and got persuaded there was a life of adventure out there if they could find it. So they spend their time chasing about at the behest of cowards who wouldn't go on a quest for anything and getting caught up in cosmic events far beyond their none too fertile imaginations. In fact, imagination is a bit of drawback for a hero. If they ever thought about what they were doing, they'd stop it and go and curl up under a bush for a good cry. They tend to be as thick as pig muck and similarly odoured. All those months stuck to a horse without the benefit of clean water.'

I wasn't having any of this. Heroes were, well, they were heroes. They did good, brave things. They dispatched dæmons and mad priests. The dispensed with fell, tomb-guarding monsters. They made the world a safer place for ordinary mortals. Didn't they?

'Don't worry. Before this is over, you'll get to meet a hero or two, I'm sorry to say. Then you can tell me what you really think. Now, it's time you prepared an infusion of dried thea leaves mixed with the fluid of a lactating cow and stirred with a cane stick.'

'You mean, make the tea?'

'That's right. But don't forget the jargon. That's what the public pays for. Now make the tea, then get off to bed. Tomorrow night's Watching Hour is when it all happens. I can't wait.' And he threw a stick in the fire which said, "Thanks".

I spent the rest of that night tossing and sweating, unable to sleep and dreading the next day's approach. My mind flickered constantly replaying the events of the last month, a month in which my life changed forever. A mere twenty-seven days and I had gone from the misery of SamBernardo's with its all-too-predictable future to meeting a mysterious armoured giant of immense significance, becoming apprenticed to a wizard and seeing my beloved Winolene. Not a day had gone past when I had not thought of her lovely face and radiant aspect. Vizagriz had said we would meet again, since the Recognition had bound her to us in some way. It was just about the only thing that had kept me going, that and my apprentice training. Together they stopped me dwelling on the implications of my next conversation with the Dark and Stormy Knight. Vizagriz had kept me busy, no doubt about that. I had learned how to make the simpler potions, mastered the business of getting in and out of the door (not a bad piece of carpentry when you got to know him, if a bit lippy) and started on the long path to understanding Extropy, the core principle of Magick.

I had also begun to read some of the more straightforward grimoires, although they were written in such flowery and abstruse language that wrestling any meaning out of them was like drawing teeth with a hand saw. Vizagriz explained that if it was easy, anybody could do it and they wouldn't need wizards. There was a union, after all.

And last, I had listened to Vizagriz, in the nights when we sat around the fire, explain the construction of eternity with its many layers of planes, realms, other worlds and wormwhorls. I sometimes felt I would never understand any of it, as it seemed to be both simple – everything and everywhere was in the same place, at the same time, all at once and you were only walking along it in a certain way – and complex, too. It appeared that every so often, or if someone made it so, various aspects of eternity would rub up against each other and the friction would weaken the fabric of whatever was holding them apart, like the elbow of an old shirt that eventually gives way to let your arm out into the fresh air. Much of a wizard's time was spent either making such portways open, shutting them for people who were frightened of what they had glimpsed through them, or putting up defences so that they couldn't happen. The door to Vizagriz's cottage was a sort of standing portway on a slack hinge that could be opened easily. Mostly it only went to places nearby so it didn't take much Extropy to open or shut it. But every so often it got itself a bit too close to a similar opening in the oxterworld or a nether-realm and Vizagriz spend whole days at times, keeping it closed and shouting at the occasional thing that tried the handle just on the off chance. We didn't get much other work done on those days and no-one could find the cottage since the door was fairly busy keeping itself locked and hidden.

I didn't make head or tail of this on most of the evenings, and my concentration wasn't helped by a fire that kept interrupting to ask for more coal or "Could you just poke this bit at the back? Ahh. That's better. Thanks", and the like.

And again, my thoughts strayed back to Winolene. I knew there was no hope of us ever becoming close – she was Handmaiden to the Fiery Swan, Vesta, which meant that she would spend the next few years reciting the rituals of the Goddess, keeping the temple fires lit, learning a couple of foreign languages and the right way to get out of a cart with your knees together and how to throw a dinner party for 600. Suitably refined, she would marry some country artistocrat or a court official and settle down to a comfortable if dull life in the Garden Suburb with regular holidays abroad and a third of a cat.

Still, I lived for the moment when I would see her again. If I could be a hero, I might throw her over the back of my charger and whisk her off to an exotic land where we would besiege a high castle and install ourselves as Margrave and Margravine and spend the rest of our lives... well, I wasn't quite sure what we would do, since our education at SamBernardo's had tended not to dwell on what possibilities there were with females, but I was sure it would be Jolly Nice, whatever it was. Occasionally I felt a vague stirring low in my stomach when I thought about her. Vizagriz had noticed this and suggested peppermint tea and a cold bath.

Eventually, I must have fallen into a fitful sleep and I woke even more tired than when I had gone to bed the previous evening. I could hear movement in another room and leapt out of bed and into my clothes. It set Vizagriz in a foul temper for the day if I wasn't up before him, not that it happened often. Much of a wizard's work happened at the dead of night and most of his customers came when it was dark, especially the ones who wanted something doing to someone else and would rather not be seen consulting a wizard about it. The door seemed to know when there was a customer on the way and made itself appear just as they were passing. I often wondered if all the doors in Hanging Basket Street did this and whether there was any jostling, or some sort of rota.

I sped to the parlour and found Vizagriz up before his habitual noon-time rising. He didn't look like he had had much sleep either. He was stirring a kettle and frying eggs, or at least, he was watching while those things did it themselves. He turned when he heard me.

'Come in, lad. Have some breakfast.'

I started to mumble an apology about my tardiness but Vizagriz brushed it aside and said it didn't matter, he hadn't gone to bed and I needed my rest, growing boy like me. This was uncharacteristically benign, especially for a morning, and I wondered what was up.

When the tea and eggs were ready I served them up and we sat munching and slurping for a while until I broke the silence.

'What do you want me to do today?' I asked.

'Tidy up, I think.'

'Tidy up?'

'Yes. I hate to say it, but it looks like I might be going away for a while and it would be an idea to get everything in its right place for once. You might wash out the cauldron while you're at it. I don't see it getting a lot of use for a bit. Now get on with it. I'm off out.'

I was slightly uneasy about this news. Tonight I was supposed to meet the Knight and get a message for Vizagriz. Surely whatever it was the Knight had to tell the wizard would involve him casting some spells or at the very least making a potion. So why was he planning to go away? The thought struck me that Vizagriz had expressed on more than one occasion his unwillingness to take any part in whatever the Knight was going to tell him and that he might skip town and lie low for a while. On the other hand, he had warned me not to miss the meeting and had also said to Master Mindador that there was no point in trying to avoid the issue. So what was happening?

I sighed and got stuck into the cleaning and tidying. At least, I thought, it would take my mind off things. It didn't, much.

Imagine luxury. Now turn up the contrast a bit and throw in a handful of sybaritic over-indulgence. And plush. Don't forget the plush. It's a strange thing, but if you took all the elegant statuary you could find, every really good picture, exquisite drapes, tapestries and floor coverings and about as much silk as would float a battle-barque, and put it all in one place, it would look, well, naff.

That is precisely what had happened in the private chambers of the High Priestess of Vesta. An excess of exuberance over taste and the use of just about every pastel shade either side of the rainbow combined to produce an effect reminiscent of the more memorable migraines that happen the morning after the lost weekend before.

Strangely, Brer Dryberg looked at home in these bizarre surroundings, recumbent on a couchette and helping himself, delicately, to a pink grape or three.

'So you see, Sister, she is perfect. Just as you said.'

'Indeed. And what of the mage? Will he play his part?'

'He already has. Two of his three conjurations have taken place. There is one left, a scrying, which happens this evening, I believe, this being a Wodin's Day and fatefully aspected. I know little of Magick and like it even less, but it is essential to this enterprise, I fear.'

'Does he suspect?'

'He knows only what he needs to know. And little does he know what is in store for him. He, too, is dispensable.'

'And the other one?'

'Ah. Him I did not anticipate. But doubtless he has a part to play or is so insignificant that his involvement will cause barely a ripple. I incline to the latter opinion. All that matters is that he does not suspect our involvement.'

'Until it is too late.'

'Precisely. Now, if you will forgive me, there is much to do.'

'I shall see to it that she attends.'

'Kindly do so.'

The day had passed slowly in the cottage of Vizagriz. I had washed everything I could find that needed it, cleaned the windows, brushed out all six corners, persuaded the chairs to move so I could get under them and put most of the pots and jars in more or less the right places, which they finished off by jostling and clattering a bit until they felt settled.

I had also watered the window box Vizagriz had started. This was one of his minor obsessions – growing mystical plants from a small bag of earth in the comfort of your own home. Vizagriz was so hacked off at being held to ransom by the apothecaries and herbalists every time he wanted some fresh spelladonna or a bit of cursely root that he had decided to see if he could turn the cultivation of such things into a cottage industry. The idea was, he could subcontract the putting of seeds into bags of soil to one of the market gardens that surrounded the city and have them sent out as the requests flooded in. Sort of a Mage-order business, he called it.

He hadn't been all that happy with the name he had thought of for this enterprise – he wanted to put a drawing of a pretty young witch on each packet and call it "Grow-Hag" but he felt it didn't quite, you know, say it all. I had suggested Abraculture and he professed himself delighted with this, so much so that he promptly forgot it had been anyone's idea but his own. As he explained to me, names were important in Magick. Because when you know the true and secret name of something you have power over it? I had ventured. Sort of, he had replied. It's called a Trade Mark and if you think dealing with a wizard is complex and fraught with hazard, you haven't been on the bad end of a writ from a copyright tortiflexer. They could sort it out once the business got going and he'd never have to actually do anything but count the proceeds.

He never got much further with it than experimenting with various combinations of soil from graveyards, peat from the Dead Marshes and Howling Desert sand but he swore the local herbalist gave him a real sideways look every time he went in as if to say, "I know what you're up to, sunbeam. and don't think you can break the monopoly". In fact Sprig, the local herbalist in question, had a wall eye and he gave everyone that same look. He couldn't help it. Nevertheless, it had to served to fuel both Vizagriz's sense of commercial paranoia and his delight at possibly putting one over a grasping tradesman, so he kept pretending he was just about to launch his marvellous product on an unsuspecting but likely-to-be-eternally-grateful world.

By the time I had finished the chores, Vizagriz was back and complaining for his supper. I had started a stew which he accepted with less than the usual quota of bad grace. After that he made the cauldron do the washing up and told me to sit by the fire for a while.

I drew up a six-legged stool by the ingle and sat, lost in my own thoughts and staring at the flames, which occasionally waved back and called 'Yoo-hoo' or something like it.

After a time Vizagriz put down the almanack he had been studying – or at least checking out the small ads for "Wizards Wanted" – and looked up. 'Ten minutes to Watching Hour, boy. You'd best be off. Now do you remember where you met him?'

'Halfway up Pally Alley, near the sign of the Neutered Newt.'

'Right. Let me know what happens. Cheerio.'

I had expected more of a send off, considering I was probably about to meet my doom. On the other hand, I was only supposed to relay a message back to Vizagriz and I'd have to be alive to do that, wouldn't I? Well, wouldn't I? Course I would. No problem. Off we go then. Wait a minute. Have I been to the loo? Best go, never know how long I ...'

'ARE YOU STILL HERE?' And I wasn't.

Picture the scene. Yes, it's the same one again – cobwebby window, dark, smoke-filled room, eerily lit blah blah, severed hands and a hexagon. Mindador cackling. But there's a subtle difference – another person is in the room with him, human this time and intact thus far.

This person is reading from a book and looks a tad uncomfortable at the proximity of the hexagon. Interior decor is not Mindador's strong point, was the thought that occurred. And the candles might be quaint-olde-worldy but they didn't add to the visibility of the crabbed, fading script in the book. Mindador sat in a rocking chair, fingers pressed together and eyes closed in concentration while the other read aloud.

'And shew unto me all manner of things, I, the great harus... haruspex, who commands all sight and all seeing, here and now, in the Eye of Wodin that seethes...'

'Seeth. See. Eth.'

'... that seeth all past, all future and the mote of time that doth separate them, O great ones, all-knowing ones, whose fingers weave the warp of the gyrations into the weft of the material world, bring unto me the wisdom of The Two, despoilers of ambition, levellers of all who would raise themselves high, look, I'm sorry, but isn't the hour up yet, only I'm due at Watching Hour choir practice.'

Mindador breathed out, hard, like he had been caught halfway through something he was quite enjoying. 'It is important to finish the passage. So that you get the entire drift. From "levellers" please.'

'Absolutely. Sorry. Levellers of all who would raise themselves high...'

As the monotonous reading went on, in a dark, sixth corner of the room a small whirlpool was starting to form. At first it blew some specks of dust around. Then it gathered speed, strength and size and took in some feathers and scraps of paper, gaining momentum as it went and becoming more visible. It changed from a milky whiteness to a smoky grey and continued to swirl ever faster, but noiselessly.

'Bring forth the Pool of Peering, the Eddy of Enlightenment, the Current of Consciousness that we may scry from its heart the knowing of imports. Imports? Like foreign goods?'

'Imports. Knowing of imports. Important things.'

'Thank you. Current, scry, heart, knowing of imports, here we are, the knowing of imports and the ways yet to be that are not yet to be but may be, and from whence cometh the light that will light our path to the days before this day and the days before us, and in that knowing, oh sorry, nearly yawned there, in that knowing...'

Hanging Basket Street is not far from Pally Alley as the crow would fly if crows were stupid enough to be caught around that part of town, but I took some of the back streets and vennels, avoiding the taverns it was best not to pass in case a flying body landed on you or you got showered by broken glass. I reached the corner of Pally Alley and stopped, peering round it to see if there was anyone or anything there. The street was empty and I made my way, very gingerly, towards the boarded-up shop that had one been the Neutered Newt. This part of Pally Alley had a lot of boarded-up places. No-one came here unless they had to so it wasn't the most profitable place for a merchant to have a store. It was highly profitable place, however, for that section of the populace that believed merchants' stores were fair game for a bit of after-hours private shopping, which also contributed to its demise as a thriving trading district.

Now, most of the buildings were cheap flop-houses or rent-by-the-week hovels inhabited by the likes of Master Mindador, recipient of Brer Dryberg's parcel on that fateful evening 28 days before.

But I was the only living thing in Pally Alley at that time. And suddenly I wasn't. Standing before me, just as before and twice as terrible, was the Dark and Stormy Knight. Again, that iron-shod voice rasped out at me in a dreadful déjà vu. 'Be you Slouch?'

'Err, if it please Your Lordship, yes. I am Slouch.'

'Slouch, apprentice to Vizagriz, wizard of this parish?'

'Yes, may't please Your Honour.'

'Bang on. At last. You will deliver your prentice-master this message. Just a minute. There's two wizards down here by the look.' He was consulting a piece of paper no larger than an official stamp. 'Bit hard to read. Wait, though. I've got Recognitions on a wizard, another wizard with a different postcode, a girl and... Nope, that's all so far. What are we light on, let's see.' The PhilosoPhax flipped open and he thumbed through a few of the pages. 'Right. Here we are. No, wait a minute, that's "Quaffing - 100 Good Places To Get Korian Lager". Ah. Quests. Right. Fine. Wizard, wizard, girl, hero, player, imp and...'

'Scribe,' said a voice at my back. I spun around and saw Vizagriz standing there, holding an identical PhilosoPhax, the one he had shown me in his library that fateful night the constellation before.

'Scribe, right. That's the one. And who might you be?'

'I might be anyone at all. I happen to be Vizagriz, the wizard who wants to know what in the oxterworld you are doing with a PhilosoPhax open at the page starting with "Quest ".'

'Quest?' I said, but nobody heard me, apparently.

'I am the Herald of Great Events. I have to know what's going on, don't I? How can I Herald if I don't know what's an Event and how Great it is?'

'Not if you're going to start shaping things, you don't. Your part in the scheme, I always thought, was to turn up and tell someone that something was going to happen, could they stay in next Moons' Day evening. Not, most definitely, not to start moving things along. What is going on?'

'This is too important, wizard. It cannot go wrong. So I have been entrusted with The Book in order that I can get the right people together in order to complete the Quest.'

'Quest?' I repeated. Nobody was listening to me, again.

'Who sent you?'

'Both of them. Now, you only have half of your other Questers and time presses. Here is your message - find the Holy Quail. That's it. I may appear a third and final time.' And with that he drew himself up straight, pressed a sigil on his armoured wrist and stood there with his hands on his hips. He stood like this, and we stood watching him stood like this, for a goodly few moments, until he said, 'Oh, come ON!' and pressed the sigil again, after which he disappeared - or rolled up would be a better description. It was as if he were painted on a kind of three-dimensional roller blind and someone had just pulled the cord. I mentioned this to Vizagriz some time later and he told me that was more or less exactly what had happened.

I was still standing, a bit shocked by the events of the past few minutes, when Vizagriz's voice pulled me back to reality. 'Come on,' he said. 'It looks like there's more to do than I thought.'

'He said there's a quest,' I gasped. 'Are we going on a quest?'

'It rather looks like it. That's what all of these Recognitions have been about. I thought my part in this was just to receive a message but no, that would be too simple. I've got go rush off on some fool's errand with a bunch of other idiots and we'll probably all get ourselves killed. Terrific!'

'A quest! We're going on a quest!' I almost shouted for joy - this was the stuff of stories. 'And Mindador and Winolene are coming with us!' I thought my heart would burst.

'Mindador will be pleased. And I doubt that Handmaiden'll be much of an asset unless we run out of easily-washable kitchenware or need a fete organised. Anyway, who said you were going?'

I stopped in my tracks. It took me a few minutes to review the list of Questers the Herald had intoned - wizard, wizard, girl, hero, player, imp, scribe. Not a mention of an apprentice or the Stooge Eternal.

Vizagriz watched me standing gape-mouthed and his face softened slightly. 'Look at it this way - did anything happen when you touched those coins?'

I had to confess it hadn't. No Recognition. No spark of light shooting skywards. No quest for Slouch.

'Then think yourself lucky. If you're not officially one of the Questers, it's unlikely you'll come to any harm. And I suppose I'll need an apprentice to wash my socks whatever happens.'

'You mean, you mean I can go on the quest?'

'Well I'm certainly not leaving you alone in my cottage. Deity knows what you'll break, clumsy oaf. Good thing you tidied up, though.'

Vizagriz turned and strode off towards Hanging Basket Street and I skipped along after, light as a feather. I was going on a quest. And Winolene, lovely Winolene, was coming too.

My elation was to be short lived. As we neared the end of Pally Alley we heard a piercing scream ring out from the window we were just passing. Had we not been there I dare say it would have gone unnoticed, or at least unheeded. A scream in that part of the Porter Quarter tended to make anyone within hearing pull their hats a little closer over their ears and walk a shade more quickly in a non-controversial direction.

'What the...,' Vizagriz said as he peered in the window and the next moment he was shouting 'Stand back, Slouch,' and blasting the door down with a bolt from his staff. We burst into the mean shack and saw Mindador, looking over his shoulder at us in a look that combined surprise, annoyance and not a little malice. On the other side of the room was Winolene, my heart's desire, holding a book to her chest and screaming. Between them was what looked like a big, dusty whirlpool, its eddies whipping everything in the room, including Mindador's robe and the hems of Winolene's petticoats.

'Not now, wizard, not NOW!' Mindador shouted but it was too late. Vizagriz had strode across the room, grabbed Winolene by the arm and raised his staff to the roof of the hovel when he suddenly stopped, gazed into the centre of whorl and exclaimed, 'You fool, Mindador. It's not a scrying pool, it's...'

The rest happened in a bit of a rush. One moment I was in Mindador's shack and the next I was either falling or flying, feeling burning hot or searing cold and myself shouting or silent. I was conscious of a whistling noise and the whoosh of wind and somewhere, very far away, a girl screaming and a panicked voice hastily reciting a chant.

And then, I seemed to be lying still.

CHAPTER THE FIFTH

In which there is much camping out, of divers kinds, and Slouch comes to realise that a Quest is not all frolics and bunting.

I lay for a while, trying to make the sounds I heard around me into some sort of sense. There was the dull thumping coming from what I hoped was my own heart. There was a groaning, keening sound off to the left. And somewhere in the distance, birds singing. The next noise I became aware of made absolute sense, however. It was Vizagriz swearing.

I opened my eyes and saw an unbroken swathe of blue. For a moment I just knew I had landed at the bottom of the sea. But as the feeling returned to my frozen limbs and I raised myself up on one elbow I could see that it was, in fact, the sky. And I was viewing it from the top of a haystack. Turning my head – no mean feat and accompanied by lots of worrying crackly sound effects – brought into sight three other pairs of legs. The purple pointy shoes sticking out of the robe and waving undoubtedly belonged to my prentice-master. The stick-like legs with studded leather boots and unmatched socks were a mystery. But the yards and yards of what appeared to be an explosion in a petticoat factory with a pair of white hose and red slippers in the middle could only be...

'Winolene!' I exclaimed. 'Are you all right?'

I scrabbled across the hay and dug about until I found something that felt like a hand and gave it as large a tug as I could muster. It was followed by a cross-looking face surmounted by an equal amount of golden hair and golden straws, so intimately intermingled that it looked like the halfway point in a goblin's spinning evening.

My mind heard words like "Oh, Slouch, my hero", and "Rescued – now I am yours forever". My ears, however, only caught "Oooooohhh! GetOFFmeyouoaf!"

I was taken somewhat aback. On the other hand, she had had a bit of a shock, poor thing, and was allowed to be a bit disoriented. I reached out my hand again to help

Winolene get herself a bit more upright, but it was slapped away. 'Ruined! My best walking-out dress. Just LOOK at it!'

Wait till you see the hair, was my uncharitable thought but before I could muster any kind of response I was assailed by Vizagriz's shouts and curses. 'I'll kill him. I'll pummel him to dust. I'll have his ears for a bow tie. I'll...'

I didn't know if I was the intended recipient of the wizard's close attention but to put myself in a better bargaining position just in case, I scrambled over to Vizagriz and started separating him from the hay. 'Master. All you all right?'

'All right? I'll be all right when I mollicate that pratt Mindador. Where is he? Let me get my hands on him!'

Mindador, by this time, has extricated himself and was sitting up, head in hands, carrying on with the groaning and keening.

'Mindador? What in the nether-realms did you think you were playing at? Where the blazes have you taken us to? Come over here and I'll pull the answers out of your head directly. I'll...' But it's hard to maintain a threatening attitude when you keep falling back into a pile of dried grass.

'Look. A ladder,' I said, more by way of calming things down than anything else. I had indeed spotted a ladder perched against the rick and headed for it. 'Come, Winolene. I'll help you down.'

'I should think so. Then you can jolly well find me a carriage to get me back to the temple and as quick as you like. The Priestess will writing to someone about this, I can tell you!'

Winolene shuffled across the hay stack and sat at the top of the ladder. 'Well?' she exclaimed.

'Yes, I'm all right, bit of a stiff neck, but...'

'I mean, HELP ME DOWN. Good grief!'

I took her hand and held it as tight as I felt was justified while she warily put her dainty feet on the rungs of the ladder and tried to get her dress and petticoats to behave themselves at the back. It took a while but she finally touched the ground and started dusting herself off, muttering imprecations about what her father wouldn't do to whoever had drugged her, carried her off and held her captive on a farm, of all places.

Meanwhile, back at the top of the hay stack, Vizagriz had got his hands around Mindador's throat and was shaking his head to see if it rattled. 'Master,' I said, 'come down. Here's a ladder.'

Vizagriz obviously decided that murder was more easily attempted if the feet were placed firmly on the ground, same distance apart as the shoulders, so he threw Mindador off and started to climb down. By the time he had checked his dignity and I had coaxed Mindador down from his perch, things had calmed down a bit. Winolene was picking stuff out of her hair and still fuming. Vizagriz was breathing through his nostrils and glaring at Mindador. The elderly thaumaturge was leaning against the ladder, wheezing and looking very sorry for himself. 'Where are we?' he asked, of no-one in particular.

'Well, call me an old silly, but as your damned whirlpool got us here I thought you might be able to tell us where here is, what happened and what you fondly imagined you were playing at, you idiot. What on earth was going on back in that rat-hole of yours? And what was this, this, girl doing there? What's she doing here? More to the pint, what am I doing here? I'll kill him, I will, I'll...'

I managed to hold Vizagriz back long enough for Mindador to get his breath back a bit and hold up a placatory hand.

'I'm sorry, I'm sorry. I don't know what went wrong. We were just reading, when this, this thing appeared out of nowhere and the next thing I knew...'

'Bollocks!' shouted Vizagriz. 'That was a wormwhorl. You don't just whisk them up with an egg-beater and a nursery rhyme. What were you trying to do?'

Mindador looked even more miserable than ever, if such a thing were possible, and slumped to the ground.

'It was just a scrying charm, that was all. The Lady Winolene was reciting some passages for me, and I thought it might be an idea to show her what the end result was, and...' He tailed off, somewhat lamely.

'Double bollocks!' He started counting off on his fingers about an inch from Mindador's unhappy countenance. 'You've got, one, an incantation of power; two, a virgin doing it; and three, let me look at the soles of your boots, come on, thought so, iron studs, three, some grounding so you don't get caught by the static. You horrible little man, you were trying Black Harry's Cyclone, weren't you?'

'No, I swear, I just wanted to look and see where the... where it went to.'

'Rubbish. That was no scrying. What was she doing there otherwise?'

Winolene suddenly realised she was the centre of attention again and rose to Mindador's defence, bless her.

'Now just a minute. Master Mindador is my tutor, so don't you go shouting at him. We were doing some Religious Instruction when you barged in, frightening people. I shouldn't but wonder if you caused, well, whatever it is that's been caused, and I'll see to it that the militia knows that you go around battering doors in at the Watching Hour.'

Vizagriz looked over at her and sucked his teeth. 'Young lady, the least you say the better. You have no idea what you're in here, or how far up to your lacy things you're in it.

This old buzzard was using you to open a wormwhorl.'

'I beg your pardon! I'll thank you not to talk to a Chosen Handmaiden that way. And tell this peasant to keep his grimy hands off my dress.'

'Only trying to help,' I protested, but I stuck my hands in my pockets in any case.

'It's all right my dear,' Mindador interjected, regaining some of his composure at least. 'I'm sure there has been some sort of honest mistake and we can sort it out. I assure you, if I though for one minute you would come to any harm from the incantation I would not have had you read it. As it is...'

'As it is, we're goodness knows where, goodness knows when and we're going to do goodness knows what,' said Vizagriz, summing up our situation admirably. 'Now, since you clearly haven't got the wits of a gnat, you better tell me as much as you know so that we can work out what's best. First, what was the incantation?'

'It was a passage from the GoodSpells. The bit where Merillion scrys his future. You know, Book of Fish, Chapter eight...'

'Verses 23 to 49. Right. And what was in your mind at the time?'

'I was just thinking of a project I have on just now. Nothing important, really.'

'Project? What kind of project?'

'More of a commission really. To find something. Nothing important, honest, just a lost trinket.'

'Fine. So the chances are, Black Harry's Cyclone would have opened up to the place where this... trinket... is lost.'

'Possibly, but I can't be sure. It was an accident.'

'My eye. You get a virgin, a cyclone, a GoodSpell and a pair of tacketty boots together and it's a recipe for something more than a squint into the middle distance. Something went wrong though, you're right about that. You shouldn't have been sucked into it, only her. And certainly not us. I don't suppose... No, even you wouldn't have been that stupid.'

'Just a minute. What do mean "only her"?' Winolene was back on the case and keeping up better than I was, that's for sure. 'Sucked into what? Come on. My father will want to know all this when he gets his tortiflexer onto it.'

Vizagriz looked up at the sky, than at the ground, then at Winolene. 'All right, I was trying to spare you this. You were duped. Black Harry's Cyclone can only be called up by a pure maiden and someone, usually the maiden herself because it saves on the staff costs if she does both jobs, gets taken by it. It's a wormwhorl, you see. A portway to another place and/or time. And it can only be collapsed by throwing a body into it. However, it seems to have got a bit out of hand, wouldn't you say, Mindador? A bit stronger than you meant? And something else went wrong, didn't it?'

'I can't think of anything. Honest.' It was a bit lame, though.

'No? I can. There are only three things that can go wrong. One is that someone else is getting a wormwhorl up next door and the two of them meet and start practising their knots. I don't imagine anyone else in Pally Alley was at it just then. So my first suspicion must be right. You haven't been... you have, haven't you?'

'Well, about a month ago I did, yes.'

'And you didn't fumigate? Honestly. You shouldn't be let out.'

'What?' I inquired. 'What else went wrong?'

'You tell him,' said Vizagriz and sat down to think.

'Well, wormwhorls can go wrong if there's any residual essence from, well, certain entities hanging around.'

'Tell him!'

'Dæmons. If there's been a dæmon in the vicinity and his presence is still palpable, it can, sort of, amplify the wormwhorl, except...'

'Except anyone with a grain of sense does a thorough fumigation after a dæmonic visitation, don't they, Mindador?'

'I've been a bit busy.'

'Well, you're going to be even busier. We'll need some water, a mirror and a needle.'

'For a spell of spatio-temporal divination?' I asked, glad to be making a contribution at last.

'For a compass. We might work out where we are, then.'

At the word "mirror" Winolene had remembered she had such a thing, reached into her voluminous skirts and brought out one of the hand varieties, looked into it and shrieked.'

'What's the matter – not The Fairest In All The Land anymore? Slouch, can you stop her doing that. It's getting on my nerves.'

'My hair,' she wailed, 'just look at my hair.'

'You look at it. We've got work to do.'

I found some water in a nearby trough and took it back to the hay stack in a broken pot that was lying nearby. I thought back to what he said about things that can go wrong with a wormwhorl. Part of me was trying to remember it for good, wizard's-apprentice reasons – everything is a lesson, Vizagriz often said – and another part was wrestling with something about his explanation, but I couldn't quite grasp it.

Vizagriz had poured a small amount of water onto the flat mirror and Winolene had managed to produce from somewhere within her flounces a pin of some sort. This was a girl who never went unprepared, I marvelled. Vizagriz was placing the pin gently on the water's surface.

'Now. I estimate we travelled for no more than a couple of minutes and we haven't been here half an hour. It was Watching Hour when we left and judging by the sun's height it's midday now. Are you paying attention, Slouch?'

I was. He had stuck his staff in the ground and was looking at the shadow

'Right. So we're twelve hours adrift either way and if I read the sun's angle aright, we're still in the Northern hemisphere at about the same longitude as Al Faq'Ahl.'

'So that means we're where, exactly?' I asked.

'Slap bang in the middle of the continent on the other side of the world. So it doesn't really matter if we head East or West since we're equally far away in both directions. North, if you look at the needle, is over there,' he said, pointing at a distant hill, 'and West across the Crocky Mountains is the Howling Desert. I don't know about you, but I'm turning right. Coming?'

And Winolene, who had just taken it all in, started wailing again.

'Who needs a Howling Desert when you've got a Princess?' Vizagriz muttered.

That jogged my memory. As we walked – Vizagriz and I in front, Winolene daintily lifting her skirts and keenly on the lookout for slipper-sucking cowpats behind and Mindador moping along behind morosely – I asked him. 'Master? I have a question.'

'Fire away. I'm not doing anything at the moment. Except starting to hemicircumnavigate the globe on foot.'

'Well, you said, back there, there were three things that could go wrong with a wormwhorl?'

'Did I? Must be right, then.'

'One was another wormwhorl.'

'Correct, if within six radii and turning in the same direction.'

'One was the presence of dæmons.'

'Certain types of dæmons, on certain days and without the benefit of exorcism, yes.'

'What's the third?'

'Ah. Well spotted. What do you need to make a wormwhorl?'

'Er, incantation, some sort of insulation or grounding and a virgin.'

'Right. We know he had the incantation and you've seen the segs in his boots.'

'And he had Winolene.'

'Spot on.'

'But she's... I mean, surely...'

Vizagriz waggled his eyebrows at me. 'There you are, then.' And he strode on.

We walked for about three hours, then rested and took water. Vizagriz proposed we spend the rest of the remaining daylight getting some food together, since we hadn't seen anything remotely resembling a settlement of any kind. The existence of the hay rick suggested someone must live nearby and that we would bump into a farm or village before too long. But we should prepare for the worst, just in case. We had also found some rough sacking hanging on a hedge and I had picked it up to use as bedding, if we ever came upon any more straw or some moss.

The countryside had changed from mountain foothills to a rolling plain, sparsely wooded and lush. Winolene had shown herself to be more of the country girl than she cared to let on and kept up with us remarkably well. Mindador still hadn't said anything but slouched along behind and sat apart from the rest of us, gazing at his feet. He did, however, snicker occasionally. It wasn't pleasant and Vizagriz had certainly noticed it, but kept quiet.

I had gathered some nuts and berries from bushes we passed and even found an old leather water bag in a ditch which I cleaned out and filled at a bright spring. Near where we stopped there was a small stream and Vizagriz suggested it might have fish in it. It did indeed, and he showed me how to lay my shirt on the bottom and yank it out when there were a few fish hovering over it. They were small and of a type I had never seen before, but they looked like they would grill up all right. I had collected dry wood for a fire and dug up a few roots which would bake nicely in the embers. I was starting to enjoy myself. Days out were few and far between at SamBernardo's and just about the only grass I had seen up close was what occasionally turned up in the porridge.

As I was impaling the fish on spits and burying the roots under the sticks that would become the fire, Winolene said something arch about wizard being able to conjure up seven-course banquets and where was the cutlery, perhaps it was just all talk and no Magick. Vizagriz had given her one of his glances and pointed at the fire which burst into flames. This shut her up for a bit while she nibbled carefully at the fish, avoiding the skin, bones, head, tail and, as far as I could see, most of the meat as well. Mindador was still sulking and sitting a bit apart but it didn't stop him guzzling his share.

I had also gathered some dry moss and leaves from the woods and stuffed the sacks with them to make rough pillows. It was a warm evening and didn't look like rain. As the sun set and the fire dwindled we all settled down to sleep with an imprecation from Vizagriz to be up and off at first light.

I sat up for while, my back against a tree and thought. Vizagriz must have noticed me taking furtive sideways glances at Winolene, fast asleep and lightly snoring and when I caught his eye, I blushed. He chuckled. I could have strangled him.

'Don't worry about me, lad,' he leered. 'If you want to move your palliasse over that way a bit, feel free, get some in before you take your oath of celibacy, I say!'

In an attempt to change the subject and cover my embarrassment, I said, 'I've always wondered about the Oath of Celibacy. I mean, it's supposed to be essential to the Craft. Preserves the magical juices and all that. But not all wizards appear to be...I mean, some of them...well, I've even seen...'

What I'd even seen was the occasional stopover by a young witch or two and the odd few dancing girls at Vizagriz's cottage, but I wasn't about to say so. They were always "Put in the guest room", as it was "too far to travel home on such a night", even if it was eight o'clock in midsummer and they lived three streets away. I had to make the beds up, but they were barely rumpled in the morning and there was a fair amount of careful nonchalance over breakfast. But Vizagriz just grinned.

'Oh, sure. There's a lot of old rubbish talked about celibacy, too. Strictly speaking, it's only us Roaming Wizards who take the Oath. The Protesting Wizards don't. The Orthodox Wizards say they do but it's more honoured in the breeches than the observance, if you know what I mean. Reformed wizards don't even pretend, they just get on with it. Even Archdruids are known to get down to the Naiad Club for an evening, and don't tell me it's because the beer's good. Because it isn't.' He sniffed.

'So, it's not true what they say then, that it saps the vital fluids?'

'It most certainly DOES sap the vital fluids, thank God. That's what it's for. But it doesn't affect the Magick. Just makes it harder to get up in the morning. In a sense.'

'But Merillion didn't...'

Vizagriz cut in. 'Oh, that one. "Merillion, the First and Only Archimage, chose none but men for his Thirteen Acolytes". I know. Didn't choose any women and didn't get married. True. On the other hand, he didn't pick any men over five foot tall either, being a bit short in the leg department himself. And you don't see a height requirement, like they have in the City Guard, only the other way round, do you? Nor did he choose any with beards. Look at the Sacred Illustrations sometime. Doesn't stop almost every wizard in creation trying to grow a corker though, does it? Anyway, how do we know he never married?'

'No wife is mentioned in the GoodSpells,' I repeated, by rote. We had learned this in Bibble class at the Catamite Training Agency.

'Probably couldn't stand the old sow and didn't want her appearing in the Great Work. Or more likely, didn't want to ruin his chances when he went on Visiting Miracles tours. Nothing puts off the stage door Sheilas like them thinking there's an ogress at home with a rolling pin and a scrying spell watching the old scrote from afar, eh?'

This seemed sacrilege to me, and I wondered whether to continue the strand of argument. He saved me the bother.

'Now, calm down. I'm not saying it's all nonsense, what Merillion wrote, or whoever wrote it for him.' I gasped at this heresy.

'Well, you don't think he had time to write all the GoodSpells himself, do you? Probably had a few amanuenses and scribes pottering about taking down every syllable like it was Holy Writ. Which it was, of course.' He coughed. 'But the trouble is, as soon as he popped his clogs - sorry, "elevated himself to a higher plane of existence and enlightenment" - every Wizard who'd been within a foot of him claimed to have the One and Only Revealed Truth and set up his own True Way, probably spotting the merchandising opportunities. It's certainly been good for the sale of GoodSpells and icons, I'll say that.'

I was aghast, and sat with my mouth open, until a mayfly decided to explore it at some speed. As I hacked and spluttered Vizagriz continued, warming to his theme, counting off points on his bony fingers.

'So, you see, that's why we have Orthodox Wizards, who can't do a spell without incense and a big hat; Reformed Wizards, who say anybody can do Magick if they just try hard enough; Reformed Orthodox Wizards, who seem to believe both of these at once; Wizuits, who want to beat the stuffing out of anyone who doesn't accept their particular view of the Craft; Wee Free Wizards, who don't even believe in singing; Methodicals, who won't make love standing up because it might lead to dancing; Seventh Heaven Witnesses, who claim there can only be 169,000 wizards but still go round like Cyclopsopaedia salesmen recruiting more; and Tonsurites, who pretend they're holier-than-thou but are really only in it for the floggings and the apprentice boys. Not that you'd know what I mean by that.' He shot me a warning glance.

'I think I do, actually.'

'There you are then. There are as many different sects of sorcery as there are fleas on a dog, and they can't all be right and they can't all be wrong, can they? So all a young lad like you can do is pick the one that suits you and defend it to the death.'

'So why did you choose a celibate order, then?' I was genuinely puzzled.

'Gets you off the hook, lad. Intrigues the ladies, because they all wonder if it's true about what's worn under the robe. But if push come to shove, you don't have to marry 'em. The Order forbids it. Took a Dreadful Oath. Fire and lightning, all that. It's sort of a non-marriage of convenience in my case.'

He settled back, comfortably, in a signal to me that the discussion was over, for now. 'Anyway, take my tip. Join the High Anglers.'

'Why them?' I asked.

'They have the nicest hats. Goodnight!'

CHAPTER THE SIXTH

In which, after a rainstorm, Slouch and his companions meet with the Faerie-folk and learn of Webs.

My weather prediction was way off. Just before dawn the skies opened and a downpour started that was so vicious it soaked us even in the few minutes it took us to gather up our pillows and head for the nearest cover. Vizagriz and Winolene ended up under a large bush and Mindador and I had headed for the same tree, reaching it at the same time. As we sat, dripping wet, under a WeeWee tree, I came to understand how it got its name. The WeeWee was really a desert tree transplanted to the temperate zones by a sadistic silviculturist and it didn't much like water. So when it rained, the tree pulled all the moisture out of the ground nearby and poured it out of its leaves as far away as possible, which in this case was not very far and all over us. Probably getting its own back. Still, it was marginally better than being in the thunderstorm. Although, I pondered gloomily, once you're wet through, there's not much wetter to get. I heard once that when caught out in the rain you should take off all your clothes and sit on them, dressing again when it's dry. Sounded like a recipe for double pneumonia to me at the time, and I wasn't about to try it now.

Beside me, Mindador was getting more terminally morose by the minute. He started to moan.

'Oh dear, oh dear, oh dear. Has it come to this?'

Clearly it had, so I said nothing. But he didn't shut up.

'What a waste I've made of my life. Such promise, Oy. Wasted! Do you know...' he turned to me, clearly grateful for an audience to bore. Misery loves company. The reverse is not true. But I put up with it. He was, after all, a Great Mage.

'Do you know that I was considered one of the most promising young apprentices in my class at the College of Knowledge? Ah? Did you know that my treatise on "Inadvertent

Finger Signals and Their Consequences for the Uninitiated" got the Top Hat for the year? Not many people know that!'

He sat, desolately picking at the frayed stars on his cloak. 'And my Levitation Group voted me Most Upwardly Mobile on two occasions! I even won a scholarship to go to the Western Continent and get a suntan!'

I stared at the ground, both embarrassed for his sense of failure and not wanting to encourage his whining.

'And now look at me!' I didn't. 'Oh, I had great plans once. I wanted to reform the whole basis of Magick.'

'What, new spells and that?' Well, I had to say something.

'No, no, research is best left to the boffins. What I wanted was to put Magick on a sound managerial footing. Organise Wizards into Group Practices, so each could specialise. You know, a Thaumaturge, a Necromancer with a nicely equipped crypt, an Apothecary round the corner where the clients could buy the stuff we prescribed, maybe a Consultant Hierophant coming in on Wednesdays. And a Receptionist, to make appointments for us. Pretty young witch to do the spade-work and the cleaning. And like that. None of this alembic-juggling and mixing your own potions, get them from the in-house Alchemist. And best of all, a decent night visit rota so we could all get some sleep and a day off now and again to watch the fruitball.'

I opened my mouth to say 'Never mind, perhaps when we get back...' but he kept going.

'I presented a paper on it at the Royal College. Had an article in General Prestidigitator. Got on all the crystal ball chat shows. But what happened? What happened?'

I didn't know what happened, but I felt sure I was going to find out. 'Nothing, that's what happened. Nothing! The Central Council said it would "Destroy the individuality of Wizardom". Said it would mean "The end of the True Generalist" and that we'd all end up being nothing but a sifting process for specialists at the local District General Coven. Said it was "Overly commercialising a noble calling", they did. Ha! As if we could all make a decent living out of curing warts and removing hexes and doling out nostrums so that love-sick kitchen maids could trap a delivery boy behind the meat locker. No, they wouldn't have it. They drummed me out! And you know why? You know why?'

I didn't know why. But I was sure I'd find out.

'All because I'm a Hebryd! Just because I don't believe Merillion had all the answers. Oh, you think there's no prejudice? Think we're all enlightened and liberal? Ha! I say Ha! And Ha! again!'

Mindador had folded his arms into a palpable sulk and pouted darkly at the universe in general. Vizagriz had once used the phrase, 'He's a well-balanced man; he has a chip on each shoulder,' and the sobriquet certainly fitted Master Mindador.

'Oh, really Master Mindador! You can't believe that in this day and age.'

He virtually spat. Not that it would have made much difference in this weather. 'Oh no? Let me tell you, sonny-boy. The Central Council are all Temple Trowellers, with their secret signs and funny hats and regalias.'

'But ALL wizards have secret signs and funny hats and that.'

'Not the point, that's not the point. Point is, if you're not IN, you're OUT.'

No arguing with that logic, so I let it pass. Years later, I discovered that what Mindador had really been drummed out for was his unfortunate part in the Death Wars Jelly Town Disaster coupled with, if that's the phrase, an unorthodox approach to oneiromancy, whereby he claimed that in order to interpret dreams, the practitioner had to sleep in the same bed as the client. He got a sound thrashing, a paternity suit and a few fang marks in his gown for that one. The trouble with catching a wizard when he's asleep or, well, not quite concentrating, is that he has no time to prepare a mystic defence, which may be another reason why some wizards are celibate.

Anyway, Mindador had gone back to moping silently, so I stared at the grass in front of me. Which was just as well, as otherwise I would have missed the fascinating site of a faerie wringing out her wings. She spotted me too, and looked up, fists on hips, jaw stuck out like a two-inch-tall prize-fighter.

''Ere! Getting a bleedin' eyeful, then? Enjoying yourself?' piped an incredibly reedy voice.

I was so awestruck at seeing a being I had up till now considered mythical, or the product of at least three quarts of mangle juice, I couldn't think of anything to say, so I moved my mouth up and down and gabbled a lot.

'It's not free, you know! Honestly. Getting so a body can't change her wet flying gear in private without every Tom, Dick and Harry copping a butchers. I dunno.'

The tiny sprite went back to beating a gossamer tunic on a twig and pinning it to a blade of grass with tiny, tiny pegs. She had about a dozen of them in her mouth, so I couldn't hear what she was mumbling.

I elbowed Mindador and pointed at the small, ethereal being. He peered over, then grunted. 'Faeries. Just what we need.'

I was reluctant to make any great noise in case I startled the wee thing so I raised myself slowly to me feet and crouch-crept over to Vizagriz and Winolene. 'Master, Winolene,' I whispered. 'I've just seen a faerie.'

Winolene snorted. 'And I've just seen a dragon flying past with a bunch of pigs following it. What was in those roots you baked last night?'

'If the lad says he's seen a faerie then he's seen a faerie,' Vizagriz said in my defence. 'Or are you telling me I encourage my apprentices to lie?' Winolene looked abashed, but it certainly didn't seem to have improved her impression of me. 'Now, it might be an apparition, it might be a glamour, but it might, just might, be a faerie. What say we find out, eh?'

'You find out. I'm wet enough without believing in forest elementals, thank you.'

'Suit yourself. Come on, Slouch. Where was it? Did it have a bluebell for a hat?'

I strongly got the impression that Vizagriz was not taking this all that seriously, either, but his reaction changed when I pointed down to where the minuscule being was rubbing her fine, white hair with a furry leaf. She stopped, looked up and sighed a tiny sigh. 'Wot, more of ya? Brought all yer mates for a gander, have ya? Bleedin' sauce!' And with that she reached down, picked up a weeny white handbag and flew off into the woods.

'Quick,' said Vizagriz. 'Follow her.' He led the chase into the gloom of the dawn forest with me close behind, Mindador following and Winolene hopping on one leg, trying to get her slippers on and shouting, 'Hey! Wait for me! Where's everyone off to?'

Faeries, it must be said, do not fly particularly fast and we had no trouble following her, especially as she glowed faintly but perceptibly in the dim dawn light filtering weakly though the murky greenwood. We had to make the occasional detour when the faerie took a shortcut through a bush, but we weren't far behind her when we burst upon the most glorious, wonderful sight I had ever beheld in my fifteen short years.

In a small glade surrounded by hawthorn and rhododendron I saw a fantastic collection of the wee folk, all singing in high-pitched but somehow raucous voices and dancing in a circle around a keg the size of a fruitball. All about the glade were fireflies, lending the light of their tails to the proceedings and everywhere small beings were sitting on lumps of thistledown, lounging in violets or perched on fungi. Right in the centre was a toadstool of the approved, mythical variety - red with white spots on it - upon which was a small creature, cross legged and belting out the words of the faeries' song.

'Oh, knees up Mother Brownie, knees up Mother Brownie, under the mushrooms you must go, E-I-E-I-E-I-O.' He was giving it rice, as were all the others dancing around him, those that didn't seem to be giving more of their attention to some fluid that was trickling out of the keg into foxglove flowers which they were passing round to others nearby.

This song clearly came to an end as the dancing sprites all let out a final "OI!" and sank to the ground. The Faerie King (as I imagined) leapt to his feet on the toadstool and shouted over the din. ''Ere. I know. Let's have a gentle one. Come on, Bella.'

A little round thing rather like an oak gall with legs waddled across to the toadstool and with, it must be said, some difficulty, hoisted itself up the toadstool. It turned to the Faerie King and said, 'All right, Dad. 'Ow's this?' The now obviously female sprite threw back her head, inflated a small but operatic bosom and trilled, 'If you were the only Sprite in the world.'

We watched this for a time, until the dawn light became strong enough drown the yellow light of the fireflies and the party was clearly starting to wind down. For the first time I became aware of my companions again and glanced across to see Winolene staring, open-mouthed at the faerie ring. 'My Deity,' I heard her say. 'I never imagined that.'

Vizagriz had also been silent all this while, but now he said, 'Time to make our presence known, not that I imagine for a moment it's gone unnoticed. Come on.' He used his staff to push aside a branch of hawthorn – never a wizard's favourite shrub at any time and one he always avoids touching if possible as it grounds the Magick – and stepped forward.

'Greetings from the outer world. My companions and I mean you no harm. Whom do we have the pleasure of addressing?'

We might have meant them harm. We might have decided to jump about stamping on them all. But if we had, the faeries didn't look like they were especially bothered by the possibility. Some of them sat about draining the last of their foxglove goblets, others were starting to disappear into the bushes. Others just stayed where they were, mopping their brows with miniature kerchiefs and fanning themselves with petals.

The one on the toadstool looked up, dropped a piece of smoking herb and ground it under his heel and said, 'Wotcher cock. Took yer time, didn't yer? Felt you lot coming last night.'

'You did?' said Vizagriz, as surprised as I was.

''Course. Felt you coming a mile off. So how's the quest, eh, Vizagriz?'

'You seem to know a great deal about us, and you have the advantage of me.'

'Sorry, manners, I'm King Pearly. Pleased to make yours. Have a noggin. Oh, you can't, it's all finished. Never mind, Mum'll put the wossname on in a minute. Nearly breakfast time, anyway. Eat a horsefly, so I could. Famished. Come on, park your bums.'

Vizagriz sat down cross legged in front of the toadstool and Winolene and I followed suit, taking care not to squash any of King Pearly's subjects in the process, such behaviour probably not going down well with royalty regardless of size. I noticed that Mindador was not in evidence, but there was so much else to think about I didn't give it a second thought. Winolene was still gaping with her mouth open like she was about to start an aria.

Vizagriz cleared his throat and nearly blew the King's hat off. 'King Pearly. So you're an Imp, I take it?'

'No, no, no. Of course not! I'm an Emp. That's how I know what you're thinking. I emp-athise. My cousin, Barry, he's the Imp.'

'Are the rest of you Emps, then?'

'You don't know much, do you? Barry's the Imp. I'm an Emp. King of the Emps, in fact. Sort of Emp-eror, really. 'Ere, that's a good one, did you hear that mum, I said... Oh, never mind, deaf as a post sometimes but lovely with it. Jacko, over there, glowing a bit, he's an Amp. Jonno, what looks so disgruntled all the time, he's an Ump. Don't cross him, he'll curdle your milk. Terry's an Omp. And Vince, he's a Yump, but he'll grow out of it.'

I was baffled. There was nothing about this lot in my Tiny Tots Book of Wee Forest Folk. I must write to the editor, I thought. I never did, though. Remiss of me, but I've been busy, you know how it is. 'Beg pardon,' I interjected, all placatory, 'but I didn't realise there were so many... different sorts of Imps.'

'We're NOT all Imps. I told ya. I'm an Emp, so's Freddy. Barry's the Imp. Jacko's...'

'Yes, yes, You said. But, why are you all, well, different?' I was really baffled now. Really.

'Everyone to their task, that's what we say. Demarcation. Strict delimitation of jobs and functions according to custom and practice, as laid out by the rule book. That's it! So I Emp-athise. Jacko the Amp, he glows and sparks a bit, give you a nasty shock if he don't like you. Jonno's the Ump, so he just goes about looking surly and pricking babies, nasty little bleeder, heart o' gold, mind, good to his family. Also referees the football matches when we beat the shit out of the Elves up Sprite Park of a Saturday. Come on you Re-eds, heh heh. Terry, he's our Omp. Not quite sure what he does, but he makes a lot of noise doing it.'

I wasn't getting the hang of this at all, but I persevered. 'And Vince, he's a...'

'Vince, my boy Vince is a Yump. Young Upwardly Mobile Pixie, he is. Never off the mobile mushroom, making deals, ducking and diving, turnin' pumpkins into coaches for the short-term hire business, that sort of thing. Knows all about the InterWeb. Got high hopes for young Vince, I have. Might grow up to be in charge, just like his dad. A real Imp-erial.'

He purely glowed with paternal pride. 'His mum says he gets it from her side, the old man being on the Woods and Means Committee and all, but I dunno as much.'

'Fascinating,' said Vizagriz. 'And you know about our quest, do you?'

'Well, I assume you're on a quest. The other one certainly is.'

The Faerie King looked about, obviously for Mindador. 'Have a word, where's 'e gone, then?'

'Good question. One of our number does seem to be temporarily not present. I think I might just pop and find him so he can present his compliments. Do excuse me. Slouch, you and your girlfriend stay here. Shan't be a tick. Don't eat any toadstools.'

'Poisonous?'

'Furniture.'

I had expected some sort of protestation from Winolene at the "girlfriend" jibe but she was still staring open-mouthed as a cluster of female faeries hovered around her saying things like. "Wouldn't catch me wearing that. Never get the stains out", and "She ought to do something with her hair. Could be quite a pretty girl if she tried", and "I dunno, bit of slag if you arst me, look at them slippers. Common as muck".

I was, I confess, enjoying her minor discomfiture as much as her bewilderment. It was good to see how easily the thin veneer of sophistication fell from Winolene when she was at a disadvantage.

Vizagriz had very little difficulty finding Mindador. All he had to do was follow the mumbling. He came across the old trickster crouching behind a bush waving his hands back and forth across Winolene's mirror, which he had obviously pocketed after the direction-finding exercise. Vizagriz watched him for a bit, then stepped in front of him, to Mindador's evident surprise.

'Oh, er, I was just, er...'

'I know what you were "just, er", and it won't work. There's no point trying to contact anyone with the old glass-glamour. It's no use here. Don't you know where we are?'

Mindador looked around as if to confirm his suspicions before speaking. 'It's a forest.'

'It's a metaphorest, you cretin. Nothing is what it seems and very little is straightforward. What do you think all that Faerie Glade bit was back there, a flea circus? We're slap bang in the middle of more raw Magick than you or I will ever get our hands round. So who were you trying to get in touch with anyway?'

'Oh, that. Nobody, just my answering service. Important messages, clients calling, that sort of thing.'

'Baloney. You're up to something, Master Mindador and I want to know what it is before I tell that lot back there you had a big collection of elf wings pinned to a board back home when you were a boy. Then you'll see what wild Magick is all about. They might be small, but they're perfectly horrid when roused.'

'Honestly, Vizagriz, I don't know what you mean. I was dropped here by accident, just like you were. Really. I mean it.'

'Uhuh. Well I mean this. I dare say you didn't mean to get sucked here, but you were definitely at it with that wormwhorl and the Handmaiden. Where were you trying to see? What could be so valuable that you would risk throwing one of the Chosen at it unless you thought you could get away with it. And what's this about a quest?'

'Quest? I don't know about any...'

'Stop it. The Boss Faerie is an Emp and he picked up our vibrations a while back. He says you're on a quest and I have no reason to doubt him. So what's it all about?'

Mindador's shoulders slumped. 'Oy Vey. I should be this unlucky. Forgive me.'

'Tell me something to forgive, and we'll see.'

'Well, the Order wanted me to find something, so I did a six-headed conjuration to find out where is was. Trouble is, it wasn't very informative.'

'They rarely are. But we might make some sense of it now. What did the Heads tell you?'

'They said:

"Seek the place where webs are woven";

"Find the weaver and ask the question";

"There is a jewel without equal";

"A man must read the words";

"It is far, but near. It is inside, but without. It is high, but deep";

"Once found, it must once again be lost, or all is lost".

But I couldn't make head nor tail of that without knowing where to start looking.'

'I see. So then you thought you'd just ask a passing dæmon, did you?'

'Sort of. I called up one I thought would know.'

'What did you give him? Any more Handmaidens that Vesta will be short of next roll-call?'

'No, no, nothing like that. The dæmon wanted an old relic, that was all.'

'Relic of what?'

'The Last Relic of Um.'

'Who was Um?'

'One of the Order, who struggled against the dæmons years ago. They still bear a grudge. When Um died the Order distributed his relics amongst themselves to keep him safe in the afterlife but the dæmons had managed to collect all the bits except one.'

'Which you were able to give them. Generous of you. And how did you get your grubby hands on it? Grave robbing?'

'No, I swear! The Order gave it to me.'

'Oh, did they just? So would I be correct in my surmise that the Order knows what you're up to?'

Mindador nodded glumly.

'And even asked you to find whatever it is?'

He nodded again.

'And – I'm guessing here but do stop me if I'm off at tangent – that piece of filth Brer Dryberg is at the heart of all this?'

Mindador sighed and spread his hands. 'He pays well.'

'He'll pay all right when I see him next. Anyway, what did this dæmon tell you?'

Mindador was less than willing to answer this question but the look on Vizagriz's face and the understated blue crackling that played around his staff persuaded him otherwise.

'All right. I may as well tell you. You'll find out anyway and I'll never get back to Al Faq'Ahl, so I suppose it doesn't matter. He said:

"Three times three times three nights from tonight, take one wizard. Spin until giddy. Raise to a high dudgeon. And put to one side". That was all.'

Vizagriz was silent for a few minutes. Mindador watched him intently as if worried the wizard might explode with rage. Eventually he rubbed his hand across his eyes and said, 'Well, you certainly managed all that. You're not going to disappoint me and pretend it was on purpose, are you?'

'I don't know. When that Recognition shot at me I just assumed it was because of the boy, your apprentice.'

'In what way?'

'He brought the relic to me the night before. So he was already linked to the gold even before you bought him.'

'Ah! Of course. So that's what threw the timing off course by a whole constellation the first time. The combination of boy and mage bent the radar a bit. Did you realise you were down for this quest all along?'

'No, I swear. I thought I would just do a scrying, see where the quest would begin and send someone off. A hero, or...'

'Or a suitably lied-to wizard. Except I turned up a bit early. Well, I've got news for you. You are in this up to the hilt. We are going to have to go through with this nonsense because it says so in the PhilosoPhax.'

'PhilosoPhax? It's really in there?'

'Oh yes, old questing buddy mine. You and I and Slouch and the drippy girl are part of a Great Event. Brer Dryberg didn't tell you that, did he?'

'No, he didn't.' Mindador was realigning himself according to where he thought his best chances of survival would lie.

'And I'll tell you what else the Herald said – yes, the Herald, he's had his oar in it. He said "Wizard, wizard, girl, hero, player, imp and scribe". Then he said I had half my required Questers – that was you, Slouch and Winolene, though I didn't really know it then. I thought the Recognition was more to do with something you might be able to tell me. I was waiting of a message from the Herald to tell me what to do next.'

'And did he?'

'Oh yes, he certainly did that. He told me to find The Holy Quail!'

Mindador gasped and put his hand to his mouth. 'You too, eh? That's what the Order wants you to get for them? Well, there's going to be a bit of competition for it. I was given to understand that the Herald was taking his orders from a very high place indeed. Higher than high. Highest possible, in fact. I don't think Brer Dryberg's got the clout that they have.'

'They? Who?'

'We'll see, Mindador, we'll see. Next thing you better do is remember as much as you can about this Quail, whatever it is.'

'Don't you know?'

'Not an earthly. But I do know it's in demand and it would be in our best interests to get to it before it becomes even more popular and we meet some competition. Anyway, we should get back. We've got something to collect.'

'What's that?'

'An imp, apparently. Come on.'

When Vizagriz and Mindador returned to the glade, things had quieted down a bit. Winolene has regained enough of her normal superior attitude to ignore the faeries and their mini-bitchiness and start looking for her mirror. She was tutting with annoyance that she couldn't find it, making do with pulling a brush through her beautiful, spun-gold, sun-gold locks and... sorry. Carried away there. She was gracious enough to say thank you when Vizagriz dropped the mirror on her lap and said, 'Yours, I think,' and carried on preening herself, fixing the lipstick and generally making herself presentable for the whatever the morning would bring.

I leapt to my feet and went over to my master. 'What was Mindador doing?'

'It's what he's done that's the problem.' Vizagriz rejoined.

'What?'

'He's only gone and conjured up a Baking Dæmon, that's all.' Then he headed off to talk to King Pearly.

Mindador was sat on a tree stump, deep in a force-ten glum. Winolene had reverted to type and was engaged in exactly what young ladies of her class and upbringing always do at moments of stress and confusion – she was collecting flowers and arranging them. Vizagriz was off talking to the miniature monarch. That left me to my own devices, so I went for a walk. I had a lot to think about.

Not that I got the chance. I hadn't gone far when I heard a rustling in the bushes and a small voice saying, 'Come on, you know you want to really' followed by a series of grunts and squeals. Thinking an animal was trapped I peered into the undergrowth and saw, to my amazement, a muskrat. It was trapped, right enough, but not by a snare or wire. It was being none-too-willingly

French-kissed by one of the wee folk. I was taken aback and stood up fairly smartly, cracking my head on a branch and yelping as a consequence. The muskrat looked up, recovered what it could of its dignity and scuttled off. The small faerie let out an exclamation of exasperated disappointment and thumped the ground where he sat. 'Typical. Never had a muskrat and the first chance I get some blundering Biggie comes in and queers the pitch. Thank you very much, I don't think.'

'"Erm, sorry", was all I could say.'

'Bleeeeedin' well think so. Haven't had a jump in days, either. Oh well, back to the wood-nymphs, I suppose. They're always game.' With that, he hoisted his moleskin britches that probably fitted the mole better and certainly stayed on for longer periods, and sloped off in a two-inch-high snit.

I didn't go for much more of walk after that but went back to the glade and sat, waiting for Vizagriz and trying to make sense of a few things.

'So, Your Majesty, it seems we are supposed to have one of your subjects along with us. I don't know why but these things are always a bit ineffable, aren't they?'

'Ineffable. In-bleedin'-effable. That is the word, my son. You said a mouthful. Never know what's doin' when that there 'Erald turns up. Do you know, dew yew knaow, he only come 'ere, wot, two, maybe three constellations back and says to me, 'e says, "King," 'e says, I mean, we know each other well, go back a long way, like that me an' the 'Erald. "King," 'e says, "I'll tell you wot's up and mark me, this is a big 'un. They've got the Right Royal 'uff they 'ave, both of 'em and it's no fun round them two when they're into one. Like a pair o' bleedin' kids they are, but there's no tellin' 'em, no tellin' 'em at all." So I says to 'im, "Come on then, give us the Ess Pee, wot's the jackanory?" An' 'e says, "They've gorn an' lorst it, 'aven't they?" Well, they 'adn't so much as lorst it, since they've never really 'ad it, 'ave they? But I knew wot he meant. Wot 'e meant was that they fancied 'avin' a sky hook at it and didn't know, not for the life of the pair of 'em, where it was at. So wot do they do? They get up a quest, that's wot, and they say to the 'Erald, "Git yoreself down below, my lad and sort us aht some Questers as quick as you like 'cos if we don't know where it is chances are no other bleeder does neither." And I don't 'ave to tell you, you bein' a wizard an' all that, there's nuffink like nobody knowin' where sunnink is to set off a fair bit of questin, is there? Yus. A large portion. It seems to me if everybody knew where everyfink was, there's be none of this larkin' abaht an' questin' would there? Stands to reason.'

'Quite. And the Herald came to see me, too.'

'Wot? 'E never did. There you are then. That's my point. Give you a map, did 'e. Nah, couldn't 'ave, on account of not knowin' where it is, wot am I thinkin'? Get a few hints, though?'

'Not really. He did say I was to put together a questing party. And one of them has to be an imp. So naturally, I thought...'

'Say no more. Say. No. More! You 'ave come to the right place, my son, no mistake. Imps are the one thing we're not runnin' out of rahnd 'ere. That and ground elder. Gets everywhere that stuff. Don't suppose you know of a good weed killer? Nah, not your line of country, is it, never mind. Imps, though. Imps I can do you. Wot, a dozen? More? Wot abaht ten? 'Ere, fink the kettle's on yet?'

Vizagriz was being remarkably patient with the King, given that he had managed to display, all in one paragraph, his inability to count, his inability to listen and his inability to keep to the point. 'He did say one imp. I'd hate to break whatever rule there might be for this business and anyway, I wouldn't want to deprive Your Highness of any more of your subjects than is strictly necessary.'

'Take the lot of 'em for me, sunshine. Pain in the throne most of 'em, know wot I mean? But look, tell you wot I'll do. I'll give ya me best imp. Well, might not be an imp exactly, but when the 'Erald said "imp" I suppose he was thinkin' a bit...'

'Generic,' Vizagriz supplied.

'Generic. Took the words right aht. Generic. I mean, we're all related, ain't we?'

'Anyone you can spare,' Vizagriz said, 'will doubtless be ideal for the quest, It did occur to me, though...'

'Yus? Wot?'

'Well, one of my companions has been doing a bit of part-time divining and it appears that we are to seek a web-weaver and ask him, her or it a question.'

'No weavin' gets done rahnd 'ere, old horse. Don't hold wiv it. That's Dwarf stuff, that, weavin'. We need clothes, we get 'em from Morrie's boys over at Dingley Dell. Lovely bit of schmutter, wholesale too.' The King lit up another smoking weed and held it backwards, cupped behind his palm. 'Talk to them. I'll set it up.'

'I don't think cloth weaving was the idea. There's other types of weaving, too.'

'Wot? Fates an' all that?'

'Possibly. But I heard you say your son, er...'

'Vince. Lovely lad, good as gold.'

'Vince, yes. I heard you say he knew about something called the InterWeb. Did I get that right?'

'Too true, you did. Better arst 'im abaht it, mind. Not my sort of thing all that tick-nologgy. Don't see wot's wrong wiv a bit of good, old-fashioned listening at eaves and whispering at windows, me. Still, Vince is your man for all that. Vince? VINCE! Git yoreself over 'ere, a bit smartish. Wizard wants an ear-bendin'. Where are ya? Come on!'

A young, smartly-dressed Yump sprang over and vaulted onto the toadstool beside his father. He looked up at Vizagriz and with a tiny index finger pushed back a pair of large (by his standards) horn-rimmed spectacles onto the bridge of his nose. 'Yeh?' he said.

'Wizard wos arstin' me abaht this Web thing you keep goin' on abaht and I said, 'Vince'll sort you aht, give you the full monty on it,' didn' I? Off you go, then.'

'If you'd be so kind,' said Vizagriz. 'I'd appreciate anything you could tell us.'

'Right, well, the Web, or InterWeb, is not so much a thing, it's more of a network. You can find out anything you want on the InterWeb, you just have to ask.'

'I see. And where do I find it?'

'Ah. That's the thing. It ain't, like, anywhere. It's sort of everywhere. Know wot I mean?'

'Afraid not,' said Vizagriz, whose head was starting to ache dully. 'Surely it's somewhere.'

'Well, you got yer local points of persistence an' you got your nodes. But wot you want is a WebMistress. She'll 'ave a terminal.'

'Ah. A WebMistress. I see. Got one handy, I don't suppose?'

'Not 'ere, no. Can't get the connections, not wivaht long distance and then yore talkin' big call charges. No, when I want to know sunnink, I ask WebMistress Schlob. She's over at Mustique Mountain.'

Vizagriz stood up and straightened his back. 'That's where we'll go, then. I assume Vince will come with us, as our companion on this quest?'

The King took a drag backwards off his weed-end, sucked in breath through his teeth and shook his small head, making the little bell on his ragwort crown tinkle. 'Couldn't odds it, guv'nor. Couldn't do it, sorry. Vince is needed 'ere. Who'd mind the precious metals tradin' an' the stag beetle races of a Frig's Day night, eh? Who'd look after the used pumpkin-coach business? Nah. Indispensable Vince is, as I always say. My right-hand pixie, ain'tcha Vince?'

'Yeh. Right. An' catch me off on some quest. Where's the profit?'

'We could,' said Vizagriz, 'be off to save the fabric of eternity.'

'Well, save me one an' all, then,' said Vince and he and his father started laughing uncontrollably to the accompaniment, in the King's case, of much coughing and "Oh, gawdstrufe" and "that's a belter".

When the merriment had died down a bit and Prince Vince had rearranged his rainbow braces the Faerie King stood upright again and wiped his eyes with the back of his hand. 'Oh, dear. Nice one. I do like a good chuckle. I mean, you've got 'ave a laugh, 'aven't ya? Still, I did promise an imp and an imp, or sunnink like it, is wot you'll get.'

'Who you got im mind, Dad? Jonno the Ump?'

'I should cocoa. I want that evil little bugger right 'ere where I can keep me minces on 'im. Be off swappin' babies and makin' cows go funny all over the place. Never sort it aht. No, I don't fink so.'

'Jacko the Amp?'

'Could be, could be, only Jacko does the bingo callin' dahn the social, doesn't 'e? Indispensable, our Jacko. Anyway, his muvver'd have me guts if I sent 'er boy off, wouldn't she. I'm not 'avin' Big Nell comin' rahnd 'ere givin' me brain damage abaht it. But an Amp is definitely wot you need, my lad. Get that soppy sister of yores to fetch Sparky, will ya?'

Vince took a small mushroom out of his inside pocket, punched it a few times and put it to his ear. 'Titania? You up yet? Dad wants a word wiv Sparky. Seen 'im? Oh did 'e just? Mucky little article. Well tug 'is collar an' tell 'im to put 'isself back in 'is trousies an' get over to the Toadstool Throne a bit smart. Right. Yeh. I'll do it. I said. When they come in, yeh. When I get 'em you'll be the first, stand on me.'

With that the Prince put the mushroom away and shook his head. 'Wot do you make of them gels, eh Dad? All I've 'ad for a week is "When's the new gossamer rah-rahs comin' in" and "Get us some silkworm tights". Fair does me 'ead in.'

'Gels. Don'tcha love 'em? Still, that's Sparky fixed up. Just the lad for the job is Sparky. Satisfaction guaranteed or yer money back.'

'Money?' said Vizagriz.

'Well, we can't just let 'im go for nuffink, can we? I mean, fink of the administrative over'ead. Fink of the management time. Fink of the replacement cost. Nah, couldn't let me best Amp go for, ooo, wot would you say, Vince?'

Vince looked up at the sky and appeared to consider all the options. 'Could be away for constellations, dad. Then there's the wear and tear. Couldn't do it for less than a piece of gold, and that's discount.'

'Piece of gold it is then. Cuttin' me own arm orf, mind. Still. Ah, 'ere 'e comes now. Sparky. Got a job for yer. Sparky's just the biz.'

'We'll see. This should cover it, plus some supplies,' said Vizagriz and took a gold Thaler from the purse. He held it out towards the toadstool and a spark of ice-blue light shot out, whirled around the approaching Amp and whizzed off into wherever.

Sparky leapt onto one leg to avoid it. 'Bleedin' 'ell. Wot woz that?'

'A Recognition. He'll do, Your Majesty.'

'Is there gonna be much of that?' asked Sparky, examining himself for scorch marks. 'I mean, I do the lectrix, usually.'

'Looks like yore it, my son. Better go an' pack. You'll be questin' wiv this 'ere wizard an' 'is happy gang. Off you go then, wot do you need, a written invitation? Gertchah.'

Sparky the Amp sprang away into the undergrowth. The King looked pleased with himself. 'Nice one. Try to get 'im back in one piece, won'tcha? On the other 'and, don't bother. Nyah-hah-hah.'

'Nyah-hah-hah,' Prince Vince joined in.

Vizagriz took his leave of the King and came back to where I was sitting. Winolene had braided the flowers she had gathered into a sort of circlet for her hair and was obviously feeling a bit more like herself. Mindador was still hunched up, peering at the ground.

'Well,' said Vizagriz. 'It looks like we have the next member of our merry crew. And we're off to Mustique Mountain, wherever that is.'

I jumped to me feet. 'You mean, an imp is coming with us?'

'Something like that. An Amp, as it transpires. I suppose he'll come in handy for lighting fires and stuff. Here he comes now.'

I looked in the direction Vizagriz had nodded and saw the woodland creature indicated skipping towards us with a small pack of luggage wrapped up in a chrysalis slung over his shoulder. 'Oh. It's him.'

'Wotcher. Are we off then? Oh. It's you.' Sparky and I had recognised each other from the muskrat incident. 'The peepin' tom.'

I started to gabble an explanation but Vizagriz cut me off and got us all up and moving, even Mindador. He had acquired a pot of honey from somewhere and a crocodile of faeries was bringing pieces of fruit, nuts and berries wrapped in large leaves and some vegetables plus what appeared to be hollowed-out giant acorn cups that might serve as drinking vessels. When we had packed these in the sacks and Vizagriz had told Winolene that oh yes, she was carrying her share and stop complaining, remember you're out, we set off from the enchanted glade.

Sparky had said Mustique Mountain was the other side of the woods and that the quickest way there was to skirt around them then follow a river to its course, so Vizagriz and I set off, followed by the Handmaiden with Sparky on her shoulder and Mindador, as usual, slumping along at the rear.

'Turn left, guv'nor and just keep on till we see the river. 'Ere, yore not a bad looker. Wot say we get up West some night, 'ave a good time, eh?' Winolene was trying her best to ignore Sparky, which is not easy when the persistent voice was right next to her ear.

Vizagriz gave me an outline of what had happened during his conversation with the King and what he knew about the InterWeb, which wasn't much. I had a question for him, though.

'Master, I've been trying to place that strange accent the imps and amps and, well, all of them have. I thought I'd heard it before and I've just realised where.'

'Oh? Do tell.'

'Your door.'

'Well, well,' said Vizagriz. 'Now there's a thing. Keep your eye on the trees round here. You might see some of his relatives.'

CHAPTER THE SEVENTH

In which Slouch meets two heroes, discovers that the World is flat, just like life, and learns something of the true nature of Magick.

The trek around the forest took a few days and nights. We supplemented our meagre rations with more fruit, nuts and berries as we found them and on one occasion caught a small deer. I had spotted it and Vizagriz threw an englamourment to stop it in its tracks. Master Mindador thwacked in on the head with a stick. We bled and quartered it, roasting as much as we could on an open fire and stashing what we couldn't eat into the sacks when it was cooled.

The nights had been warm and dry enough to sleep in the open, just on the forest margin but we tended not to stray inside it too much. As Vizagriz explained to us, a metaphorest is no place to get lost. Nothing is as it seems in a metaphorest - trees may not actually be there, but just give the appearance of trees and sometimes shift their meanings. I mentioned him at one point that is was hard to see very far into the metaphorest. There seemed to be something in the way. 'You mean, you can't see the wood for the trees,' he said and I had to admit he'd got it in a nutshell, at which point a nutshell dropped on me. Moreover, Magick doesn't really work or is at best unpredictable in the metaphorest, he said. That dealt with Winolene's almost constant whining about the ability or otherwise of wizards to conjure up carriages, boudoir tables, cosmetics, decent food and proper toilet arrangements. I doubted that was the only reason he didn't make much use of his Art. Still, Winolene was a country girl by upbringing and sturdy with it. Her airs and graces had subsided a bit and she was on the verge of actually not minding the walk.

Mindador continued to mope around and Sparky kept up an almost constant line in patter until Vizagriz shut him up with a fortune telling as to what his immediate future would hold if he didn't give it a rest, quest or no quest.

The amp was by any standards a filthy little beast. Apart from the incident with the muskrat, we knew fine he had often slunk off in the dead of night, in search of other small rodents to do unnameable things with, to and up. While we sat around the campfire, we were often aware, at the fringes of our hearing, of squeals of mammalian outrage and tiny, high-pitched sighs of ecstasy. Sparky returned soon after, with a smirk on his face like cat that had got to the vet's to find a sign saying, "Closed - Gone For Vasectomy".

One evening, he came back into the firelight circle rather sharpish and settled down on a log, muttering to himself that adders had "no sense of adventure". And the next night I glimpsed the heart-wrenching sight of a pair of dormice sitting just outwith the range of the lambent firelight, with expressions of deep longing on their faces. A magpie spent a whole day circling above us as we travelled, dropping twigs from its beak; and if you've never seen a weasel try to look coquettish, believe me, you haven't missed much.

We were followed, for hours on end, by pining pine-martens, wistful weasels and the occasional sad squirrel - although Sparky didn't have much time for squirrels after the time he came back a bit slowly, rubbing a part of his small but well-utilised anatomy and declaiming that squirrels were a bit literal-minded for his liking.

However, if nothing else, Sparky's nocturnal ramblings and the entertaining spectacle of various rodents having screaming, jealous rows gave me something to ponder over on the long march West. Was love never simple? How could I win over Winolene? Or was there some impenetrable emotional barrier between us that Sparky seemed able to vault with all manner of four-legged and furry creatures?

At least it kept my mind occupied. Let's face it, Mindador was as much fun as a wet Wodin's Day and Winolene just sniffed haughtily every time I tried to start up a dialogue and confined her replies to the barely civil.

Vizagriz, on the other hand, was most expansive, as if he were actually enjoying the quest. He took the opportunity of the long march to school me in some of the simpler spells associated with household chores. "Cantrips for camping trips" he called them, and I'm sure there was a joke in there somewhere. By the eighth day I was a dab hand at heating up water without a fire. Sparky took this hard, regarding it as his particular fiefdom, this being according to custom and practice. But I ignored him, which is very easy when there's a discrepancy in height of more than five feet.

But my Magick progressed! Vizagriz made me practice a good way off from the forest edge. On one occasion I managed to get some water to work itself up into a lather. And I even persuaded my clothes to dry themselves after a summer shower by vibrating like fury, only losing three buttons in the process. Vizagriz expressed himself extremely pleased with my progress, although he said I couldn't afford to get cocky and I wouldn't truly understand extropy until I could unboil an egg. But he awarded me a gold star for my report card. I already had three - Elementary Alchemy (with a special in nerve poisons), Warts Ancient and Modern, and Essential Divination. One more and I could trade them in with the Sorcerers Apprentice Society for a signal ring, a secret code book, a cap badge and - more importantly - a Grade I exemption from the College of Knollege entrance exam.

At this rate I could graduate at, oh, 65, but Vizagriz assured me that things would pick up a bit now that I had mastered the basics, and could even take on clients' simpler requests when we got back to Hanging Basket Street in Al Faq'Ahl. If we ever did.

To my own chagrin, though, I hadn't proved so good at conjuring food out of thin air as Winolene wanted. One the one occasion I tried it the steak was wooden and nearly pierced Mindador through the heart, except he ducked in time; the cup of Hospice wine had a passing resemblance to a sample from a horse with diabetes; and the dessert had all but melted with the heat by the time it materialised. The metaphorest effect, again. But Vizagriz wasn't disheartened. "Practice makes parfait", he would say. "You'll crack it yet!"

What he wouldn't let me try was the old stand-by - turning base metal, in my case a copper dinar - into silver. "These spells are tricky", he would explain. "They have a tendency to rebound, and you can get home to find the stash of gold in the sock under the mattress has turned to syrup. No fun, that!" He was right, too. I didn't like syrup.

I did come to understand, however, what Magick was about. Vizagriz explained to me more about extropy. It seems that some philosophers have posited a universe built purely on the laws of physics with no Magick (though such a thing is barely imaginable, and used simply as an example to prove how ludicrous the non-existence of Magick truly is). This world would operate by the transfer of energy from one form to another, with the loss of some energy as entropy on the way. Such a world would eventually run down. Everything would end up as uniformly-distributed heat and the whole of reality would eventually disappear up its own fundament. Such a universe is clearly impossible, since it would have a finite beginning and an end - some sages have gone so far as to propose an initial birth explosion (the Big Pang) and an eventual death in randomness of an even temperature (Deep Heat). Not only that, but a universe constructed on those lines would be no fun at all. As Vizagriz said, you couldn't even bend a spoon without using trickery.

But in a properly-constructed plane of existence, the natural tendency of matter and energy to get more and more disordered is balanced by the extropic principle on which Magick is founded. The lost entropy reappears as extropy - matter and energy created apparently out of nowhere. This happens spontaneously in any case, as when things go bump in the night, when screws disappear from their boxes only to turn up in another drawer weeks later, and when articles of ladies underwear mysteriously manifest themselves in gentlemen's pockets, defying rational explanation.

What wizards do is act as a focus and a sort of earthing mechanism for all this extropy. And if they didn't, Vizagriz said, there would be hell to pay - all that natural ordering tendency running loose, causing furniture to move around and frightening the horses.

No, he explained, wizards perform a natural and valuable function by siphoning it all off and putting it to good use. But it had to be used judiciously. Every time an extropic transformation happens, there is a local time-effect. As Vizagriz said, there's always a price. One of the consequences of eternity being constructed the way it is, and what other way could there be, is that energy and matter are really two aspects of the same thing: matter determines the shape of space and space and time are much the same. Didn't make a lot of sense to me at the time, either. But it works like this, he explained.

The reason extropy can be used to manifest things, transform one object into another and generally make material appear out what appears to be thin air, is that energy is a sort of fore-shadowing of matter. Matter, in turn, is energy slowed down and made to behave for a while. All energy has the potential to be all matter and what a wizard does is impose a sort of template on whatever extropic energy is about at the time. In a metaphorest the extropy is a bit tied up keeping things as they appear to be and there isn't a lot left over for your everyday sorceries.

But matter takes up space. Where there is matter, space - a naturally empty place - has to move out of the way a bit and keep its elbows in. So there's a bit more space than there should be, cramped up a bit tighter than is comfortable. It is, Vizagriz said, the natural tendency of space to get as much legroom as it can and it resists the material. It does this in a number of ways. One is by occasionally shuffling things about so it can stretch a bit - which is why places often seem further away than you remembered last time, or a road doesn't go quite where it says on the map, especially if the kids are screaming, "Are we there yet?" in the back and the wife is going on about sense of direction, the lack thereof, should have turned left but no, you have to try these stupid little cart tracks just because you once went to a tavern up here with your fishing mates. Another way space gets its own back is to hurry up time around an object. Time has to get past the object so space says, "Come on, there's a bit more of me here, get past this way" and time, being an obliging sort of quality, does just that.

Time, for its part, is a bit single minded. It just goes round and round. In one of Vizagriz's simpler books - The Ladybug Book of Time And Relative Dimensions in Space by The Doctor, with 43 Illustrations - I had read that eternity could be viewed as sort of oscillating rubber band. Everything that had and would happen took place along the band. Being a bit wobbly, the band moved about a bit, sometimes stretching (which is why Sun's Day afternoons, summer evenings and geography lessons seem to go for ever) and sometimes getting a bit close to other bits of the band. At these times there is the possibility of transfers between bits of the band, hence seeing the past and future and moving between them. All the possible moments are there on the band and time sort of moves along it at a reasonable canter but if one time gets close to another time they can become a bit mixed up and, fully worse, sometimes get into a knot.

Now imagine not one rubber band but a whole bag of them, representing the other realms and planes, all oscillating away like billy-oh and bumping into each other. That's why portways happen. Wizards, thaumaturges and scryers can sometimes force one of these bumpings-into and sometimes they just wait until one is due along so they can make the best of it. The oscillations and bumpings are reasonably predictable with a bit of hard sums and knowing the aspects. Occasionally a wizard overdoes it and a band breaks, lashing its ends about and getting caught up with others. Vizagriz said that was called a split infinity, something to be avoided at all costs.

That's the potted, five minute account, of course. Try Stephen The Hawk's clavicle, A Brief History of Rubber Bands if you want the long version. Can't make head nor tail it myself and it would have benefited from a few pictures.

What all this means, though, is that when extropy is invoked, time hurries up a bit nearby, like a stream sworling round a stone. This has an effect, not on the greater totality of existence, but on the person doing the extroping. Wizards and other Magick users age a bit faster than the rest of us, and the more Magick they do, the more they age. Not that don't live as long – they get their allotted span. If the rubber band has them down for 70 gyrations, that's what they get. They may age 200 gyrations in the process, mind, which is why they all look old, have bad tempers and tend to be a bit whiffy. Ever seen a young one? That's my point. They're all dead keen when they start, manifesting hither and yon, scrying like nobody's business and transporting themselves about like there's no tomorrow. Except there is, and it comes on them a bit fast. After a couple of years of hard-at-it magicking they wake up one lunchtime to find they're middle aged and had better slow down before they start losing their teeth, this knee's giving me gyp, I need to go more often nowadays.

Also, there is a limit to time's compressibility, or rather the more squeezed and stretched it gets, the more it resists – that rubber band effect again – so there's only a certain amount of extroping that a wizard can to within any given time span. That's why some spells take a long while, why some require more than one mage and another reason why a lot of Magick happens at the dead of night when there's not much else going on time-wise. It's also yet another excuse wizards have for not doing Magick when it is isn't strictly necessary. It wears them out.

I tried to explain this to Winolene one day when she was going on about there being two wizards here and neither of them can whistle up so much as a picnic basket. Wizards only use Magick when they have to, because they get older in the process. Quicker the better, she retorted. But Vizagriz suggested that it wouldn't be too hard to fix things so that she aged fast for a while instead of him so what did she fancy, a ten-course dinner with attendant footmen, glass slippers and a nice refreshment tent? She was quiet after that and went berry-collecting with a bit less mumping about it the next afternoon.

However, none of this appeared to be getting us any closer to our quest. I had sort of assumed we would turn up somewhere, biff a dragon, grab a jewelencrusted goblet and leg it, trolls pursuing us noisily but to no avail in the far distance, then transport ourselves home for a nice cuppa and "Here, remember that bit when you turned round and there was this huge serpent staring at you? Laugh?" That sort of thing.

But a quest seemed to go on for ever. True, we were heading for this Mustique Mountain and WebMistress Schlob, whoever she was, but we hadn't reached the river Sparky kept saying was "just around the next hill". It never was, and I realised that a sense of geography is somewhat different when you're the seeing the world from the approximate position of a mouse and generally do your travelling on the back of a mistlethrush. The whole place looks a bit different from above, I imagine, and not quite so spread out as when you're having to walk it.

It was getting dark and I suggested we might park ourselves in a copse I had seen over to the right. No, the left. Funny, I could have sworn it was on the right a while back. Must be catching Sparky's problem. Vizagriz agreed and we headed towards it.

We were down to our last bit of venison and hadn't come across much by the way of fruit recently – the metaphorest had gone all coniferous on us which, Vizagriz said, was its way of saying it was pining for something.

We got ourselves up small knoll towards the copse and I set about collecting firewood. Strangely, there wasn't any. The ground lacked the anticipated profusion of dead branches, leaf litter and twigs. Vizagriz had noticed this too. He also pointed out that the flowers weren't as randomly distributed as you might expect. They were in neat, round clumps, mostly of one type or where there were more, of the same colour. 'Somebody's looking after this place,' he said, 'I hope it doesn't mind trespassers.'

'Should we go somewhere else?' I asked.

'No point. If whatever it is knows we're here it's left us alone so far. If it doesn't, chances are it may not come by.'

I could see a fair number of holes in this logic but before I could politely point them out he continued. 'Anyway, whoever or whatever takes care of this wood has a tidy mind and can't be all bad. Ravening dæmons and fire-breathing monsters aren't usually dab hands at weeding nor do they typically have much time for pansies.'

All the same, it was going to be an eerie night. I decided the only way to get a fire going was to break off some of the lower branches and uproot a small bush or two. I did that and the fire was bit smokier than I'd have liked. Sparky was nowhere to be seen but he rarely ate with us – it doesn't take long to get through one raspberry and some beech mast. The atmosphere round the old campfire was more subdued than usual and Mindador had gone back to the private, manic cackling with the occasional thumping of the head with the heel of the hand. What was it with him?

After we had polished off the last of our supplies Winolene actually talked to me for about five minutes without slipping in an insult. She said the place reminded her of her sister's garden and she hoped to have a nice lawn one day, maybe a dog to go with her time-share cat and some decent wrought-iron patio chairs. I ruined the mood by asking what a patio was, some kind of meat paste presumably, and she gave me a withering look. I excused myself to go and stir the fire a bit and she started collecting daffodils.

It was nearly dark when Vizagriz sat bolt upright from his slump against a tree bole and shushed us all to be quiet and keep still. He got to his feet and reached for his staff, mumbling a protective spell. Mindador also got up and started making intricate hand gestures. I could see nothing untoward but when Winolene asked, 'What's the matter,' Vizagriz held out his arm to indicate she was to keep close to the fire and between him and Mindador.

Slowly, as the sky darkened, I became aware of a faint, blue light shining and blinking through the trees and the distant sound of crunching, like someone walking slowly but purposefully. When a deep voice said, 'Elloelloello!' I almost jumped out of my skin. We all whirled around to the direction the voice had come from and saw before us a stand of trees where there had been far fewer last time we looked. 'What's goin' on 'ere, then.'

Vizagriz upped his murmuring to a full chant and started waving his stick. The voice from the trees said, 'Now then, now then, there's no need to go brandishing sticks about, is there? You just put it down and we'll say no more about it. Evenin' Miss. These people bothering you?'

This was obviously directed at Winolene who looked on the verge of letting out a world-class shriek except that it was competing with a strangled gurgling somewhere in her throat. The voice continued.

'So what have we here? Oh dear oh dear! Starting a fire in a public place. Vandalism.

Aggravated flower-collecting. And various other offences against the Parks and Gardens Act. They'll throw the book at you. Three months without the option, I shouldn't wonder. Anything you say will be taken down and may be used. Right. Names.'

Vizagriz had obviously got enough of a warding spell up by this time as he relaxed a bit. 'I am a wizard and mage of Al Faq'Ahl. These travellers are under my protection. My colleague there is a potent thaumaturge, the boy is my apprentice and the Lady is a Handmaiden of the Fiery Swan, Vesta. May we have the pleasure of your names, by way of return?' I noticed that Vizagriz hadn't actually given any names as such.

'Wizard, thauma-thauma-sorcerer, apprentice, Vestal, er, Handmaiden. Right. Now, what are you all a doing of hereabouts? Come on! These are serious charges.'

Vizagriz seemed to have caught a glimmering of what was going on. 'Are you some sort of guard or militia?'

The trees seemed to stand a bit straighter all of a sudden. 'Twenty years in the Force, all of us. Not many can say that.'

'Well, you certainly keep this place very nice and guard it well. Keen on a spot of gardening?'

'Oh, you know. You do what you can to make the place look attractive. Nothing the public likes better than a well-presented militia station, is there. And it's no trouble really.'

'I see. So how many of you are there?'

'Six, counting the Sergeant.'

'May we see you, have a chat face to face?'

'You can see us. You're lookin' straight at us. What's up? Been taking something we shouldn't have, wacky baccy, bit of E? Best to get it of your chest. It'll all be taken into consideration.'

'You are... the trees?' Even Vizagriz was surprised. Mindador, however, was flapping and clucking agitatedly.

'Vizagriz, Vizagriz, I've heard about this. It's the Enchanted Copse. They were a city militia patrol in Glesca but they raided a sabot one night and got in the way of a transforming rapture. They were turned into trees. But I never imagined they were still around.'

'Well, well, well, we are a bit of a grass, aren't we? What did you say your mate's name was, Vizagriz? Write that down, Constable.'

The wizard was visibly put out by this. 'Oh, thank you very much. Give away my name, why don't you, especially to an englamoured evergreen!' Mindador muttered that he was sorry, it just slipped out, but Vizagriz wasn't listening. 'Look.' he said. 'My companions and I are Questers. We are on a perilous mission entrusted to us by The Two.

We are merely passing by and hoped to spend a night here in shelter. If we have done any damage, we apologise and we'll try to put it back. Sorry about the fire, okay?'

'That's more like it. Don't know what The Beak will have to say, mind. Bit harsh on vandalism, she is. Anyway, I don't hold with this questing business. You're the third lot we've had recently with that story. Makes a change from "I was keeping it for a friend" I suppose. You've got better manners than the others, though, I'll say that.'

'Others? What others?'

'Perhaps you know them. Two big lads, right tearaways, armed to the teeth. They didn't stay long. Gave PC 29 a right hammering with a double-headed axe, mind. They're for a sudden trip down the stairs if I ever catch them again. Hats with horns on. Leather jackets. Ring any bells? '

'I'm afraid not. We're on our own. As far as I know.'

'The other one was by himself. Looked a bit of a loner. Hood, funny hands. Didn't get much of a chance to see him properly. Asked a couple of questions - always happy to oblige, of course - and he went off.'

'Which way?'

'Pardon?'

'Which way did this loner go off?'

'You are an inquisitive wizard, aren't you? And here's me thinking we were asking the questions. You're still in trouble, you know.'

Vizagriz obviously considered the placatory attitude was still likely to be the most fruitful. 'Look, I'll tell you what I know. We have been asked to get back something that is lost or stolen. We have to return it to the rightful owners. There are obviously others after it too. I didn't know that, but I suspected it would happen. The quicker we find it, and before anyone else if possible, the quicker it'll get back where it belongs.'

'Ahah! Recovery of purloined property! That's more like it. Sort of loss adjusters, are you? Undercover?'

'That sort of thing. Now, we have to catch the other lot if we're to get the goods before them. Do you know where they were all headed?'

'I don't, but DC Douglas will. He's the one with the info.'

'Is he?'

'Certainly. He's Special Branch.'

'Of course he is. Should have seen it coming. Can you ask him?'

There was a sort of gentle soughing, like wind through branches. Vizagriz had relaxed a bit and Mindador had stopped gesticulating. Winolene had been mercifully quiet throughout the entire episode. I was still as confused as ever but at least I was taking it in my stride. 'Master,' I whispered. 'Who are these other people they mentioned?'

'At a guess? Couple of heroes and somebody up to no good.'

'Heroes?' I was thrilled. Winolene turned when she heard it, as well.

'Could be wrong, mind. Could be two fruitball hooligans and a travelling icon salesman. Except...'

'Yes?'

'Except they all mentioned a quest. When questioned.'

The trees seemed to have come to a decision and the rushing sound had stopped. 'Me and the lads, we don't think you're bad sorts. Funny taste in hats, though. Still, we've decided to let The Beak see the evidence and make a judgement. Stay here.'

There seemed, after a moment, to be slightly fewer trees in front of us than before, then I heard a rustling of wings and an owl flew down perched on a low branch opposite us and cleared its throat.

'All rise,' said the enchanted copse voice. 'Pray silence for the Bench, The Magistrate Minerva presiding.'

The owl looked at us all with slow-blinking eyes and arranged its feathers, settling down. 'Carry on, Erl-Sergeant,' she hooted.

'Thank you, Ma'am. We were proceeding, well, nowhere really, when we came upon the four accused making what appeared to be a fire. The young lady was vandalising the flower beds and the young man had broken some branches. When challenged, their leader brandished an offensive weapon, to wit, a stick. The other one made menacing gestures.'

'And what are the charges?'

'Going equipped. Threatening behaviour. Aggravated defacing. Flowergathering with intent to arrange. Speeding in a built-up wood.'

'Speeding?' the owl whooed.

'We might not offer evidence on that one, Your Honour.'

'I see. And what is the defence? Who represents?'

Vizagriz had either been through this sort of thing before or had got the measure of it. He rose to speak. 'May it please the bench, I will represent us. Vizagriz, wizard in good standing and Immediate Past President of the Sages of the Purple Ride.'

'A Purple Rider, eh? Very well, you may proceed.'

'Your Honour, we meant no harm. We are on a quest and inadvertently strayed into this place. We have reason to believe that a crime has been or is about to be committed, and we intend to stop this happening and to restore a rather valuable item to its owners. If I might suggest an adjournment, we will undertake to return and present the evidence to the court.'

'Good idea. This Bench will hold itself in recess until then. However, you are bound over and bailed to return. I will not take kindly to any more nonsense. Is that clear?'

'Perfectly, Your Worship,' said Vizagriz and bowed. The owl, however, was not finished.

'And you, young man, I take it you have a trade?'

I was dumbstruck at being addressed by a nocturnal bird but Vizagriz nudged me. 'Er, yes, may't please Your Worship. I am indentured to the wizard as his acolyte and apprentice.'

'Glad to hear it. What about the girl? Does her family know she's out gadding with the rest of you?'

Winolene let off a full court curtsey and said, 'I am avowed to a temple, Your Worship, and I have to accompany the wizard on his quest.'

'Community service, eh? Good thing too. What about him, the odd-looking one?'

Mindador didn't manage to say much of anything beyond mumbling his name and the fact that he was also a mage. Of sorts.

'Don't like the look of him. Funny eyes. Good mind to hold him over till next session.'

Vizagriz spoke up again. 'If I may speak on his behalf, he is central to our quest. He has certain knowledge which we will need if we are to apprehend the malfeasants and fulfil our commission.'

'Told you he was a grass,' a quiet voice said from the direction of the trees.

'Very well, then. Erl-Sergeant. have you any objection to my conditions?'

'None, Your Honour.'

'Good. Court adjourned.'

'All rise,' the enchanted copse said again, and off flew the owl. 'Got away with that one, didn't you? Still, you had a good brief. No hard feelings.'

Vizagriz stood up and walked over to where the voice cane from. 'So. Any idea where the others were headed?'

'We've heard from DC Douglas. He's been in deep cover, posing as a shrubbery down the hill a bit. They went off towards the inn.'

'A tavern!' said Vizagriz.

'A bath!' said Winolene.

'A bed!' said Mindador.

'Achoo!' said Slouch. I was getting a chill.

Vizagriz took directions then suggested we got some sleep and set off before first light. 'Mind how you go. Evenin' all!' the copse said.

Winolene wasn't for it. She obviously had her mind set on that bath. 'Do we have to stay here? It's creepy.'

'Oh, I think we'll be quite safe. All these guards around your sleeping-chamber? Answer to a Handmaiden's prayer, I should have thought.'

With that, we all settled down. Then I realised – where was Sparky? A muffled squeal from the bushes and a shout of "Oi! What do you think you're playing at. Put that rabbit down!" answered my question. A faint blue light headed off into the distance and when all was quiet, I snuffled myself to sleep.

CHAPTER THE EIGHTH

In which Slouch learns more of the nature of Magick, and of oxcart drivers. He also learns about beer, tavern-owners' daughters and fights in hostelries.

When we emerged from the enchanted copse next morning, having carefully disposed of any breakfast litter and making sure we didn't step on anything other than grass, we followed a stream until noon, when we reached a cart track which wound away in both directions.

'Wonder where this road goes?' I mused.

'Looks like it stays right here,' opined the Amp, who was turning into a real smartarse and feeling a bit pleased with himself after his amatory exploits the previous night. The fact that he'd evaded capture only seemed to add spice to his adventure. I might have to step on him at some stage, I thought.

Vizagriz put his head up an sniffed the air. 'Probably goes to a village. Most roads do, after all. It's what they're for. Anyway, the copse said there was an inn nearby. With any luck there'll be a cart or wagon along in a minute and we can get a lift. I'll just consult the time table.'

He raised his arms beside his head, his fingers extended like claws, and opened his eyes wide, which gave him the appearance of a startled deer. But I knew a scrying spell when I saw one. Vizagriz often did this the night before horse races.

But Winolene wasn't having this. 'Hold on,' she said, 'you don't mean that carts run along here according to a schedule, do you?'

'Probably not,' Vizagriz admitted. 'But since all events are predestined, I can peer into the near future and see if any carts are predestined in the next little while. If they are, we wait; if not, we move on until we get to somewhere that carts are predestined. All right? Now if you don't mind, I'll get on with it.'

But Winolene still wasn't happy. 'No, just a minute, I did Philosophy at school, you know, and events can't be predetermined because if they are, there would be no point to any action since the outcome would be set in advance, and then, and then, there wouldn't be any point to this quest. Or anything. I mean, you could just look ahead a bit, see what was going to happen, and then we could either go through the motions or just forget it accordingly. Can't be!'

It was the most she'd said since we started. Vizagriz put his arms down and rubbed his eyes. 'Well what they probably didn't tell you at Roe Dean or wherever, but which every wizard knows from the cradle almost, is that reality is conditioned locally and for short times by the totality of recent events. Small events don't make much of a ripple in the fabric of things, but Great Events reset the clock. That's why we can't see all that far into the future, because it hasn't been fully determined yet and is a bit far along the band.'

I don't know if she got the rubber band reference, but if not, she didn't let on.

'However, I don't think the arrival of a cart can reasonably called a Great Event, not unless it flies here, and I don't see any other Great Event going on in the neighbourhood, so the chances are I'll be able to suss out the schedule of carts and wagons, right? Now if you DON'T mind...,' and he went back to staring again.

Winolene was poking at the ground with the toe of her now rather tatty slipper, somewhat withered by the blast. 'The sisters at the temple say we're all responsible for our own actions and that we have to propitiate Vesta and through her The Goddess else no good will come of it. Can't be predestined, then, can it?' But no-one was really listening. We all wanted to know what was happening to our cart or wagon. All except Mindador, who as usual was prepared for the worst.

'I'll bet there isn't one. Never is when you really want one. Then three come all at once.'

Vizagriz ignored this, him being in a trance and all, and after a few minutes he breathed out, blinked and put his hands down. 'So what's the answer?' Mindador asked petulantly. 'Every cart for miles in the repair shop, I suppose?'

'Actually, no.' Vizagriz said tiredly. 'There should be one in about half an hour, give or take.'

'Give or take? Whatever happened to accuracy? Oy!'

'What happened to accuracy, friend Mindador, and why I was away so long, is that things are a bit fuzzy, almost as if there were indeed some Great Event round the corner. If I didn't know better...,' he squinted off down the track and back towards the metaphorest. But he let it drift.

'Anyway, I suggest we wait for it. Slouch will make us all a nice cup of thea leaves, and we can hang on here. It's as good a place as any, and I'm still knackered from dealing with that stupid enchanted copse. Can't get much sleep when there's militia nearby, arboreal or otherwise.'

I busied myself collecting twigs for a fire, which were more in evidence here than they had been the night before and to my delight Winolene, who hadn't said much to me for a while, came with me and got some leaves and moss together. The Amp spent a frustrated few minutes trying to set light to this fairly soggy mixture but he finally managed to get it to take, largely by shouting at it and jumping up and down a lot. I collected some water in the now-empty honey pot, threw in a few thea leaves and got the cups out.

We were just settling down to drink the infusion when, wouldn't you know it, an oxcart loaded with hay rolled around the nearest bend. There was a fair amount of flurry and swearing while everyone gulped the scalding liquid and I put the beakers away. Vizagriz stepped out in front of the cart. He made one of his imposing wizardly gestures and said, 'Hold, good Sir. I, Vizagriz the Magnificent would like to speak with you.' Magnificent. That was a new one. Still, we were in the country where they're impressed by these things.

When the cart rolled to a halt beside us, I looked from ox to driver and couldn't see much difference. The carter was short, squat and ugly, with a big round bald head and a pugnacious face that looked like a pit bull with a grudge. He surveyed Vizagriz, who was still holding his imposing stance.

'Wot?' he offered.

'Ah, a fine morning to you, good carter. I wondered if we, that is, my companions and I, could solicit your aid in this, our Noble and Holy Quest. We would travel with you to the nearest village or town, or settlement, even, where we might obtain lodgings and sustenance.' Wizards feel they have to talk that way to strangers. Part of the image, but they can't usually keep it up for long.

For his part, the carter looked around us as if weighing up the trouble if he said yes against the trouble if he said no. He rubbed his stubbly chin with a big paw, and the ox lowed softly as if to say "I know damn fine who's going to be taking the strain on this one, squire".

'Well, it's against the rules you know, taking passengers. More than me job's worth, really.'

Vizagriz patted his pouch ostentatiously. 'We understand that this would put you to inconvenience, and would acknowledge that fact with recompense in the form of specie,' he said, grandly.

'I was thinking more of cash, meself,' the carter explained. 'I mean, it's a good distance, out of me way really. I was going home, after all. But I suppose so. We could say, mebbe, oh... five florins?'

'Agreed!' said Vizagriz.

'Each,' added the wily cart driver.

'Oh, come on! You can't count the sprite here, he takes up less room than my hat. Mindador is on the pension, and as for my apprentice, he's never a full fare. He's barely started shaving!'

Behind me, I heard my beloved Winolene titter and I could have strangled someone, possibly myself.

'Call it a Thaler the lot, then,' Vizagriz offered. 'Done,' said the carter, and we certainly had been. 'Swilbury suit you?'

As we piled into the cart, Mindador muttered, 'I knew a straw cart would come into this. I don't suppose it occurred to anyone that two wizards could have persuaded him to take us to the oxterworld and back for free.'

'Why didn't you suggest it, then?' I asked, reasonably.

'Not my money, is it? Anyway, I'd probably have had to stay awake to watch him,' and true to form, he settled down in a corner with a pile of straw, pulled his cowl over his eyes and started snoring.

The journey took about four hours and was no hay ride. At least, it was a hay ride as far as the fact that we were riding, and we were in hay, but you know what I mean. Winolene sat as far away from me as possible, which is not very in a small cart, but I got the message.

Worse still, we were subjected to a constant monologue from the driver, who let us know exactly what he thought about mythical beings, heroes, dæmons, witches, politics, the way the country was run, every known form of sport and a great deal else beside.

'I mean, you're a wizard, right?' he addressed Vizagriz who had sat up front with him and was certainly regretting it. 'So you tell me, am I wrong, or what? And as for them Hebryds, they're all the same, it's nobbut Thalers, sesterts and dinars with them, and they keep it all to themselves. And what about them immigrants from the dark continent? I'd send them back, me, right away! Wouldn't even let them off the boat. They only come across here to have lots of babies and get some free Magick. I mean, what's the point of a National Mage service anyway? If people can't afford to save up for their Magick, they shouldn't have any. Sponging off the state like that! I'm private, meself. If I want a potion or a hex lifted or a note for a few days off, I pay for it. I've got pride, me! 'Ere, I had that Gandalf in the back of me cart once...' and much more in the same vein.

Mindador was still asleep, which was a blessing in the light of the anti-Hebryd references, and rolling them home good-oh. Winolene was sitting back with her eyes closed trying to pretend the World wasn't there. The Amp was amusing himself alternately leering at Winolene in his smutty little two-inch-tall way and making cat's cradles out of electrical sparks between his fingertips. I was gazing off into the middle distance and thinking about Winolene, as usual, wondering why she didn't like me, as usual, and getting a headache. The carter just droned on and on.

' ...so what I say is, what's the point of a quest if there's no dragon's treasure at the end of it? A Magick ring at least. Listen, I had them Halflings in the back of me cart once...'

Vizagriz put up with this for a while, muttering "Hmm" and "Yes" and "You don't say" and "Absolutely" and "Mmhmm" every few minutes until, on the pretext of getting a clay pipe out of his pack, he made a few mystic passes, cast a limited Wall of Deafness around all of us, winked at me, and settled down to puff at his tabac. The rest of the journey was uneventful except for the bit where the Amp set fire to the straw and no-one else noticed, what with us all being temporarily deaf. But we dealt with that, and it even livened up the trip a bit.

Vizagriz had set the deafness spell on a timer, and it lifted just before we reached the village. It meant we had to endure a few minutes of Jon the Carter boring on. But the welcome sight of people and buildings distracted us. I did notice, though, that the various market stalls, which I would have expected to be busy selling food, were a bit bare. Must be the end of trading, I rationalised.

The cart drew to a shambling halt outside an inn called the Frog and Hatstand and our driver stepped down. The ox found something fascinating on the road and started chewing it.

'...anyway, what I say is, I don't mind paying taxes, not like some, but if I can get a few florins buckshee, where's the harm in that, eh? You're probably the same. I'll have that gold Thaler now, if it's all the same to you. Got to get back to Barsoom. Nice place, Swilbury, but not what you'd call alive, know what I mean?'

As we unloaded ourselves off the cart – which involved waking up Mindador, prodding me to say we had arrived, me being off in some private world of my own, and offering Winolene a hand (which she ignored) – Vizagriz took the gold Thaler out of his pouch and handed it to Jon the Carter with, I thought, surprisingly good grace. If there's one thing your average wizard likes more than a good lunch it's hanging onto the gold. I waited for the Recognition and thankfully, there was none. I could not imagine being stuck with the rabbitting carter for the rest of the quest. His ox wasn't much company either.

The carter accepted the coin, bit it and grinned. 'Anyway, that's the inn. I highly recommend it. The Landgrave's called Mukk. Good mate of mine. Just tell him Barsoom Jon the Carter sent you and he'll see you all right.' He spun the Thaler in the air but as he caught the coin, it took a googly spin, bounced off his hand and landed among the straw in the back of the ox-cart. As we collected ourselves together and went into the tavern, Jon was scrabbling around in the hay looking for his earnings. We left him cursing and throwing hay about. I wanted to help, but Vizagriz whispered, 'Come on,' grabbing my sleeve and propelling me into the swing doors of the inn. Mindador hung back a bit, as if he wasn't quite sure what he would find inside.

The Frog and Hatstand was pleasant enough, with a roaring log fire and just enough customers to attest to its popularity without suggesting it was packed every night. It looked like just the sort of place we could have a day's rest and some decent food, and maybe Vizagriz would let me try some of that beer stuff he was so fond of. He strode up to the counter, which was being polished by a large rubicund man with a white towel tucked into his breeches.

'All hail, Landgrave, and a Wizard's Blessing on all here!' Vizagriz intoned, just so that everybody would get the point. 'My companions and I are on a Holy Quest, and would fain sojourn at your most excellent hostelry for a night or two, ere we once more set off on our appointed task.' He looked around grandly, and indeed some of the custom looked to be impressed. A wizard was not a common sight away from major towns, there not being much money in provincial practice. The Landgrave, however, had clearly seen it all before and wasn't going to be upstaged in his own place.

'Aye, Sir wizard. If you and your fellow Questers are indeed of good faith and well-meant, welcome to our humble tavern, and welcome again! We have the finest ale, food that is plain but wholesome and filling, and beds that are clean and well-aired. No credit, as a refusal often offends.'

Vizagriz had met his match in this one, I thought. But he rallied. 'Then we are content to bide with you, Landgrave. Pray have rooms made up: one for myself and my apprentice; one for Master Mindador, a most puissant thaumaturge; and one for the Lady Winolene, Handmaiden to the Fiery Swan, Vesta.'

'Hoy!' exclaimed a small voice from below the bar. 'What about us mythical beings, eh?'

'Oh yes. Remiss of me! Put some wadding in a shoebox for my friend the Amp, there's, a good fellow!'

'You've got an Amp?' This had impressed the Landgrave and the customers, who all started pretending to stand up and rearrange their trousers nonchalantly or going to the bar, but really trying to get a better look at our two-inch tall sprite. Mine Host sidled out from behind the bar counter, heading for the taproom and kitchen. 'My daughter, Abigal, will see to your accommodation. Please be seated at yon table near the ingle and I'll bring you ale and food presently.'

'Kindly do so, and in that order!' ordered Vizagriz.

At the thought of food Mindador looked a bit more composed, and we settled down in wooden seats near to the fire. As Winolene arranged her skirts before sitting down, she caught Sparky trying to glance a quick peek up her petticoats, which didn't improve her mood. He grinned, winked, and limbered onto our table to perch on up-turned beer mug.

By the time we were settled, the Landgrave was back and asking what ale we'd like. 'Apart from my own brew, of which I am most proud, and call Hatstand Winter Oilchange, we have a wide range of beers, some from as far away as the next Countdom.'

'Ahah!' exclaimed Vizagriz, livening up. 'And what would you recommend, good Landgrave?' he asked in his ingratiating best. This was the most animated I had seen him since the time he caught his beard in the toaster at Muffin Tide.

'Well, Sirs and Lady. There's some as likes the ale from the Ruddy Dells. Others again swear by the Best Courage. Yet more, though their opinion is not wholly uniform, hold mainly to the Spearbreaker. For myself, I am partial to the Fat Porter. Draught, not so much the bottled. We also have a wide range of imported lagers.'

'Not the lagers, I feel, they encourage loutish behaviour. But the ales sound most excellent. Bring them all, good host, and we will give you our judgement as to their relative merits! The lad is on halves. I am not.' Vizagriz smacked his lips and rubbed his hands together.

Winolene gave a tiny cough. 'Ah yes, how rude of me,' Vizagriz added as the ales turned up. 'The Lady Winolene does not partake of the giggle water, this being one of the vows of her calling, but no doubt you have some unfermented fruit beverage which would please her palate.' The Amp crossed his arms and cleared his throat. Vizagriz gave him a look, and added, 'and you might find a thimble for our faerie friend. Oh, and Landgrave – please take this gold Thaler as a deposit for our stay and sustenance, and as a token of our good faith. We're on expenses.' I was as surprised as the Landgrave at Vizagriz's unaccustomed generosity, until I happened to glance out of the window and caught sight of Jon the Carter flinging armfuls of hay about, looking for the coin that quite clearly Vizagriz had managed to spirit back from him, cheeky beggar. I looked over at my master, who merely raised his eyebrows and set about parting an ale with his nose.

I confess I took to the beer after the first few mouthfuls and had got used to the bitter taste. When we had all sunk a couple, and Vizagriz had given me a cautionary frown about not overdoing it, the Landgrave returned with his towel over his arm, all ready to be the waiter. 'Would you be ready to order food, Sirs, Lady and, er, Your Ampship...'

Vizagriz smacked his lips again and licked his moustaches. If there's one thing a wizard likes more than a gold Thaler, it's his dinner. And no-one could deny he (and the rest of us, come to that) deserved it after the rigours of the past few days.

'So, Landgrave Mukk, what gustatory delights can you tempt us with, this fine evening? Eh?' The hand rubbing started up.

'Well, we normally have haunch of venison, ribs of beef, mutton stew and loin of pork.'

'Splendid! That'll do for a start.'

'Ah! I did say "normally". We don't actually have anything except pork. I'm afraid it's all off just at the moment. Except for the pork. Just at the moment'

'Why? Lot of trade recently? Not paid the flesher?' Vizagriz laughed, nudging Mindador, who grunted.

'Ah, no, great wizard. But all the cattle went down with Brain Sponge and the deer had mange.'

'The sheep?'

'Husk'

'Ah! Well, no matter. The pork will do fine.'

Mindador went pale. 'Not for me it won't.'

Vizagriz looked at him, then nodded in understanding. 'I had forgot. My friend Mindador does not eat of the pig. You presumably have chickens, or other game birds? A pigeon or two?'

'Afraid not, sirs. The chickens and woodcocks all got fowlpest. Pigeons have been at something of a premium since then and they're keeping their distance.'

'They would. But no doubt Mindador will be happy to make his repast, just this once, on fresh fruit and good country vegetables.'

'Yessss...well, that would normally be all right, but there was a bad blight this year in the orchards.'

Vizagriz patted Mindador on the knee. 'Looks like it's potatoes and pickled cabbage, old horse!'

'Sorry, we finished the horse last week.'

Vizagriz was not going to be put off his good mood and ordered the pork - pork chops, pork loin, pork sausages, pig's blood pudding, trotters, chitlins and boiled potted head. 'Finish this lot and there'll be nothing left of that pig but the squeal,' he announced and started tucking into the various platters as they arrived. Winolene also displayed a hearty appetite and proved the value of a good finishing school in teaching gels to eat substantially but in such a way that nobody notices they're troughing it down. Mindador made the best of his pickled vegetables and potato soup, remarking that at least it was hot, for a change. I just got on with it although my stomach felt like it might call it a day before I did.

The inn had started to fill up, this being a Satyr's Day evening I supposed, and various parties ensconced themselves near the bar, against a wall or in dark recesses as was their wont. When we had made a complete fool of all the dishes set before us and Vizagriz was leaning back, patting his stomach and grinning, the Landgrave reappeared to tell us that our rooms were ready. In a corner by the window a canary was singing to the approaching twilight.

'Isn't this pleasant? Off you go, Slouch. See that all's well, will you?. I'll have the bed farthest from the draught.'

Winolene asked if she might have hot water, towels and any form of soap whatsoever. The Landgrave rejoined that his daughter would be happy to give her whatever requisites were typical and that she could have a tub drawn in her room if that was her wish. She all but cheered at this, then remembered herself and said that she thought that would probably just about do and set off upstairs to see to it.

I followed her but not as quickly as I might have done and with considerably less accuracy than I was accustomed to. The stairs appeared to move about a bit and didn't go quite where I expected them. The whole thing was a good deal funnier than it justified, too. My head seemed a bit fuddled. Vizagriz was calling for yet more ale and slapping Mindador on the back, who looked less than delighted at this attention and said something about some people being more pickled than the cabbage. I didn't understand this but chose not to worry about it.

At the top of the stairs - eventually - there were three doors open. Through one of them I could see someone flinging sheets about and plumping up pillows. I went in and said 'Is this where I'm sleeping?'

The bed maker turned around and smiled and my head almost burst. I don't know what it is about the countryside but they certainly breed healthy-looking girls. This one was obviously Abigal, the daughter of the establishment and she had rosy cheeks, a full head of dark curly hair, green eyes that flashed with her white smile and, well, her dress didn't so much cover her as try to hold in various bits that seemed to have a life of their own.

'Are you the apprentice? Ooh, father didn't say you were handsome.'

'Arghlblrrghflxbwmph,' I said, or something similar but I was cut off by the sight of her bending forward across the bed to smooth the quilt, affording me a deep view down a canyon that wouldn't have disgraced the Crocky Mountains. She sidled round the bed and stood about as close to me as my own skin which felt all prickly as if looking forward to the competition.

'You'll have a good sleep tonight, won't you? If sleep's what you're after! The beds here are very comfortable. Especially mine. Anything I can... get you?'

I was trying my best to get the back of my brain, which knew exactly what it was I might want, to tell the front what it might be called in words, when there was a steely voice from the doorway.

'When you've finished distracting Slouch, perhaps you could see to that tub I was promised.'

'Winolene! I was just, I mean the young lady was, that is, she was just getting everything ready for me.'

'I can see that,' Winolene spat and stood to one side as she made sure Abigal left the room. Abigal gave me a wink as she did so and said, 'My room's just above yours in the attic. Knock me up if you need anything.' Winolene said "Humph!", threw me one of her special hands-on-hips glares and slammed the door.

Confused? Certainly I was. Had Abigal just been nice to me because I was a guest? Was Winolene angry because her bath was getting cold? Or was she... No. She couldn't possibly be jealous, could she? I lay back on one of the beds to think about it and watch the roof spinning but closed eyes seemed the better part of valour and I imagine I dropped off quite soon.

'Anyway,' I said to the Dikkeadh, 'I said, "What you really want is a Sphere of Substance with a bit of Warding thrown in. Shouldn't take more than a couple of days if I can have some help with the entrails," and he said that would be fine, so what I did, and this is the really clever part, I used the first half of Blagdon's Erupting Crystal with that bit from Faust's Fancy, you know, where you twist the lizard's head off and, oh you know the one I mean, and chucked in some soap powder. Well, you have never seen a bubble like it - grew and grew until it enveloped the entire city and it held for seven days and nights. Kept the Hordes of Hoggath away, I can tell you. Surely you remember?'

'I remember all right. I also remember when it burst and everyone got covered in slime.'

'Minor side effect. Nobody minded really.'

'They minded when it started to eat through the walls of their houses and they couldn't get if off their hats. Were you on a kick-back from the milliners' guild or the builders' merchant?'

'Oh, it wasn't as bad as all that.'

'Yes it was. Everyone said "Vizagriz will never work in this city again". It was about that time you developed a sudden interest in transcultural transmogrifications and went of to the dark continent for couple of years, wasn't it?'

'Coincidence, Mindador, coincidence. Anyway, as soon as I got back - and a fascinating trip it was, I must tell you about it sometime ...'

'Yes, you must. Sometime. I'm off to bed.' Mindador hoisted himself none too steadily and started to slide his way out from behind the table. 'Mind you, how I'll ever sleep with all that sour cabbage and...'

The door had opened and a tall, dark-cowled figure entered the inn. The face was obscured and the hands were folded into the capacious sleeves. There were no feet to be seen and the new entrant moved across the inn like a bat on casters. Heading for the darkest recess the figure got seated and picked up an empty tankard, waving it at the Landgrave in a signal he understood. A clean, full replacement was picked up by his daughter who had finished her upstairs duties and was doubly busy trying to fulfil the customers' requests for ale and repulse their requests for whatever else they felt might just be on the menu, weaving and avoiding grabs and pinches, giggling as she went. This time, though, the Landgrave caught her elbow and signalled that he would take the drink across. The atmosphere had subsided from a raucous babble to a quiet susurrus but when the visitor spun a coin out from within the sleeve and nodded once at the Landgrave when he put the tankard down the place slowly regained its previous level of noisy enjoyment.

The patrons had obviously decided that there wasn't much more to be seen and went back to their card game, laughing and grabbing at Abigal as she passed who skilfully bodyswerved every one of them.

Mindador, however, had seated himself again and was fiddling with his robe as if in the grips of some inner turmoil. 'Vizagriz,' he muttered.

'Yes, what is it? Have I told you about...'

'Listen Vizagriz. I haven't been entirely honest with you.'

Vizagriz pulled himself up, shook his head, muttered an incantation containing words that sounded like "enzyme" and "dehydrogenase" and was instantly as sober as teetotal judge during Lent at a temperance meeting.

'I know, Mindador. I'm well aware of that. Time you levelled with me then, isn't it?'

'You see that tall, dark person who came in a few minutes ago.'

'I didn't, but I do now. What about it?'

'I think "It" is right. I'm not sure that's human.'

'Come on, Mindador. You know more than that.'

'Right. Yes. Sorry, Well, it's like this...'

All of sudden there was a crash, two crashes and the doorway was filled with huge, painted tribesmen, each bearing a massive two-handed sword and a grudge, by the looks. The second crash must have been the back door giving way as more tribesmen appeared from the kitchen entrance, one of them holding Landgrave Mukk by the collar with one hand and a struggling scullery-boy with the other. The entire inn went silent, and not just the customers. Chairs stopped creaking, floorboards were quiet and even the canary in the corner was keeping schtumm in case anyone noticed him.

The dark stranger rose from the recess and stood in the middle of the floor. 'Landgrave. Some drinks for my guests. And perhaps these... wizards... would join me?' The voice was a low, hissing growl and there was no knowing what type of tongue had formed the words, the hood being impenetrable still.

The tribesmen started to file up to the bar or position themselves strategically around the room, one to each table, one by the window and two at the foot of the stairs. Mukk did exactly as he was told, sensible man that he was, and plonked full tankards in front of the savages.

Vizagriz remained seated but Mindador oscillated between upright and sessile as if he couldn't decide which was the more dangerous – staying where he was or making a bolt for it past the painted warriors. Vizagriz pulled Mindador down and elbowed him. When Mindador looked him, he nodded down at his fingers, which were making a complicated gesture beneath the table top. Mindador swallowed and nodded. Then and only then, did Vizagriz stand. 'I will happily drink with anyone, when I know his NAME!'

At the last, shouted word he pointed at the figure and a gust of wind blew the hood off. All the tribesmen took a step forward but the now-revealed visitor held up a restraining arm. 'Wait,' she said. 'Why should not friends see each others' faces while they share a flagon or two?' The voice was the same, low rasp but it belied the countenance which was that of a handsome, redheaded Northlander woman. The hood off, she also discarded the cloak to reveal what were obviously artistocrat clothes designed for far riding – a fine brocaded shirt under a slashed kid-leather jerkin, green trews and brown leather thigh boots polished to a high gleam. Her waist was girt with a fine filigree belt clasped by a buckle of gold centred with an opal. She had no weapon save a ceremonial dirk thrust into a silvered horn sheath.

'Forgive my Kuntz bodyguard. Their zeal may be excessive, but it is refreshing in these faithless days. Now, wizard. Your drink.'

'Your name, stranger.'

'I? I am Nazrat. And you?'

'Just "wizard" will do for now.'

'As you wish. Landgrave, a flagon of wine.'

Vizagriz accepted a cup from Mukk but left it untouched. 'Your henchmen made quite an entrance, Nazrat. Did they have to come in both ways at once? Or were they worried they might get left tied up in the cart park?'

The tall women threw back her head and laughed, shaking her fiery red hair. 'Oh, very good, wizard. You realise, if I were not here to control them they would have run you through for a remark like that.'

'If you were not here to control them, I doubt they could find their own backsides using both hands and helping each other!'

'Do not test their loyalty to me any further, mage. There are limits to what even I can stop them doing.'

'Perhaps you could stop them stinking the place out. They smell like they sleep with pigs, and I don't just mean they share a sty.'

That finally did it for one of the savages. He roared, raised his huge sword and brought it down on the nearest games table, neatly bisecting the wood and ruining forever one old man's chances of a grand slam, redoubled. The redhead shouted a single word of command in a guttural foreign tongue and the tribesman went back to merely growling.

'Come, wizard. You have tested my mettle enough. Are you ready to discuss business?'

'What business could simple wandering wizard have with such a captain of men? Need a wart cured? Saddle blisters playing up?'

'I think you know, wizard. We seek the same artefact, do we not? A certain valuable bird? I can assure you, I will get to it before you do, so we may as well join forces. I can further assure you that the rewards of joining with me are far more tolerable than the penalties of opposing me.'

'That may be,' Vizagriz replied. 'But the pleasure of travelling in your company is less attractive than the prospect of what may befall us when the quest is fulfilled.'

Again the tall woman laughed. 'Come, come. Wizards have protections, I'm told. How could these simple Kuntz hill-dwellers threaten your safety? They are, I assure you, in mortal dread of your magicks. Had they not been, they might have used your head for a fruitball long before now. They have been following you for days.'

'Really? Then they must have been very bored indeed. And if they were following me how is it that you reached the enchanted copse before we did?'

'Ah. I said they were following you. I, on the other hand, was some way in front. However, I was able to retrace some of your steps and find out what you know. You are heading towards a mountain are you not, to consult with a Web?'

'If you know this, why do you need us?'

'I know about a mountain. I do not know which mountain. They did not have time to tell us.'

'Who?' Vizagriz asked, and in answer the woman threw handful of what looked like dried leaves onto the table. On closer inspection they were the broken, lifeless bodies of six faeries. One of them was King Pearly.

'You fiend!' shouted Vizagriz. 'Mindador. NOW!'

A flash of light, a pall of smoke and a loud bang covered the next few seconds in confusion. Four of the tribesmen fell back, holding their faces and shrieking. A further four at the bar were dispatched by Vizagriz who blasted one with a burst of flame, vanished a second into oblivion and hit the other two on their heads with his staff. Two of the remaining four rushed toward the wizards and the others rushed up the stairs.

Just at that moment there was a further crash and the windows shattered as two more warriors burst in through the inn's windows. One rolled forward and sprang upwards to thrust his sword through a tribesman's stomach. The other newcomer landed on a table, vaulted upwards and in falling brought his two-headed axe down on the last tribesman's head, cleaving it almost to his collar.

'Upstairs!' Vizagriz shouted.

I had missed all of this, of course, being asleep, but I was dragged back to consciousness by a piercing scream that went straight through my head and bounced off all the walls. My first thought was "Winolene!" I leapt out of bed, rushed next door and saw the Handmaiden standing upright in a tub, covering herself inadequately with a small flannel and a lot of shrieking. Before her was the hulking form of what looked like a huge, hairy ape. The Deity knows what possessed me but I rushed at the massive shape and propelled it towards the window. Its own momentum must have done the rest, as it tripped on the bed leg and carried on to crash out of the window into the yard below. I had barely started breathing when another scream made me spin round to find another hulk framed in the doorway. I could see now that these were not apes but-fur-clad savages. This one was clearly going to avenge his compatriot's plunge, but he was momentarily distracted by the sight of Winolene at her ablutions, albeit yelling her head off at the same time. The hesitation was enough because as he raised his sword to cut me in two a blade appeared between his ribs and disappeared again, leaving a spreading stain on his furs. As he fell forward he revealed the grinning face of a warrior clad in sheepskin and sporting a horned helmet. 'Evening, love. Nice bath?' the face said.

Winolene spun around to face me, covering not quite enough of herself. 'Well, don't just stand there you oaf. Hand me a towel!'

The rest of the evening in the inn was a bit more subdued. I had rushed downstairs after helping Winolene cover her embarrassment, a task she felt took rather a long time and one I felt hadn't lasted quite long enough. I had also dragged the dead savage out into the passageway so she could close the door. But I was anxious to see what had been going on and if Vizagriz was all right. The sight that greeted me down in the tavern was gory in the extreme. Five savages lay quietly steaming from burn marks, like they had been struck by lightening. Two others were conscious but bound hand and foot. A further two were in various stages of disembowelment or decapitation. There was one still seeping blood upstairs and a look out of the shattered window confirmed that the first-floor plunger wasn't going to be having breakfast.

Abigal was all but hysterical, saying over and over, 'The poor faeries, the poor faeries,' until Vizagriz showed her a handful of dead leaves. I heard him say, 'Tell her, Sparky. What happens to faerie-folk when they die?'

'Dead faeries?' I asked

The Amp appeared from a parting in Vizagriz's beard and said, 'They just fade away.'

'That's right,' said my master. 'When Nazrat threw those bodies on the table, Sparky was hiding in my hair. He told me that they couldn't be faeries – the bodies just wouldn't last that long. Then I knew it was an illusion and that we were in the presence of potent Magick. Mindador had a blasting spell cocked and ready and he let it go when I gave the signal.'

'Nazrat?' I inquired.

'That got some of them. I got a few more and these gentlemen seem to have dispatched the rest of the Kuntz.'

'Kuntz?' I interjected.

'I don't know how or why they got here, but it was in the nick of time, I'll say that. Unlike a hero to actually be of some use.'

'Heroes?' I queried.

'But Nazrat seems to have disappeared in the melee. I didn't even see her go, which makes me even more nervous.'

'WILL SOMEBODY PLEASE TELL ME WHAT'S BEEN GOING ON?' I demanded and everyone fell silent.

'Ah, Slouch. Took care of things upstairs, did you? With a bit of help, I believe. Good-oh.'

Then he explained to me the proceedings of the last half-hour while the two heroes helped the inn's patrons to drag the various corpses outside into the yard.

Quite a lot of the furniture was scorched or shattered. Mukk, the Landgrave, was in deep shock at the damage. Abigal had cheered up a bit with the news that the dead faeries weren't real, and was giving the heroes free drinks and a lot of attention. Vizagriz and Mindador were deep in discussion and I got a severe tongue-lashing from Winolene, now dressed and downstairs, on correct behaviour in ladies' boudoirs. She seemed to have forgotten that I had saved her life. One and a half times. Gratitude? Women!

Vizagriz took Mukk to one side and called me over. 'I'm sorry for the destruction. My companions and I accept it's partly our fault. Now, I could pay for it, but I have a better idea. Your real problem is not getting new bar stools, it's getting the custom back. Occult battles tend to flatten trade for a bit. But I have an idea. Tell everyone here to let the locals know there was some trouble tonight but that it's all cleared up. Won't happen again. And tomorrow there'll be free wizardry here at the Frog. Bring their warts, their cows that won't calf and any frogs they want kissing. And a fireworks show for the kiddies. Believe me, you'll sell more ale than you would in a fourteennight. Sort of a benefit. All right?'

That seemed to lift his spirits somewhat and he and Abigal plus the kitchen boy who had nearly stopped quaking set about clearing up the debris and swabbing the blood off the floors. The two heroes, however, were content to get stuck into their freeman's and chuck the empty tankards at the two bound Kuntz, as Vizagriz had called them, propped up against the bar and looking surly, worried and battered. Various locals spat on them bravely as they left for home, forgetting that for the majority their part in the fracas had been to hide in the privy. In later years the anniversary of the event was celebrated by a "How many can we cram into the earth closet" competition, but the record for that night was never broken.

Eventually, after all the patrons had been persuaded to go home, Mukk bolted the doors, (Vizagriz having magicked up some new, complete windows for him out of the debris) and went to bed, leaving us Questers alone with the heroes. Winolene retired with a headache. Mindador was still shaken by the experience and retired. Abigal had long since been sent upstairs by her father, Sparky offering to light her way like a candle. The little pervert never missed a trick. Vizagriz and I sat down opposite the two rough-clad warriors and poured them another flagon each of wine. I started to give myself one but my stomach thought better of it and I filled a tankard with water from Mukk's butt behind the bar.

I was completely in awe of the two swordsmen and didn't say much but had a good chance to examine them closely. So this was how heroes dressed for real. They were fairly similar in look and costume and were of a disparity in ages that might have made them father and son. They both had their hair in long braids and each sported one of those bushy mustaches that makes the wearer look like he's half way through eating a hamster. Horned helmets lay on the table beside long, steel swords and a double-headed axe. They kept shorter, curved swords stuck in their broad leather belts which went round sheepskin jackets. Under his jacket the younger one had a shirt that seemed to bear two large initials – C. P. Probably his name, I thought, or a protective sigil.

'So, gentlemen. Good thing you turned up when you did,' Vizagriz said, pouring them drinks.

'Oh, we've been tracking that lot for days,' the older warrior replied. 'Lost them at one point near some talking woods but we picked up their trail again and they came here. We were going to wait till they went to sleep and bonk them about a bit but when we saw the fight starting – well! Couldn't miss a rumble like that, could we?'

'Well I'm glad you did,' Vizagriz complimented. 'You certainly saved the Lady Winolene's neck and a few other bits I imagine. I'm grateful.'

'We'll see how grateful she is in a minute,' the hero said and leered.

'I don't know, you were doing not badly yourself, wizard,' the younger one said. 'The lad here got one as well. You'd probably have managed.'

'Now, now, Rongwei. That's not Stage Four. Come on, what are the stages in a battle?'

'Right, no, I know this one. Okay. First, lay about yourself regardless.'

'Correct. Next?'

'Check all other rooms, floors, passages, crypts, holes in the ground or similar places of concealment and polish off the stragglers.'

'Right. Three?'

'Quaffing. Rapine and wenching if available. Accolade of the natives.'

'Yes. We'll do the community relations module next year but quaffing is fine and there's time for the other. And last but not least...'

'Divvy the treasure and boasting.'

'Good. Nice one. So, take all the credit. Now where did we go wrong tonight? Come on, it's constructive criticism time.'

'Okay, let's see. Should have come in one at the back and one at the front,' said the younger one, Rongwei.

'Except...'

'Except there was a chance for a dramatic entrance.'

'There certainly was. How about the entrance itself, then?'

'I dunno. I felt I could have landed a bit better. You know, not so much rolling.'

'I felt that too. I did. A five-point-eight for technical merit but somewhere in the high fours for artistic ability, I'm afraid. Mind you, it was lucky that barbarian was in your way. You nearly got the dartboard.'

'You don't miss a thing, do you Egric?'

'That's my job. Now, if our friends here will just hand over all their valuables, we'll pop upstairs and see if these two nice young gels will help us with the middle bit of stage three, shall we?' The younger hero blushed a bit at this and seemed reluctant to go.

Vizagriz had let this exchange carry on longer than I though he might have. He seemed enthralled. 'This is fascinating. Am I to understand you're on some sort of training scheme?'

The elder of the two spoke up and extended a huge paw to shaken by Vizagriz talon-like hand. 'Sorry, should have said. I'm Egric, External Supervisor brackets Pillaging Experience Placement close brackets, Conan Polytechnic. Rongwei here is in his third year and heading, if I'm not giving too much away, for a very creditable two-one. Depends on his thesis, of course. Got the practical off pat but not one for handing in the essays.'

'Fascinating,' Vizagriz said again.

'Yeh,' Rongwei chipped in. 'I'm doing a dissertation on "Dialectic Materialism As An Alternative To Blind Violence In The Sacred Quest". But I'm hoping to get a job as a temple guard eventually.'

'He does himself down,' Egric interjected. 'Got a Blue for Mayhem and was Captain of Visigoths. He'll go far.'

Rongwei muttered into his tankard a bit and blushed again. A blushing hero. Not what I had imagined.

'Whatever,' Egric continued, draining his tankard. 'As I was saying, the only bits left are collecting the loot and the wenching. Hate a loose end, me. Hand it over.' He extended his paw towards Vizagriz who demurred.

'You want our valuables, do you? Bit risky that, trying to take a wizard's money. We tend to be a bit possessive. You understand.'

'Nothing personal. Rules and that. Way it's always been.'

'Hmm. I wonder, however, if you would accept this?' From his hand he flicked a gold Thaler. It spun in the air and just before it hit the table it let off a fwoosh and zipped a blue flash at Rongwei which circled him twice before zooming up the stairs and away.

Egric had leapt to his feet and had the short, curved sword out. Nippy on his feet for such a big fellow. Vizagriz placated him, though. 'Now, now, it's all right. That's a Recognition spell. Seems you're bound with us in our quest.'

'Quest? As is Sacred Quest?' Rongwei interjected now that the shock had passed. 'Here, Egric, that's just what I need for my thesis, isn't it?'

Egric replaced his sword in his belt and sat down far more slowly than he had jumped up. 'Could be, son, could be. But I'll need to know a lot more about it first.'

'I wish I could tell you more,' Vizagriz said, taking off his hat and laying it casually over the gold coin now lying sedately on the table. 'We appear to have been gathered together to find something called the Holy Quail and...'

'Holy Quail! That's what them Kuntz were talking about, wasn't it, Egric?'

'Yes,' Vizagriz confirmed. 'They seem to be after it too, or at least their leader was.'

'Leader?' Egric queried. 'Tall bloke in a long cloak?'

'Sort of,' Vizagriz answered. 'Not a bloke, though. Rather striking lady-type person. Red hair. Gave her name as...'

'Red Sonja!' Rongwei interjected, clearly fascinated at the prospect of meeting a legend.

'Nazrat, in fact,' Vizagriz disabused him. 'And not all she seems. More than she seems, really. Uses illusions. Has a voice like a wood saw. Wouldn't be surprised if she's actually an it. Dæmon to be precise. Now, how did you come across them?'

It transpired that Egric and his pupil Rongwei had been heading for a pre-arranged bit of pillaging across the Howling Desert. There were some cities there that offered work experience to student heroes. They went and beat up the neighbours, sacked nearby temples, found bits of lost treasure for them and generally did all the left-over heroing that wouldn't otherwise get done. A good deal all round from which everyone benefited.

Egric and Rongwei had been surprised one night to come across a band of Kuntz hill-tribesmen so far from their homes in the Crocky Mountains and had crept close to their encampment to find out whether they were worth engaging. Given that there were twelve of them they felt a bit of intelligence-gathering would be a suitable first step. They had heard the tall person talk to the savages about a mysterious artefact called the Holy Quail and how, when they found it, everything would come to a sorry end. They, the Kuntz, would have their way with anyone they fancied and could take over the known world or some similar, typical promise.

The heroes had then overheard the tribesmen discussing it – Egric had a smattering of Kuntz picked from his days ravaging the hill forts round the base of the Crockys and had gathered that their plan was predictably simple, straightforward and stupid. They would follow the tall stranger until the artefact was found, take it for themselves and go home. What they would then do with it wasn't even considered, but how much sophisticated thinking would you expect from a race which can't count above eight without taking its boots off?

Egric and Rongwei decided that following the Kuntz would be a good idea. They had missed them on a sharp bend at one point and got ahead of them, reaching the enchanted copse just before the Kuntz's leader. Waiting for the Kuntz to catch up they had seen the tall figure conjure up some sort of apparition and ask it a question which seemed to involve a recipe of some sort. Next thing, they were at the inn and giving it rice with the swordplay.

Vizagriz considered all this for a while then shared his thoughts with the rest of us.

'It is as I suspected,' he concluded. 'Nazrat is a dæmon or at least in concert with dæmons, and Baking Dæmons at that. They want this Holy Quail and what you say about "everything coming to an end" makes sense, too. For some reason the Baking Dæmons have decided to dupe my fellow traveller, Mindador, into thinking they're helping him with his quest for this Holy Quail, which he fondly imagines he's doing on behalf of an Order of monks back in Al Faq'Ahl. For our part, we seem to have been sent on this wild quail chase by The Two who feel the object is theirs, for some unspecified purpose, and a fair amount of cosmic arm-twisting has gone on to get all of us together at this point in time. I feel, gentlemen, that our quest is really beginning!'

I was up to speed with most of this except the references to Baking Dæmons and The Two continued to elude me. I might have asked Vizagriz to expound if I hadn't fallen asleep on my arms at the table.

And the next day was a bit busy.

CHAPTER THE NINETH

In which Slouch takes part in a circus, gleans more of the nature of heroes and meets a Web Weaver.

Next morning, after a substantial breakfast of fruit in a kind of thick, soured milk, hot rolls and a bitter drink called khoffi that grew locally, Vizagriz held court outside the Frog and Hatstand. The word had gone round as he had instructed and it seemed like the entire countryside had turned up for a free peek. The inn was as busy as it could be and Mukk had to take on extra staff to cope with the demand. I helped him out, ferrying empty tankards and goblets back to the kitchen and rinsing them out. Other than that, I went about gathering provisions for the rest of our journey.

Abigal was alternately carrying out trays of drink and food and flirting with Egric. I wondered how she had the strength given the amount of tossing and turning I had heard from her bedroom above me during the night. She obviously hadn't got a lot of sleep, poor girl. Probably the strain of it all.

Vizagriz was consulted by a constant queue of peasantry for whom he cured warts, gave advice on crop blight, lifted the odd hex and generally did the sort of small-time country wizarding that could keep a nice little practice going. If I ever qualify, I thought, I might like to set up in a place like this – fresh air, a pleasant inn to go to of an evening, nothing too demanding in the necromancy department. Quite a good life.

Mindador had been persuaded to set up a sort of booth affair and did fortune telling with the aid of a scrying sphere he conjured up for the purpose. I went to listen in for a while and heard a great deal about tall, dark, handsome strangers, messages concealed behind pictures and how a lady dressed in pink with a paintbrush in her hand was going to be lucky. Cowherds, harvest workers and someone whose house had a green roof would be celebrating too.

The two heroes joined in with the fun, doing strong-man stunts, giving the children rides on their backs two at a time and judging the egg-and-spoon races. They won the arm-wrestling hands down, if you'll forgive me.

Some farmers' wives had brought cakes, pies and jars of preserves and they were all buying each others' in the sort of circular economy that keeps small places going.

A popular event was throwing mud, glaur and old vegetables at the two Kuntz whom Egric and Rongwei had placed in the stocks for this purpose. They growled and howled for a while but eventually subsided into a sullen acceptance that said 'This is bad but I know what's going to happen to us after it's over so I might as well enjoy this part."

The braver individuals paid a dinar to look in Mukk's barn at the bodies of the Kuntz dispatched the night before, strung up for display. They would be ritually burned the next day when the local Freer would come round and intone prayers for their souls, much good might it do them.

Sparky was nowhere in sight but there was a bit of a flurry around the Kiddies Pet Show.

Even Winolene appeared to enjoy the day, going about looking at the horses and talking to some of the better-off landowners about harvest festivals, pageants and dinner parties. They seemed to regard her as a tad exotic, her coming from the other side of the globe and a large city at that, and she was happy to give it the sophisticated bit for their edification. She was even consulted on a couple of matters concerning the arrangement of flowers, which surely made her week. Vizagriz had asked her to look out for a string of sturdy ponies and she had found a few good ones - round, bright-eyed things they were - and haggled with the owner so much he finally all but gave them away to stop the earache. She tied them up behind the inn with Egric and Rongwei's horses and gave them each some hay and a bag of oats to be getting on with.

Dogs barked, cattle were bought and sold, old friends renewed their acquaintance and swains disappeared into the woods with their beloveds, coming back a bit flushed and nonchalant a couple of minutes apart.

Towards evening, just when he judged that everybody had had almost exactly enough, Vizagriz finished off the proceedings with a mystical pyrotechnics display that had all the children ooh-ing and aah-ing and sent them off tired but happy. Every child below ten got a small coin or a tiny toy found in their ears and the whole occasion was judged the most wonderful success, must do it more often, we ought to make it an annual event, let's get a committee together, ciao!

When the rush had died down and only the locals were left in the inn, each one telling the others exactly what he'd have done to them Kuntz if only Fred there hadn't got in the way, Mukk expressed himself extremely pleased with his testimonial. The Frog had taken more cash than it normally saw in a month and he was sure its fame would spread. He even tried to hand back Vizagriz his gold Thaler which the wizard, surprisingly, declined, saying that if Mukk hadn't been meant to have it he surely wouldn't have been able to hold onto it. This puzzled Mukk but he took it in good part and bit the coin just to make sure.

The Landgrave had even bought some beef from a farmer whose cattle hadn't suffered the Brain Sponge (yet) which Abigal fried up and served with fresh vegetables, to Mindador's relief and delight.

The two heroes had brought their own supplies, not least a Snarler they had trapped a few days back and was just high enough to roast, which Egric persuaded Abigal to do. They got stuck into this, chewing the meat but eschewing the vegetables. "Real men don't eat greens," Rongwei had said to me, leading me to a series of conclusions about the heroic temperament and the regularity of their bowels which I won't bore you with.

I had sat myself between the two heroes in the hope that they would tell me tales of derring-do and put me right on certain continuity errors I had found in the illustrated stories, way back. But Egric was more concerned with getting as much Snarler meat and ale inside him as he could manage - 'Never know when you might next get a decent meal or a night's sleep, so take as much of both as you can,' he advised - and winking at Winolene who avoided his gaze the whole evening and sat in haughty silence, breaking it only to ask Mukk for another cup of water.

Rongwei had other ideas, if you can grace them with that title. He was not so much gnawing the Snarler bone as making love to it, but he broke off between great gulpings and chewings to wave the meat-shredded object at me and make philosophical points. It was not a pretty sight. What he was saying was no less outrageous, either.

'The World MUST be flat. Everyone knows that.'

'Why? That's stupid.'

'Well, if the World is flat, then it's like a dinner plate, yes? With a rim on the outside to stop the water falling off and a sort of dip in the middle where the gravy, er, the Middle Sea sits, yes?'

'With you so far.' I wasn't really.

'But if the World ISN'T flat, then the dinner plate isn't flat either. All dinner plates must be spherical, like a ball, and your peas will roll off and fall into your napkin, right?'

'Er...'

'Is your dinner plate spherical?'

'Well, no...'

'And do your peas fall off?'

'No, I can't say they do.'

'And when you put your fork into a carrot, does the plate roll away and bounce on the floor like a fruitball?'

'No. I can honestly say that has never happened to me.'

'So your plate is flat. With a dip in the middle.'

'I believe so. Yes.' I felt I'd missed something. And I knew for certain that Rongwei was missing something too. A few marbles, perhaps.

'So if the plate is flat, and you agreed the world was like a plate, then the World is flat too. What's good for one is good for the other.'

'But, no, hang on...'

'Ah, you were going to say "Maybe the World is round but just appears flat because of the way we observe it", weren't you?'

'Was I?'

'Yes, and if that were the case, then balls...'

'The very word I had in mind,' said Egric.

'No, listen, balls would also appear flat, just like dinner plates and you wouldn't be able to kick them. Kick the balls, that is.'

'Which I'd like to,' added Egric.

'So the World MUST be flat.' Rongwei concluded, and sat back, self satisfied grin on his features, the smug bastard. Trying to think of a place to start unravelling his train of thought, I felt like a man with a stone in his shoe – he knows it's there, but he can't quite find it, and it's damn irritating.

'QED,' Rongwei added, to rub salt in it.

'What's that mean, Kyew Ee Dee?' asked Egric, not really bothered.

Rongwei's brows furrowed momentarily. 'I'm not entirely sure, but it's what philosophers say when they get it right. I think it means "Quiet, Egghead Deliberating".'

We all turned in early, except Vizagriz and Mindador who got themselves into a corner for a quiet discussion to which no-one else was invited, apparently. I tried to get to sleep but there was a lot to think about, which kept my head awake when the rest of me was dog tired.

My attempts to drop off weren't helped by Abigal apparently having a stomachache, which I imagined accounted for the "oh, Oh, OOOOH" noises coming from above. Poor girl, She didn't get a lot of rest, but she seemed to look well enough on it.

I was no clearer on what the Holy Quail was or why some many people wanted to get their hands on it, nor why this particular group of people seemed to have been fingered for the task of finding the damn thing. What part would Winolene, for instance, play in the quest? For that matter, what part would I? I remembered Vizagriz's reference to the Stooge Eternal and was none too pleased by that. Was this to be my contribution to Destiny? And why couldn't Vizagriz just Magick up a scrying, like Mindador had done, see where we were supposed to go and manifest a flying carpet to get us there? Moreover, who was this Nazrat I had missed the night before?

It was nearly Watching Hour when my brain gave in and curled up for a doze, about the time that Abigal finally stopped moaning. I must get one of the wizards to give her something for that, I thought as I drifted off.

We were up and at it by dawn. Winolene had managed to get something more appropriate for riding than her acres of petticoat and while I fed and watered the ponies Vizagriz took his leave of Mukk. The heroes were looking a bit liverish and said they'd catch us up. Mindador was eyeing his pony suspiciously and the pony in question was giving him the same back. I loaded the spare animal with our provisions and got them all round the front, ready for the off. Sparky was sitting between the ears of one of the ponies having decided that the other end wasn't much use to him given the disparity in sizes.

As we mounted – Winolene easily, me with a bit of circularity, Vizagriz by virtue of an immobilising spell and Mindador with a great deal of swearing – I remembered what I had meant to ask Vizagriz.

'Master,' I said. 'I think Abigal's got a bit of a problem. Do you have a nostrum that would make her feel more comfortable?'

'Oh, I think you'll find Egric's given her one and she's all the better for it,' he replied.

'Does Egric know about women's troubles, then?'

'Almost certainly. He's probably caused a good few in his time. Giddyap!'

With that, we started off down the track, out of Swilbury and towards Mustique Mountain.

Sparky expressed himself confident that we weren't far away from the river we had to follow but we'd heard it all before. By the time we stopped for lunch, the heroes had caught up with us. They told Vizagriz the slightly disquieting news that the Kuntz had gone from their stocks and the locks were still fast. Vizagriz mused on this for a bit and announced that we should get a move on, no time to waste. We went at a fair old canter for the rest of the day, slept in the lee of a hillock that night while Rongwei and Egric took turns on guard and set off again the next morning.

Mindador had just about got the hang of staying on but his pony had a tendency to pull up sharp and explore the botany every so often, which usually catapulted the old mage onto its neck. I tried to start up the occasional conversation with Winolene but she confined her responses to the monosyllabic and to issuing occasional instructions about the management, care and feeding of equines. It was towards evening that Sparky suddenly jumped up and down excitedly on Vizagriz's shoulder and pointed into the far distance. Sure enough, we could see the tell-tale sparkle of what could well be a river and hidden in clouds there did indeed seem to be a mountain. We estimated that we would reach it by next nightfall and headed towards a stone circle that would offer some shelter from the wind that was starting up around us.

Again, we cooked supper, settled the animals, organised a watch rota with me involved this time and Vizagriz made a few muttered incantations around the ring of stones before having a quiet word with the two heroes then getting his head down.

I was on first and sat upright against a henge of sorts, listening to the various snorings, snufflings and coughs that sleeping people make.

I had no idea that I had dropped off, so soporific was the sound of ponies and people breathing quietly, that I started a bit when I felt a hand on my shoulder. Rongwei come to tell me it's his turn, I thought. I was rudely disabused of that when another hand was clamped across my face and I was yanked backwards out of the circle and onto the grass, with a blade at my throat. I opened my eyes to see the horrible sight of a Kuntz tribesman about a handspan away.

I was quickly and roughly tied up, gagged and thrown over a shoulder, the owner of which loped off along the plain with me aboard. I was terrified but could do nothing about my situation except hope it would resolve itself soon. After half an hour or so I was unceremoniously dumped on the ground and my gag – but not my bindings – torn off. My captor propped me up against a blasted tree trunk. Before me was the other Kuntz and a tall, striking women with read hair. I say she was striking because she was striking me. This must be Nazrat that Vizagriz and the heroes had talked about, I realised.

'So, you've brought me a whelp, have you?' she growled in a low, grating voice. 'No matter, he'll do for the moment. Tell me, boy, where is it that you're headed?'

I was dumbstruck by fear and winded by my landing so I couldn't say anything. This won me another cuffing. 'Come on, we know you're aiming for the mountain. Why? What's there? Is it the Quail?'

I shook my head as if to say I didn't know but this only served to earn me another cuffing, this time from the savage.

'Leave him. If you beat him senseless, we'll get nothing out of him. I have other ways.' In Nazrat's hand there was a lash. I knew exactly what she meant. At SamBernardo's it had figured strongly in the curriculum. I was trembling and not really capable of speech. Nevertheless, Nazrat hunched down and tried me again.

'You're pretty, you know that, boy? There are certain friends of mine who would find you toothsome. I don't mean these hill-dwellers – they would just disembowel you and you'd die in a few hours. What my friends would have in mind is something a bit more drawn out and certainly involving a long marinade. Now, I can spare you that. Just tell me what you know and I'll dispatch you quickly. The only thing we have to agree is whether you tell me now or after I've flayed most of the skin from your body. Doesn't matter to me. I've got all night. I do think, though, you ought to think carefully about how you want me to spend it.'

She stood up again and barked something at the Kuntz who both grunted and sat down sullenly, as if they'd been left out of something for bringing the wrong kit and had to watch from the sidelines. I had no idea what to do. The little I knew about our quest probably wouldn't satisfy Nazrat – she'd think I was holding back on her. By the time she realised I'd given out everything I could, I wouldn't be in any sort of fit state and she'd probably take out her rage on me with some foul torture. Or there was that oblique reference to cookery. Cookery! Vizagriz had said something about Baking Dæmons. I had no idea who or what they were but I was fairly sure I was talking to one now, or would be doing so in the not too distant future. What I needed was a miracle. What I expected was to feel a burning sensation quite soon. What I didn't expect was that it would start in my wrists.

There was definitely heat behind my back and a smell of something being singed. Was I imagining it because of my predicament? I had my answer soon enough – a tiny voice whispered in my ear, "Keep quiet, I'll get your ropes off. Vizagriz says tell her anything you like, just keep her talking. When I give the word, run for it." Sparky! The little Amp was cutting through my bonds but keeping the voltage down so as not to make too much light or noise. I kept as still as I could.

Nazrat had finished her conversation with the two fur-clad monsters and was standing above me again. 'Decided to talk?' she asked. I nodded quickly.

'Good for you. Sensible boy. We'll try to get this over with as speedily as possible, then. Shall we?'

Again I nodded.

'Fine. Let's start with the Holy Quail, then. Where is it?'

'We don't know. We were told to head for Mustique Mountain and consult a web spinner. That's all I can tell you.'

'I see. And who sent you on this quest? The Order?' Nazrat rasped.

'You mean, the Order of Penitent Martyrs of the Flesh? I was in their care for a while.'

'Were you, indeed? So you're part of Mindador's effort right enough. How did you come to be in this place?'

'Mindador conjured up a maelstrom of some kind and we fell into it. I brought us to near here and we've been travelling ever since.'

'Towards this mountain. So who is the web spinner?'

'We don't know, honest. All we know is that we have to ask a question.'

'What question? Do tell.'

'We don't know that either.'

Nazrat laughed, horribly, a rough, gargling laugh that made me shudder all the more. 'Oh, please. You're not really trying, are you? Why would anyone go to ask a question if they don't know what question to ask? You're holding out on me, boy. I have a solution for that.'

Nazrat stood up and raised the lash above her head, I closed my eyes, ready for the all-too-familiar sting of leather, when a number of things happened at once. One was a high voice in my ear saying, "NOW!" The second was me leaping to my feet. The third was a glimpse of Nazrat looking at her lash, which had caught fire. The next was Egric putting a sword through one Kuntz and kicking the other away with his foot. After that it got a bit confused. There was some swordplay which ended with the other Kuntz lying down holding the backs of his legs and howling, a few flashes which illuminated Nazrat and Vizagriz standing facing each other with their arms raised and me running straight into the tree I had been tied to, knocking myself cold.

When I came to it was almost day. There was enough light to see that Nazrat was kneeling on the ground, surrounded by spinning loops of flame and what looked like a glass tube, except that it kept changing colour and didn't seem to be all that solid. Egric was standing over me saying, 'He'll be all right.' Vizagriz was in front of Nazrat, sweat popping from his brow and chanting.

'Once again, I conjure thee, foul dæmon, by all the power at my command and by Hok, by Lyne and by Sinquer, give up to me thy true form, they true name and thy true purpose, then return to thy fiery pit and return no more to this demesne. I bind thee and command thee, tell me these three things, then shalt thou be released. First, show me thy form!'

The swirling bands spun ever faster and within them the red-haired women slowly mutated into a red-bodied dragon with small, ineffectual-looking wings and long, highly efficient claws. A tongue lashed out and licked the air, if there was any, within the cage of fire.

'Now thy true form is before me, reveal unto me they name, by all the mysteries of Shed!'

The sinuous tongue flicked a few times and the great maw opened to form the word, "Patisse".

'Thy form and thy secret name are before me, a most potent mage and commander of thy destiny. Shew me thy purpose ere I fling thee back whence thou wert spawned. By all that holds thee, give me thy intent!'

At this the dæmon threw back its massive, reptilian head and laughed the same rasping laugh I had heard Nazrat use. 'NEVER!' it shouted and with a bang the fire bands blew apart and smoke drifted in the place where the worm had lately been.

Vizagriz murmured a few more abjurations, twirled his staff a couple of times and sprinkled a handful of powder around the site of the conjuration. Then he sank to the ground, clearly exhausted. 'Put years on me, that has. Literally.'

'Master!' I gasped. 'Are you all right?'

Vizagriz took a while to answer but eventually he struggled to his feet and clasped me on the shoulder. 'Yes, lad. I'll be fine. I'm older but I'm none the wiser. Still, you did your part well. Sorry about that.'

'It's okay. I wasn't harmed, really.'

'What the wizard means is he's sorry we had to use you as bait,' Egric grunted, sticking one of the Kuntz's iron weapons into the ground, I imagine to disperse any residual Magick and prevent a rematch.

I was startled. Had they really done that? Vizagriz looked me straight in the eye. 'There was no other way. I had to get Nazrat - Patisse, rather - off her guard and how better than let her think she was winning? You were in no danger. Egric and I would have stepped in had things got any worse.'

I was shaking. I felt betrayed! Could my prentice-master really have used me as a lure? More to the point, was there going to be any more of it? I looked at him accusingly. 'Well, I hope you got what you wanted!' I spat.

'As a matter of fact, I didn't. It's better that we know the true name of that monstrosity and knowing a true name is never a bad thing. But I couldn't hold her long enough to wring any more out of her. It's never the same when you bind them. Conjure them up from scratch and you have a chance. But she's a strong one, that.'

'You should have asked Mindador to help you out if you couldn't manage it,' I said, not without some venom. At this, Vizagriz merely snorted and stood back. 'Anyway,' he said, 'that dæmon won't bother us for a while. Not here, at least. I may have managed to send her far enough away that we never see her again, but I wouldn't count on it. I think she may have jumped before she was pushed. Come on. I'll make the breakfast.'

I was still hurt and confused as we walked back to our stone circle to find a worried-looking Mindador and Winolene and a couldn't-care-less Rongwei who was feeding his horse. He looked up. 'Hello. Go off all right then?'

'Sort of,' Egric replied and in their usual heroic way, they dropped the subject.

Winolene, however, was clearly concerned about me and went so far as to look at my wrists and tell me to sit down and have some thea. At least I was getting attention from her and that made me feel better.

Mindador flustered about trying to look as if he had something to do and he didn't go anywhere near Vizagriz, who sat down with his eyes shut and didn't move for a good while. Finally, he raised his head and announced, 'I think I should share with you all a bit more of what's happening. And I'm sure Mindador will want to tell you a few things himself. Won't you?'

The old Hebryd nodded briefly in agreement and came a bit closer. Vizagriz breathed slowly for bit, as if deciding where to start, and how.

'As you know, we appear to be on a quest. None of us asked to, except Mindador here, but we're in it. For my part, it seems I was picked by The Herald or his superiors, all of whom you might try to avoid if you've got any sense. Mindador was actually working on someone else's behalf, but we'll come to that. We were supposed to have two wizards, a girl, a hero, a player, a scribe and an imp along, and we've nearly managed it. We seem to have doubled up in the hero department so all we lack is a scribe. But appointed Questers do have a habit of turning up when they're needed, so no doubt a scribe shall present himself. I have no idea what part we are all supposed to play in this. Why Winolene is along, I don't know, except that she will have some purpose at some time. Egric and Rongwei? Well, they've already shown their worth and will do so again, I have no doubt. Anyway, being heroes, they'll go along with more or less anything, no offence.'

'None taken,' Egric responded. 'Good exercise for the lad, here.' He punched Rongwei on the chest, dislodging his horned helmet.

'Fine. Sparky knows where the Mountain is, sort of. Slouch – I don't know. He wasn't on the Herald's list, but that doesn't mean he's not involved. Perhaps he did his bit last night when he let us get hold of Nazrat for a while. Perhaps his function was to help save Winolene's life back in Swilbury. Maybe his contribution is yet to be made. What we do know for certain, though, is that we're not the only happy band of travellers looking for this Holy Quail.'

'You mean that she-dæmon and the Kuntz?' I asked.

'Them, certainly, although the Kuntz are a bit depleted. However, they may not be the only ones. We'll have to see.'

'Well, I just wish I knew what the Quail thing was,' Winolene chipped in.

'So do I,' said Vizagriz. 'Mindador?'

The old freelance thaumaturge stepped forward and cleared his throat. 'The Holy Quail is an object of great power. It has the form of a golden bird studded with jewels, all of which have some mystic properties. It has been lost for aeons, but suddenly it is in demand. I was asked by, by...'

'Say it!' Vizagriz ordered.

'By the Order to find it.'

Winolene and I both gasped at the same time but she gave voice to our thoughts. 'You mean, Brer Dryberg knows about this? Then, when he sent me to you. he must...'

'Yes, yes. I'm sorry. It was no accident that you were with me when the scrying went wrong. Only a, well, a pure maiden could peer into the pool and see where the Holy Quail might be found. But it went wrong and we were sucked into the eddy.'

'And it went wrong, precisely why, Mindador?'

'Because, because I had conjured up a dæmon to tell me how to find it.' Mindador was nearly in tears.

'If it's any consolation,' Vizagriz offered, 'I think you weren't completely in control of things that night. I have a feeling the dæmon was bit more co-operative than you had any reason to expect because he and his kind wanted us all here and it was a happy coincidence that you chose to call on them when you did. I think they must have boosted the whirlpool when we arrived and got us all here on purpose. Or if not the dæmons, then some other source of power. Forgive me, Mindador, but I don't think you've got the strength to open a cupboard at times, never mind a portway that takes people half way round a planet.'

'Yes,' Mindador admitted in a small voice, 'you're probably right.'

'So, this dæmon of Mindador's told him to spin a wizard and send him somewhere else, albeit in a rather oblique and metaphoric manner. You might say he was that wizard, or it could refer to me. There was mention of a cart of straw bringing us together. That it certainly did. What was the last bit?'

'He said, "Empty onto a flat surface, then leave to cool overnight. Next day, put in a high place." I think that was it,' Mindador said.

'That sounds to me like a cold plain with a mountain in it. Egric might able to confirm this, but my if my geography isn't too awry that might be the Wastelands of Sinne.'

'Could be,' admitted Egric, from around a Snarler bone he had been keeping for a quiet moment. 'But it's about three days from here even if we get a shift on.'

'Never do it in a day,' Rongwei confirmed.

'We'll see,' Vizagriz added mysteriously. 'This may not be the "flat place" he meant.'

'So what do we do?' I asked.

'We consider. At the very least we're up against Baking Dæmons. We've met one, or two in Mindador's case.'

'Baking Dæmons,' I piped up. 'You've mentioned them. What are they?'

'They are the worst, the very worst of the oxterworld races. They exist for only one thing and that is to bring an end to everything. They claim they're not in a hurry so they have all eternity to achieve their ends and they're so thick they don't realise that's exactly how long it will take, by definition. However, they seem to have speeded themselves up a bit recently.'

'But why "Baking"?' I persisted.

'Ah. That's not their name for themselves. As far as they're concerned it's The Great Ones or The Dark Family, but Baking Dæmons fits and it's sort of stuck. Merillion was probably the first to give them the handle. He fell out with them pretty badly just after he performed the Miracle Of The Five Thousand when he had his acolytes gather up everyone's dog-ends and gave everyone a packet of ten to take away. The reason for the name is three fold. First, they have a penchant for cookery, especially of their victims. Slouch will have heard a reference to himself as a component of a fricassee that Nazrat had planned.'

I shuddered and nodded.

'Second, they take names when they poke through into our realm which reflects their particular favourite dish. Nazrat calls herself "Patisse" though that's no more her real, true name than mine is Vizagriz.'

That last bit was a surprise to me, but it made sense when I thought about it.

'Third, this End of Everything that they have planned is called, at least by them and those that consort with them, "the Final Great Oven Cleaning". You'll gather from this that they can be a bit single-minded.'

'So why the Holy Quail, then?' Egric mumbled around his chewings. 'Do they want to spit-roast it?'

'They may well. It's probably tied up with this heat death of the universe in some way.'

'So what's our next step? Wastelands of Sinne or Mustique Mountain? Not that I mind, just it would be nice to know.'

Vizagriz thought for a moment. 'I'd say the Wastelands, which Mindador's pet dæmon seemed to think was the place where it would all happen, except that Mindador did another conjuration – been busy, haven't you? – which indicated we were to seek a web spinner. The Faerie King told me there was such a being on Mustique Mountain and Sparky is supposed to take us there. But I still don't know what this Web is or what we're supposed to ask it.'

'I think I can help you there,' said a voice above us, and we all sprang to our feet.

CHAPTER THE TENTH

In which Slouch and the Questers learn more of Webs and Weavers and hear something to their advantage, mostly that they are not on the menu.

It's not often that you come eye to eye with your worst nightmare. Eye to eyes, I should have said, because our eavesdropper was the proud possessor of eight of them. Not to mention an equal number of legs. Perched on top of the henge was the biggest, hugest, blackest, most panic-inducing spider I could ever have imagined. I tended not, in fact, to imagine spiders since they were my pet hate, but reality had saved me the trouble in this case. Would we be eaten? Would one of the wizards blast it into kingdom come? Would I ever move from this spot and manage to get my mouth shut again? A sorry end for all of us, it looked like, as the fangs nipped open and shut, dribbling slightly, and the vast, hairy body bobbed up and down slightly on its legs, not far above us. The only incongruity, and I'm amazed I was able to take it in, was the fact that it appeared to be knitting a long scarf out of silk.

The others were as stunned as I was and some of them sprang into action. Winolene let out a piercing scream that I was by now becoming quite familiar with. True to form, and a bit more usefully, our two heroes shouted a gargled, blood-curdling war-cry each and leapt at the thing, swords raised. I saw, from the corner of my eye, Vizagriz raise his hands in preparation, as I thought, for an explosion of Magick. In fact, my master pointed at Rongwei and then Egric and froze both of them to their respective spots, where they stood like toy soldiers or figures in those statues to forgotten warriors that dot the parks in the city.

'Wait!' Vizagriz shouted. 'I don't think we're in any danger.'

At that, the two swordsmen collapsed to the ground, still in their frozen poses, and rattled slightly. They slowly relaxed and started to twitch where they lay. 'If I'm not mistaken, you would be a Web Mistress?'

'That's right. Got the biggest Web around here, that's for sure. Want to see it? Terribites of space. Loads of bandwidth, Mind you, having the hardware helps.'

It took a while for things to calm down. Sparky, knowing exactly what dangers there were for a two-inch high morsel, zipped off and hid in the saddlebag. I recovered my power of movement and went over to Winolene in what I hoped everyone would take for a protective gesture but which, happily, also took me further away from the horror above us. Mindador was sitting, cross-legged, on the ground, battering the side of his head with his palm and muttering. Why did he do that? Egric was shouting blue murder at Vizagriz and Rongwei was rubbing his legs. However, when it seemed that the wizard had been right and the spider stayed exactly where it was, everyone was placated. Not happy, but placated. Vizagriz had, by this time, moved a bit closer to the beast and was speaking to it. Gives me the shivers just to think of it, even now.

'All hail, Web Mistress. We are on a quest and were advised that one such as you might help us in our search.'

'I'll try,' the spider said, quite reasonably. 'What do you want to know? Not that I can guarantee an answer, mind. All knowledge is in the InterWeb, but you have to know what to ask and where to search. Fancy a go? Ever seen it working?'

'We would be honoured,' Vizagriz responded. 'What is the InterWeb?'

'It's not really a thing. more of a network. Anybody who's got a Web Site can join in and we all talk to each other, share information, that sort of thing. Of course, the information has to be there for it to be available, but you generally find there's something about almost everything lying about in some Web or other. I'll get one up, shall I?'

With that, the spider started to spin a massive net-like structure back and forth across the top of the henge. We're being hemmed in, I thought, and this is the entertainment before dinner. Throughout the weaving back and forth, the spider kept up a steady monologue, interrupted by Vizagriz when he didn't understand the jargon, which was often.

'I just have to get some HTML up.'

'HTML?'

'High Tension Message Lines. It's the way the Web works. I string up a few in the right configuration – I'm using HTML 3, by the way, and not everyone's silk can support it, but anybody with any poke in their Web should be up to speed. Now, I'll just finish it off with a couple of Sig lines.'

'Sig? Like sigils?'

'Like signature. How will anybody know who I am or how to respond if they can't read my Sig? There you are. One home page. Now let's fire it up!'

The spider scuttled into the centre of the huge net and thrummed the strands slightly. There was a sort of high, thin whistling coming from it, like the keening of a night bird, but steady and flat.

'That's just me sending a general message to say I'm here. Called eeeee-mail.'

The spider was clearly listening intently for any changes or modulations in the note. When satisfied - and the thought kept coming back to me exactly what constituted a satisfied spider and what part I might be playing in that process - the eight-legged monstrosity sat back and announced, 'On-line. Now let's ask your question.' Then, in a loud voice that startled all of us and set the ponies neighing, the spider put its mouth parts near the web lines and shouted 'YAHOO!'

Even Vizagriz was jolted as the noise echoed off the henge stones. The spider seemed to realise this had been a bit of a shock and looked round at us. 'Sorry, but that's the searching call. Everybody's Webs for miles around will be resonating now.'

'So am I,' admitted Vizagriz.

'Right. Good. So, what did you want to know?'

The wizard straightened up and said, 'See if you can find out anything about an object called the Holy Quail, would you?'

The spider strummed the lines, occasionally moving to another strand and listening to the responses that made the silk oscillate. After a few minutes, the movement ceased. 'Right,' the Web Mistress said, 'there are four thousand references to "Holy", hundreds to "Quail" and a couple of announcements for new Webs. I think we ought to narrow this down a bit. Come on, the more keywords you can give me the more I can direct the search.'

'All right,' said Vizagriz. 'Try this. I am Vizagriz, a wizard of Al Faq'Ahl. We're on a quest to find an artefact of great power which is some sort of jewelled bird. It may be somewhere in the Wastelands of Sinne, but it may not.'

The spider was thrumming away and occasionally spinning a new line as Vizagriz spoke. After what seemed like an age, there was a low, zinging sound, and the Web started to vibrate. 'Bit slow today. Must be a lot of traffic. Or maybe there's a conference in progress. Nothing chokes the bandwidth like real-time chatting. Oh, look!'

'What?' Vizagriz asked.

'Now that's interesting, It's a male.'

'What?'

'A male spider out there, using his own handle. They don't usually.'

'Why not?'

'Well, most Web Mistresses are female - goes without saying, really, males haven't got what it takes, technically. But every so often ones gets into it. However, most of them use female handles so nobody can tell.'

'Why?'

'Pestering. Spot a male out there and some Web Mistresses are likely to bombard him with eeeee-mail, try to find out his location, that sort of thing. It can get very abusive at times. I've seen some of it. We call it Virtual Mate Munching. Anyway, if they don't want bothered they shouldn't announce themselves. Their own fault really. Bring it on themselves. Ah, now, here's something.'

The spider was silent for a few moments, then said, 'I've found a reference – oblique, I'll grant you, but it's there. Seems there's something called the Gnomion that will tell you what you want to know, but it's not on-line so I can't read it. Also a word that begins with a Q but seems to be garbage after that. Corrupted. There is a link, but it keeps coming up "Error 404". Judging from the address, I'd say, yes, it's somewhere in Sinne. Is anyone else after this thing?'

'I'm afraid so,' said Vizagriz, who was very much afraid so. 'Why? Does the Web tell you that?'

'Sort of. This site's been visited a few times recently. Let's see if I can find out where from.' There was a bit more fiddling, then an answer. 'It's been accessed from a Web over at Mustique Mountain.'

'Ahah!' Vizagriz nodded his head, 'We were originally directed there, but found you instead. It seems that one of our competitors has followed the same route and found the Web Mistress we were told to consult.'

'What was the name, of this Web Mistress, I mean?'

'Schlob, I believe,' Vizagriz answered. 'Why?'

'Well, I can call her one-to-one and see what she knows. Shall I? Might take a while.'

'By all means,' the wizard answered, and came over to where the rest of us were standing, which was as far away as possible from the knife-like jaw pincers. Vizagriz took a moment to apologise to the two heroes, but they didn't seem especially bothered. Egric, having decided there wasn't any danger, was eating as usual, and Rongwei had taken out a picture of a young girl and was gazing at it. Despite the shock she'd had, Winolene was sufficiently interested to ask about it.

'It's my fiancée,' Rongwei replied, a bit wistful. 'She's a temple-dancer back in Cimmeria. We met when she was at training school and I had a part-time job as a bouncer at one of their hops.'

'She looks nice. What's her name? Do you miss her?'

'Thanks. Sharon. Yeh. I mean, all this questing and tomb-breaking and that, it's fine, and I want to get my degree, but I'd be just as happy in a nice, safe job somewhere. You know, steady wage, bit of night security work on the side. Then we could settle down.'

'Don't you want to be a hero, then?'

'Oh, it's fine, but it's not much of a life at times. All that chasing about, away for years on end, some of them chained to a galley-oar. No, I'd prefer something a bit quieter, I think.'

'What does Egric say about that?'

'He's just my Supervisor. All he wants is for me to pass the practicals. Then I can do what I want.'

'What about Sharon? Does she want a career?'

'At the moment. Technically, though, she's a temple virgin. They have a sort of limited sell-by date, know what I mean?'

Winolene obviously knew exactly what he meant, being in the same line of country, and it obviously set her thinking. She was quiet for a while.

I had become worried about Mindador. He was still rocking and mumbling, occasionally battering his forehead with his fist. I started to walk over towards him, but Vizagriz pulled me back and put a finger to his lips. 'He'll be fine. Just leave him alone for a while.'

'He doesn't look fine. What's the matter with him?'

'Head dæmons.'

I was taken aback. Had Mindador brought dæmons with him. Was that the source of all our misadventure? Why didn't Vizagriz do something about it?

'Don't worry. He's just got a few odd bits of dæmon in his skull, that's all. They're not dangerous, just a bit annoying.'

'They look more than a bit annoying from here. Where did they come from?'

'Well, when you spend as much time poddling about in the darker realms as Mindador seems to, you occasionally bump into minor dæmons and bits of them stick when you're off your guard. It's the metaphysical equivalent of going out for a few beers and waking up with a tattoo. It's a pest, but not so much that you can be bothered getting them taken away. Eventually they'll wear off and he'll just be left with a bit of a scar in his mind.'

'Won't that be bad?'

'It'll itch a bit, but with everything else, I don't think he'll regard it as much of a priority.'

Mindador did seem to be a bit more calm and was just sitting, staring at the earth in a depressed fashion. 'See what I mean?' Vizagriz pointed. 'Back to normal!' Then he got to feet and went over to the Web Mistress to see what was happening.

The spider was looking a bit agitated, running back and forth across her Web and plucking strands. Vizagriz saw her distress and asked what the matter was.

'Strange,' she said – I had come to think of her as a she, and it didn't cheer me up given what I knew of the gustatory habits of female arachnids. 'I've tried both eeeee-mail addresses and Schlob's Web Site, but I can't get any response. It seems she's down. Can't understand it. It must have been working earlier today. I'll try a back door.'

Vizagriz drew in a deep breath. 'It's possible one of our competitors has got to her. We've been followed by a dæmon called Patisse, or sometimes Nazrat. Any mention of this?'

'I can't get anything at all. Look, I'll send out a newsgroup message and ask everyone to keep their pincers peeled. If I hear of anything, I'll let you know.'

'How?'

'There are Webs everywhere. Even in your cottage.'

'What?' Even Vizagriz could be astonished at times.

'You're Vizagriz, right? Al Faq'Ahl? I tapped the Web Site of a house-spider in your kitchen cupboard. Small thing, but chatty.'

'Well... what's the news?'

'Not much. Your table and chairs are arguing, if that means anything to you.'

'I thought I told you to clean the place up!' Vizagriz growled at me, clearly annoyed at not having realised this networking had been going on under his huge nose all this time. He was obviously about to launch into me when there was a loud "NO!" from the Spider, who fell back, shaking.

'What is it?' I asked.

'Hell, hell, damnation, bother and flies bottoms!' the spider exclaimed as the Web dissolved around her. 'I've caught a virus!'

'A what?'

'Whoever put a spoke in Schlob's Web obviously left a nasty there, too. I found a way into her core and I was downloading her activity log so I could get a handle on the problem when this thing came through. Sod!'

'Can't you weave another one?'

'Oh, yes. It's that easy! Don't you see, any Web that's been in contact with Schlob – or me for that matter – will have this damn thing in it now. I can't reconnect until everyone else has spotted it and disinfected. That's us all off games for a while, I'm afraid.'

'You mean we can't get any more information?'

'Nope. That's your bundle. Wasteland of Sinne, Gnomion, something beginning with a Q.'

'I'm sorry. That was our fault.'

'No, I'd have caught it at some time. Why do people do this?'

'Probably to stop us getting anywhere.'

'Right. It's still not on, though, is it? I've meant to install one of those Solomon's Minds guard programs but I've never got round to it. Bet your boots I'll be putting one in tomorrow, though.'

Vizagriz had obviously been pondering the implications of the InterWeb. He scratched his head, rubbed one foot with the other and stuck the end of his staff in his mouth. It's combinations like that which leads the naïve public to believe Magick is all about hand signals.

'Listen,' he said. 'Could I... sorry, we don't even know your name. What with all the goings-on and such.'

'Quite right.' The spider declared, and curtsied with all legs at once, an effect rather like up-ending a bag of spanners. 'Remiss of me, too. My name is ÿtsë-wwïtsçë.'

'Indeed. Er...'

'That's in our language and orthography. You can call me Kylie.'

Vizagriz made a deep bow. 'Kylie. Charmed. It occurs to me that now we have met, we might want to keep in touch. You appear to have the perfect conduit for communication. Is there any way we can ensure the continuation of this delightful acquaintance?'

Don't you just hate it when people go all smarmy after the first date?

'Silly of me,' Kylie said, and waggled her mandibles. Not a pretty sight. 'I should have thought. Here. Hold out your hand.'

Now, there aren't many societies I've come across where spitting into someone's groin is considered a friendly greeting, but Vizagriz took it on the chin. No. He didn't. He took it in the groin. Just about the last-turkey-in-the-shop area there appeared a small cobweb, glistening in the sunlight.

'Um. Thank you,' was all he could manage.

'I call it a lap-top,' Kylie said. 'Mind you, I can see how it wouldn't be very convenient all the time.'

'No. Fair comment.'

It's a small-scale, micro-miniaturised version of my personal organiser.

'It's certainly personal,' Vizagriz muttered, still peering at his nethers.

'If it doesn't suit you there, such it somewhere else.'

'Such as?'

'Any other flat surface.'

I had a sudden inspiration. 'Winolene. Can I have your mirror?'

'Hardly the time,' she spat, while fossicking around in whatever secret recesses gels have in their flouncies and handing me her hand glass, 'to be concerned about personal appearance, not that you ever are.'

I ignored the jibe, took the mirror and gave it to Vizagriz, who pressed it against his groin and visibly cheered up when the conweb transferred itself to the glass.

'Ah,' he said. 'Keep it there, then, shall we?'

'Palm-top,' Kylie smugged. 'With fully reflective screen.'

'And how does one use it?' Vizagriz asked, peering at the refracted colours as he twisted it back and forth in the light.

'Ping.'

'Pardon?'

'You send a "ping" command.'

'Of course. Just remind me, now. How, on this particular device, does "ping" work? Not familiar with the model, you know.'

He was making it up, I could tell.

'Just give it a ping. With your finger.'

The wizard plucked a filament of the web and let it fall back. There was an audible "ping" noise. The web strand right under Kylie's abdomen vibrated. 'Ooooh. Naughty! Web titillation. I'll need a filter for you, won't I?'

'What?'

'Never mind. Watch this.'

With that, Kylie performed a complicated dance on her web and the smaller version on the looking-glass resonated and started to reform itself into recognisable characters, which looked like "Saucy! (:-} Call me!".

'You've got the idea,' Kylie said, settling back on the still-thrumming web. 'If you want to send a message, just ping. I'll respond in your language.'

'Ah,' Vizagriz exhaled. 'I meant to ask. How in Deity's name do you speak our tongue?'

'Amazing what you can pick up on the web,' she explained and performed another intricate fandango on her threads. The mirror pulsated with the twanging of the small cobweb, and formed itself into tiny characters that I couldn't understand. Vizagriz looked at them, chuckled, and showed them to Mindador, who guffawed out loud.

'Oh, that's a good one. "Depends how long your string is, the Bishop said". Very funny.'

Vizagriz was also succussating. Look it up then.

'Excellent. Can you do any other runic alphabets?'

'Automatic translation, a built-in function. Do you a nice Mandarin.'

'Not hungry, thanks,' Vizagriz said, gasping.

'And you've seen the Joke-a-Day facility. Also full scheduler and appointments calendar. Miracle of miniaturisation.'

'Look,' said Vizagriz, wiping his eyes with his sleeve. 'You've been very helpful and we've put you to a lot of trouble. Is there anything we can do to repay you?'

'Well, since you offer, I am a bit peckish. Must have been your pun on the small orange.'

'We don't have any flies, I'm afraid, but I know a spell that could conjure up a few million. Ideally, it needs an animal's head and a small, fat boy with glasses.'

'Oh, I'm not much of a fly hand. They're a bit fiddly when you're my size. Got anything more substantial? Not a lot of protein around this place.'

You've heard the expression "being eyed up". Think about it when there's eight of them.

'I think I can help you there,' Vizagriz said and walked over towards me. Here it comes, I thought. This is my part in the quest – dinner for a big arthropod. I started to edge backwards. I was just about to bolt for it when Vizagriz held me by the shoulders and gave me a reassuring pat. Then he left the stone circle for a moment and returned, leading a pony. 'Slouch!' he ordered. 'Get the packs off this thing, will you?'

Winolene had spotted what was happening and came rushing over to remonstrate. 'You're not going to... I mean, you don't... You'd never...,' and other half-finished utterances came from her outraged mouth as she tried to wrestle the bridle away from the wizard.

'I certainly am. Or would you like me to suggest an alternative? We still don't know why you're with us. It might be that you'd make a great egg-cocoon when you're hollowed out!'

This gave Winolene pause for thought, and she let the pony go. She wasn't happy about it, mind, and I could see it would rankle for a while.

We left the poor animal tied to a rock in the henge as the spider waved a foreleg and shouted, 'Coo-eee!' and we gathered ourselves together for the journey to Sinne. As we mounted and Vizagriz consulted the heroes as to the best direction, I tried to cheer Winolene up by telling her that it was all for the best and that we were even closer to the end of our quest now.

'I don't care!' she pouted. 'That was a terrible thing to do to the poor little creature!'

'It certainly was,' Egric agreed. 'I was looking forward to a bit of it meself.'

That shut her up, and we moved off across the plain.

Rongwei and Egric got at least a mile without one of them saying, 'So. What did the Bishop say, then?'

Vizagriz told them, after which there was fully five minutes of chuckling, none of which I was privy to. Grown-ups!

The next days passed without incident. They were, frankly, rather boring. When he wasn't riding off to check the way, Egric was always either eating or asleep. Rongwei was no conversationalist unless you got him onto dialectic materialism, and that was definitely no fun either. Mindador mooched along at the back. The Lady Winolene maintained a sullen silence. Sparky kept himself to himself after the first night when he came off second best to an ossifrage. Even Vizagriz was feeling restive and started arguments with almost everybody, even the normally placid Rongwei. It was during one of his monologues about the different approaches to conflict espoused by Higgle, Marcus and Lemming that Vizagriz lost the place with him.

'Oh, do give it a rest! Heroes are supposed to be the strong, silent types, not constantly rabbitting on about some rubbish they get spoon-fed at Hun Tech. Go off and slaughter a sand-serpent or something if it keeps you quiet.'

Rongwei was huffed and muttered for a while about how he was only trying to improve his mind and heroing wasn't all thud and blunder, didn't everybody realise there was a need for a more thoughtful approach at times. 'Anyway,' he sniffed, 'it's Conan Poly; not Hun Tech. Not anymore, since we merged with the Regional Militia Centre and the Priest & Temple-Dancer Training College.' Then he went on a bit about not being one for mindless violence, really and any sand-serpents around here were all right in his book if they kept themselves to themselves. Egric said they were tasty and went off to look for one.

The weather was getting decidedly chilly and we were slowly ascending in altitude. It was at the crest of a hill one night, when we were about to stop and cook supper that Mindador spotted something down in a valley through the mists that had started swirling around us. 'Look,' he said, pointing. 'There's a building of some sort down there. Or it could be a pile of stones. Hard to tell in all this weather.'

We all peered and certainly, there was something grey and squat down below us. We resolved to head for it the next day and found a hollow in the hillside that would afford some shelter from the frosty air and the wind that was just getting its breath for a good old blow.

Blow it did and the night was cold, dank with the mist and miserable, even huddled round the small fire we had made from shrubs and heather that died after a few hours and wouldn't relight no matter how much Sparky swore at it. None of us got any sleep except Egric who snored for the first half of the night then swapped with Rongwei on guard for the rest and chewed his way noisily but steadily through an entire leg of something.

Come dawn and a quick, cheerless breakfast, we started off downhill towards the stone structure, or whatever it was. The going was slow even for the sure-footed ponies that led the way for each of us. The mist was getting worse and the cold was intensifying with every step. As a result, it was almost the next evening when we reached the valley floor and could re-mount. Winolene insisted we feed and water the animals before proceeding and as we had stumbled across a small spring it seemed as good a time as any to stop and take stock.

'We had better press on,' Vizagriz suggested. 'Whatever that building or cairn is it will give us shelter. If there's anyone in it we can ask them for directions.'

'We could slaughter them and get a good kip inside for a change.'

'Or, as Egric suggests, politely ask for a night's accommodation.'

That settled, we moved on. As we approached the grey shape it resolved in our vision to be a rough, stone-built structure that backed into a low hillside with a slate roof and no door. Vizagriz stopped us some way off and went with Rongwei and Egric to investigate. When they returned it was to report that it seemed to be some sort of disused mine or cave entrance and that we could shelter inside it.

We got Sparky to set light to some pitch torches we had brought from Swilbury but had never had a chance to use, being mostly outdoors since then, and set a fire with some timber that Rongwei said he had found lying around, clearly part of the structure in the past.

I kept hearing soft, low grinding noises just at the fringe of my hearing but I dismissed them as imagination or the effect of my ears thawing out. I could not have been more wrong. It was in the depths of the night that the sound suddenly amplified itself to a threatening rumble and we all leapt to our feet, looking around us for the source of the noise.

'Quick,' Vizagriz shouted. 'Outside!'

We immediately complied, but were too late to get to the entrance before there was a crash and a shower of rocks as the doorway caved in. Above us the roof was creaking ominously. 'Back,' Vizagriz ordered and we retreated about ten yards into the hillside, Rongwei and Egric having the presence of mind – or was it training – to grab two of the torches before they flung themselves after us. The entire structure had collapsed, neatly filling the mine entrance with tons of rubble and large boulders.

The dust settled, the rumbling stopped and we all recovered our breath. It was

Winolene who spoke first. 'Rongwei,' she said, in a voice that contained a barely-suppressed fury. 'Exactly where did you get that wood you brought for the fire?'

'It was just sort of lying around.'

'Just sort of lying around and propping up the ceiling, was it?'

'Well, I had to knock a few bits out to get at them, but they weren't in very securely.'

'Secure enough to keep the roof up for another THREE HOURS YOU IDIOT!'

Vizagriz wasn't in any mood to be placatory either. 'She's right. That was about the daftest thing I've seen anyone do since the last really daft thing. Egric? What do we do?'

'Just a minute. I'm getting this down,' the elder hero replied, scribbling in a little notebook. What was he doing? 'I've got to note this. Failure to observe the health and safety rules, endangering others, not obeying one of the central principles of life - if you're not sure don't erk about with it - and generally behaving in a truly exemplary manner. There!'

'Exemplary?' Vizagriz exploded. 'What's so exemplary about burying us under a ton of countryside and cutting us off from our transport and our supplies?'

'That's what heroing is all about, isn't it? Little people do the right things and do them safely. Heroes barge in, tear things apart, put everyone in jeopardy and sort of move the plot along. This'll go down well on his report card, I can tell you.'

There followed a good five minutes of shouting and bad language with Egric supporting Rongwei, Vizagriz giving out more synonyms for "berk" than any thesaurus had ever heard of and Rongwei trying to get a word in edgewise and being told to shut it by both of them. Mindador and Winolene sat in identical knees-round-ears postures just letting it all wash over them. It was Sparky who finally made them stop.

'Look,' he said, reasonably. 'I can see that there's a lot to discuss here, but it'll wait until we're outside, won't it?'

'That's the point, you stunted tablelamp. How do we get outside now that mince-for-brains here has dumped half a mountain on the doorstep?'

'Well, it's up to you, squire, but for my part, I intend to follow the draught.'

'What? A draught? I can't feel anything!' Vizagriz said, sniffing the mine's air with his eagle-like beak.

'Well, if you don't mind me pointing it out, you're not the size and weight of a feather, are you?'

True enough, I had to concede. Anything that tipped the scales at just over two ounces was likely to be a bit sensitive to the gentlest of breezes. Thinking about it, Vizagriz calmed down and said, 'All right. But I'm still furious. I'll want to talk about this again, for quite a long time, in a loud voice and without hesitation, repetition or deviation when - if

– we ever get out of this tomb. Rongwei, you first. If there's dangerous insects, large holes to fall in, spears coming out of walls, big balls of stone flying down ramps at us or any of that, you will have the honour of seeing them first. Now move it!'

Rongwei seemed strangely pleased to have been accorded this singular honour and set off with a torch at a fairish pace.

For my part, I had found the word "tomb" ever so slightly unsettling.

Egric took the rear and I walked in front of him holding the second torch. I had offered Winolene my free hand, which she batted away with a tutting. Sparky sat on Vizagriz's shoulder behind Rongwei and Mindador shuffled along after them.

We were an hour or more walking through the gloom and I had to admit I could feel a faint breeze. As Vizagriz had said, the fact that we could breathe at all was testament to the fact that there must be an air-flow so we were probably doing the right thing. Whether there was a hole big enough for us all to get through was a different matter but he was sure we could use Rongwei's head to batter one out if it came to that.

It is possible to get rather disoriented in a dark, winding tunnel, but I had the distinct impression that we were travelling uphill ever so slightly. Given what I remembered of the topography of where we had come from it would seem that were heading deeper into the hillsides at the other side of the valley. We stopped to rest once and I rolled a smooth pebble both ways along the mine shaft, Sure enough – ahead was up and back was down.

It was an unknowable time later that the torches started to sputter and go out. When they both finally failed we had to rely on Sparky to put up a small flare every few minutes to check our progress. I hesitantly asked at one point if there wasn't some globe-of-light spell that would do the trick and got growled at for my pains. The rock around us was full of iron, apparently, and there's no chance of Magick working without lots of back-shocks in those surroundings. It wasn't explained to me quite so politely, but that was the general drift.

We carried on, Rongwei using his sword like a blind stick, waving it from side to side and tapping the ground with it, until he suddenly came to a halt and we all bumped into each other like a row of whippets in the mating season. Sparky let up a flare and Rongwei said, 'Can I hear something?'

'How would we know that, dumbo?' Vizagriz spat. 'Shush and let me listen.'

We all listened and, sure enough, there was the sound of rushing water in the far distance. And something else, too, like gas escaping from an alembic during one of Vizagriz abortive alchemical experiments. There was nothing to do but carry on. Maybe my eyes were now accustomed to the dark but I was sure I could see a faint glow up ahead. More by way of hearing my own voice than anything else, I said, to no-one in particular, 'I wonder what they mined here. Iron?'

'This is no mine,' the voice of Vizagriz answered from the darkness ahead. 'Where are the ruts in the ground where the carts took the ore to the surface? Why are the walls perfectly smooth? And why is this tunnel absolutely circular like it was bored rather than hewn?'

'So what is it then, if it's not a mine?'

'I think you'd call it a burrow,' came the answer.

'Then why the building at the entrance?'

'Very typical. That's where the priests would live.'

'Priests? Worshipping what?'

'Whatever made this burrow.'

'Well, anything that could carve a tunnel like this must be...' I tailed off, realising exactly what the next word was.

'Huge. Exactly. Couldn't keep it to yourself, could you? So now that you've scared everyone half to death with your inane theorising, perhaps we could move forward and hope to Deity that whatever lived here is long gone.'

Another few minutes and we all saw what was definitely a dull shining. As we approached it, the tunnel started to twist and turn and it was clear that what we were seeing was the reflection off the smooth walls of daylight coming from not far away. It also had a rainbow-hued quality. The rushing water sound was louder, too.

Rongwei was first around the last bend and we could hear his voice saying,. 'It's all right, there's fresh air here and a sort of chamber and GOOD GRIEF, LOOK AT THE SIZE OF THAT!!'

CHAPTER THE ELEVENTH

In which Slouch and his companions on the Quest enter the Tomb of the Unknown Lunch and confront their worst nightmare. Again. Why does it have to be snakes?

As we joined Rongwei around the corner we could see a domed chamber perhaps forty paces across with a flagstone floor, lit by the dwindling daylight filtering through a round entrance that looked out into midair and the distant hills. In the middle of the chamber was a plinth of carved granite on which rested a book in an oil cloth wrapper. Off to our right was another tunnel like the one we had travelled along. But what really caught our attention was against the far wall – a pile of jewels, gold and silver coins, pearl necklaces, carved statues and close-worked daggers with opals and other stones let into their hilts. On top of the mound of valuables was a huge, white diamond, many-faceted and pouring out rainbow-coloured light onto the chamber walls.

'Look at the size of that diamond!' Rongwei repeated, as if to convince himself.

'Well, well,' said Vizagriz. 'What do you know. Treasure.'

Winolene gasped, Sparky gasped, Mindador gasped and I gasped. Egric grinned. 'So. The lad did the right thing, eh?'

'Wait a minute,' the wizard cautioned as Mindador and I started off towards the fabulous heap of precious items. 'Is it real, or illusion? Hand me a stone or something.'

I looked around on the floor but there was nothing there. I felt in my pockets and found a piece of dried bread I had been keeping for my pony and forgotten about. 'Would this do?' I asked, tentatively, not at all sure what it might be wanted for.

'Admirable. Now let's see.' Vizagriz took the stale bread and threw it hard at the treasure. It hit the wall just above a mound of rubies and fell onto them, continuing to skitter and bounce down until it came to rest on a silver casket. 'Fair enough,' he announced. 'It's real. Rongwei, give me your knife.'

The bemused hero handed over his weapon and Vizagriz threw this too. As it hit the coins and jewels it gave off a loud report, produced a blinding white flash and instantly vaporised.

'And it's protected by a spell. Wonderful.'

I was disappointed. 'You mean, we can't get at it? I thought you said Magick wouldn't work here with all the iron about.'

'I said you can't go throwing Magick about where there's iron. That knife was iron and look what happened to it when it moved through the magickal field. Moving Magick through iron would have had the same effect, probably on us. Anyway, whatever enchantment's on that treasure is static not current.'

'Can you cancel it?' I asked more in hope than expectation.

'Nope. Mindador?'

'Shouldn't think so. Probably been here so long it's seeped into the very stones. Take an age to lift that spell, even if we knew what it was. Plus what Vizagriz said about the iron. Oy! So near, yet so far.'

'Oh, come on!' Egric blurted out. 'There must be some way to counteract the spell. We haven't come all this way just for a look-see. I haven't, anyway!'

Vizagriz was thinking. He clearly wanted to get his hands on the trove as much as any of us. 'There is a way, yes. Perhaps two.'

'What?' everyone else said at once.

'Ask whoever cast the spell in the first place to lift it...'

'But there's no-one here,' I pointed out, helpfully.

'At present, no. Or, the second way, read that book.'

We had all forgotten about the tome on the plinth, so absorbed were we in our private fantasies about how many tropical islands, dancing girls, twelve-course banquets, palaces, ball gowns or compliant hamsters we could each buy with our share. Vizagriz held his hand out to Mindador. 'Got any iron filings on you?'

'I think so,' the elderly mage said and fished about in the depths of his robe until he found a small pouch and handed it to Vizagriz.

My master strode over to a point between the plinth and the treasure. As confirmation, he sprinkled some of the iron powder towards the treasure and watched it sparkle as it burned in the magickal aura that surrounded the pile. Then he repeated this with a pinch over the book. Nothing. Convinced, he picked up the volume, took it out of its wrapping, opened it, ran his finger down a page and announced, 'Bugger!'

'What?' I said. 'Doesn't it say anything about the spell?'

'No idea. It's in gibberish. Or some other language I don't know. Rats!'

He handed the book to Mindador who also had to confess he couldn't make head nor tail of the symbols. Egric, who had a certain facility with the spoken versions of various tongues took a cursory glance and agreed that whatever it was, it was indecipherable to him.

'Not even so much as a diagram. Still, we'll hold onto it. Never know, might be useful under a table-leg or something,' Vizagriz said and stowed it inside his clothes. 'So, it appears we can't do anything about this lot. A pity. Especially if the Holy Quail is here, but I don't think it will be.'

'Why not? Isn't this the end of our quest?' I asked.

'I don't imagine so. Mindador, run it past me again – what did Dbyrne's Talking Heads say?'

Mindador recited the results of his divinations. 'They said "Seek the place where webs are woven" and "Find the weaver and ask the question". I think we've done that bit.'

'I agree,' said Vizagriz. 'What next?'

'It was. "There is a jewel without equal" and "A man must read the words" I think.'

'Right. We assumed the "jewel without equal" referred to the Holy Quail, but it might well be that diamond. As for a man reading the words, chance would be a fine thing.'

'Excuse me,' I said. I had heard something.

'Let's have another look,' Vizagriz suggested, getting the book out again.

'Erm, I think...'

'Quiet, Slouch. I'm trying to concentrate.'

'But I just...'

'Will you give it a rest? I'm trying to think of a way of getting these words to make themselves plain to me.'

'Sssssssssssssss...'

'And don't hiss. If you can't keep silent do something useful like...'

'That wasn't me. It came from that tunnel over there!'

This got everyone's attention and we stood, rooted to the spot, while we watched the massive head of what must be a vast serpent slide from the other passage, its tongue licking the air and its huge, slitted eyes staring at us in quiet, sure malevolence.

Winolene let out her customary shriek and Egric and Rongwei instinctively moved to either side of the chamber so as to attack it from both sides at once. Mindador gabbled and gnawed his knuckles. Sparky buried himself in Vizagriz's hair while the wizard backed off, slowly, his face aghast.

The head moved to and fro as if tasting us, which was no doubt the next step. Egric made the first rush but was met by a blast of foul gas that spewed from the snake's mouth, making him fall to the ground, retching and gasping, rubbing his eyes and writhing in agony.

Then it spoke, a spine-chilling, sibilant whisper that echoed inside the domed chamber.

'Who disssturbsss Quaxialcaybl from hisss sssluuummmbersss?'

Winolene fainted clean away and Mindador was immobile with terror. Rongwei was at a bit of loss what to do, but edged round slowly to where Egric was lying, reassuring himself that the older hero was incapacitated but would be all right when the effects of the vapour had abated. Vizagriz was also in a quandary. Normally, he would have let off some Magick, but couldn't, given the sorcerous capacitance of the tomb. As it was, he motioned to me to get back while he thought of something.

The serpent scanned us all with his eyes and tongue and repeated his challenge. 'Who daressss enter the lair of Quaxialcaybl?'

Vizagriz spoke, which was the only thing he could think of to do.

'We mean you no harm,' he said, in a neat reversal of the prevailing situation. 'We have been sent to retrieve the Holy Quail. Give only this to us and we shall leave you in peace and never return.'

'The Holy Quail? Why do you sssseek thissss? Who ssssent you?'

'We are on a sacred mission from The Two. Do not seek to impede us or we will be forced to take the Quail and destroy you. But render it unto us and you will come to no harm by our hands.' I will say this for Vizagriz – he did not lack nerve.

'The Holy Quail will never leave the Tomb of the Unknown Lunchchch! Sssssss.'

It was Sparky who provided the distraction needed. While the rest of us just gaped and trembled, the little Amp jumped from the wizard's shoulder, sprang towards the serpent and, landing on its head, delivered a spark right between its eyes before leaping away again. While the snake head reared and spat in pain, Rongwei jumped in and lifting up his sword with a two-handed grip, plunged it up towards the throat of the serpent, driving it right through to the skull. The vast head swayed and bucked for a moment, then crashed onto the floor.

We all breathed for the first time in minutes but abruptly stopped again when the voice continued from what looked like the slain head. 'There wassss no call for that, now wassss there?'

Rongwei wasn't to be put off. Which only proves how stupid he really was. He walked up to the recumbent head and poked it a bit. 'Anybody in there?' he inquired.

'I will rend the fleshshsh from your bonessss!' the voice continued from within the tunnel. 'I will crushshsh your bodiessss and ssssmear them acrossss the wallssss!'

'Oh, now just a minute,' Rongwei said. 'Who's talking here? It's not this snake head, is it?'

'I am Quaxialcaybl, death-sssserpent of the Tomb of the Unknown Lunchchch! Ssssee me and dessspair!'

Rongwei wasn't having any of it and he continued his diatribe while all looked on, open mouthed. He spoke directly to the mouth of the tunnel now, reasoning that whatever was producing the voice was really in there and not within the defunct saurian. 'Now look, Quax – can I call you Quax? - you see, you've got this Holy Quail thing, and we'd sort of quite like it. Really. And let's face it, you don't do anything with it, it just sits here in the Tomb of the Unknown Lunch... er, excuse me, but shouldn't this really be called the Tomb of the Unknown Warrior or something?'

'When they're outssssside, they're warriorssss. When they come insssside, they become lunchhhhhh,' hissed the dark voice.

I swallowed, then nearly threw up as I remembered that the serpent must have done a fair bit of swallowing too in its time. I wasn't going to want any Snarler chops for a while after this, I thought. But Rongwei carried on.

'No, you see, you've got it, and we want it, and that's all right because you don't use it, whereas, er, whereas if WE had it, we could use it to good purpose and stop the End Of Existence And Everything. See? We don't want it for us, but for, well, everybody.'

'But I don't WANT to stop the End of Existencccceeeee. I want ruin, and death, and darknessssss and eternal night,' the voice wheezed, horribly. He had a point. But Rongwei was into his stride on the philosophy now.

'No, hang on a minute. If you want the End of Existence, right, that means there won't be anyone or any, er, thing for you to be horrible to, I mean, exercise your dark demesne over, and that won't be much fun, will it?'

'Welllll.....'

'And, and, and what's more, if you're PART of existence, then YOU probably won't come out of it awfully well, will you? I mean, I mean, it could be the end of you, too!'

'QUAXIALCAYBL WILL ENDURE! THE DEATH SERPENT WILL SSSSSURVIVE!'

'Ah, but can you be sure of that? I mean, really, really, REALLY sure? Chances are you're going to get it in the neck too. See what I'm driving at?'

If a silence can sound uncertain, that's how the silence sounded. Finally the voice hissed, 'The Death Serpent will endure. Quaxialcaybl is the darknessssss!'

'Ah, well, if you're at one with the darkness, then when it comes, you won't be able to tell the difference between you and, like, anything else, will you.'

'Sssssss,' the dark tunnel said, or hissed, rather.

'So all round, it's not much of a deal for you either, is it?'

'Oh, sssod it!' the Dark One ssssaid.

I made a mental note to congratulate Rongwei on taking those courses on dialectic materialism at the Poly and on his personal assertiveness module. In the meantime, I was still absolutely sure we were still going to be Lunch, and nothing Unknown about it, either.

'Come on,' Rongwei coaxed, as you would a dog that won't bring a ball back. 'Who's in there, really? Come out, we won't hurt you.'

There was a sort of resigned sigh and the head started to vibrate. This is it, I thought, it's not dead and it's getting itself together for a final lunge.

But the vibration was due to the footsteps of the small, dumpy creature that now emerged from the tunnel. It had a short beard, rosy red cheeks and a cross expression.

'Bloody typical. Never fails on anyone with an ounce of brains, that Death Serpent bit. But along comes a thick hero and the whole thing's up the spout in five minutes. Who's going to pay for the repairs, that's what I want to know!'

Mindador had found his voice again. 'A Gnome!' he exclaimed.

'Yes? Never seen a Gnome before?'

'Well, no, actually. Pictures, yes, but never in the flesh.'

'There you are then. Now, if you don't mind, you've had you bit of fun and caused some damage. Would you mind getting off and let me do the necessary? Don't slam the door in your hurry.'

'Now just a minute,' Vizagriz chipped in. 'You terrorise us, make the poor girl there swoon with fear, paralyse my apprentice, hurl some poison at Egric and you expect us just to say "Nice one" and "Cheerio"? I don't think so.'

'She'll be all right. Nerves. And your friend will recover with a bit of a skin itch as soon as the mustard wears off.'

'I ought to blast you to your boot tops,' Vizagriz threatened.

'But you can't, can you?' the Gnome replied as he was checking the snake head for damage. 'You've seen what Magick can do in here – oh, congratulations on that bit with the knife and iron filings, by the way. Most people just charge at the treasure and end up as a sort of puddle.'

'No, I can't do it, I'll grant you. But Rongwei there could put you to the sword as soon as wink, couldn't you?'

'Could I?' Rongwei wondered. 'I'm interested in philosophic alternatives to violence you know and...'

'OH FOR PITY'S SAKE! Just do stop that!'

The Gnome was wiping his hands on an oily rag. 'Oh, I don't imagine he'll do it. For one thing, how are you going to get at the treasure if I'm not here?'

'You mean, we can take the treasure?' I said, coming to my senses after a long time apart.

'Well, that's what you want, isn't it? I mean, that's why you came. And it's sort of the rules. Defeat the serpent, take as much treasure as you can carry. Not much point me guarding it if nobody tries to have a go, is there? I mean.'

'We haven't come for the flaming treasure!' Vizagriz said through gritted teeth to a chorus of "Oh no?" and "Why not?" and "Speak for yourself" from the rest of us.

'No, we haven't. That's not why we came. We seek the Holy Quail!'

'Yes, you said. Out of luck then, aren't you? It's not here.'

'What? All this trouble and it isn't...'

'Not here exactly. Not far, but not here. No.'

'That sounds a bit like "It is far, but near. It is inside, but without. It is high, but deep", doesn't it?' Mindador mused.

'Yes. Something along those lines. Good divining, whoever did it.'

'Well, where is it then? Eh? Eh?' Vizagriz was getting to the end of his tether.

'Ah. When you leave here, look due East for a big mountain with a hole down the middle. That should be the place.'

'Right. Fine. Well, we'll just do that then, shall we? Another wild quail chase, no doubt!'

'No, it's there all right. And I should know, because I made it and I put it there, see? Me and the Brothers.'

I was intrigued. 'You made it? What does it do, then? That's the bit we've never been quite clear on, except that in some way it's tied up with the End of Existence and that sort of thing.'

'What does it do? We've never been quite sure. Happens sometimes - you make something and in the process it takes on a life of its own. Whole more than the sum of the parts, as it were. That's partly why we hid it. Too much interest in it, considering we thought we'd made a sort of wall ornament.'

Vizagriz sat down rather heavily. 'I do not understand ANY of this,' he admitted. 'Just who the hell are you, anyway?'

The Gnome squatted down cross-legged opposite him. 'I may as well tell you, I suppose. Don't get much company. You see, me and the Brothers, we were toboggan manufacturers but we decided to get out of the business.'

'Why?' I asked, right on cue.

'It was going downhill. One of us, forget who, might have been Doc, found the Gnomion in a second hand bookshop that sold books by the yard as wall furniture. He was really looking for How To Smarten Up Your Burrow or back-issues of Gnomes and Gardens. In the Gnomion, which had been written a long time ago in the days when Gnomes could really make things, I mean really make things, there was the description of the Quail. It looked worth doing and we felt we could knock out a line of them. However, we got some of the enabling spells wrong. Not our fault. There was a page we couldn't read properly because the mould had got at it and I confess we misinterpreted the odd flyspeck as a full stop.

When we finished the damn thing, it started manifesting all these weird properties and ethereal beings began to turn up to ask if they could have a shufti. In particular, it became quite clear that whatever we'd made had some kind of accidental link with Eternity and could be used for a variety of less than savoury purposes. Well, that was a bit hot for us to handle, so we chucked it.

Doc was devastated. The Death Serpent thing was his way of capitalising on it and getting the pique out of his system. He figured that if people were going to want to see it they ought be given a bit of a hard time. Liked a laugh, did Doc. So did Happy. Grumpy, though...'

'Can we forget the family and get to the next bit? Please?'

'Well, I miss them.'

'I won't miss you,' Egric growled. 'I'll hit you full square.'

The Gnome sniffed, ignored him and continued. 'So, anyway, we set up this place as a reception area, as it were. Carved it out all nice and round, smooth walls, lovely bit of carving, that. It worked, as well. Some priests came, at a loose end after their deity was demoted or something and set up shop at the tunnel entrance. Demanded tribute from the surrounding cities, passing caravans, that sort of thing. Hence the treasure. Twisted little sod at times, our Doc, now I think of it. Later on we found him a Cyclotherapist called Frood who explained to him that everyone has a deep-rooted desire to sniff bicycle seats and that if you lie down on a couch until it goes away, you'll feel better. Can't see it myself but it seemed to do the trick with Doc. He's making racing bikes now and never been happier.

As for the other six of us, we found that although we had got rid of the Quail we were sort of bound to the flamin' thing and we took it in turns to carry on this Mystic Guardian bit. I'm the last. I must confess, though, I've had about enough of it. I think I'll chuck it in when you've gone. Go back to tunnel boring. I do a good tunnel, you'll have noticed.'

Vizagriz had been leaning with his chin in his palm and gazing at the Gnome. Now he spoke. 'Marvellous. Bloody marvellous. We come all this way to find something that's still hidden and we get threatened by a fake snake put there by a bunch of Gnomes who want to frighten people away from a thing they made but don't know what it does and haven't got any more. Does that sound plausible to you?'

'Well,' the Gnome conceded, 'there is a philosophy that says we're all part of a big game of some kind in a giant machine and other people out there are making us move around in it, constantly searching for things that don't really matter.'

'Don't be stupid,' said Vizagriz. 'Even if there were a grain of truth in that, who'd waste their time playing a daft fantasy game with no satisfactory resolution, on a machine? Doesn't make sense.'

'Or a book,' Rongwei chipped in. 'Some philosophers say we're all in a book.'

'Oh, right. I'd like a word with the author in that case. But who'd be warped enough to think this lot up? No, let's stick with Kayyam's Razor and assume there is some sense in all this and bloody well get to the end of it. Now. Where's this Gnomion?'

'Oh, that's long gone. Fell to dust over the millennia. Silver fish got at it. You might find the manual useful, though.'

'You mean this?' Vizagriz pulled the tome out of his robes and threw it between them. 'Can you explain it to us? I presume it's in Gnomish or whatever.'

'Ah, no. That's part of the problem. After we'd made the Quail we figured it would need a user's manual, but that's not our sort of thing, see? So we subcontracted the writing to a race of yellow Dwarfs who live on the Islands East of the Sun. When we got it back we found they'd done it in a lost language called Askey, and one of us who could read it said there were a lot of misspellings in it, which makes the incantations a bit risky. It's also full of jargon like "initialisation string" and "interface protocol" and such. The grammar is bad. It's unintelligible. We had a go at the Dwarf specialists but they said the jargon was perfectly understandable to those who wouldn't need to use the damn manual anyway. You're welcome to it.'

Vizagriz re-wrapped it in its oil cloth covering and put it away.

'We had a prophesy that said "A man must read the words", though,' Mindador chipped in.

'Good for that man, then,' the Gnome said breezily. 'As far as I'm concerned the flippin' Quail never worked and the manual is about as much use as a chocolate fireguard. But you're the Questers, so it's all yours.'

'I'm afraid not,' came a low, rasping voice from the tunnel entrance we had lately come through. 'I'll take that, if you don't mind.' I was jerked back to the here and now by the sight of Nazrat, the tall redheaded avatar of Patisse, standing there with a new band of Kuntz behind her.

Vizagriz shot to his feet and, completely forgetting himself, let off a blast of Magick that reverberated around the chamber, rebounded off the treasure pile and shot back at him, bathing the wizard in a green, flickering haze and lifting him clean of his feet before dropping him on the floor, to all appearances dead.

In the momentary confusion and possibly as a result of the display of power, the Kuntz momentarily retreated back into the tunnel, giving Egric, now recovered, time to jump his feet. Nazrat seemed dazed and blinded, probably being more sensitive to the magickal resonance which had floored my master, and she reeled about, moaning.

Egric shouted at Rongwei to join him at the tunnel entrance and for all of us to get behind them. The Gnome had scuttled back behind the snake's head and was gone. Mindador, however, was heading for the treasure. I saw him reach for it and, thinking he had forgotten the protective spell canopy that overlay it, I shouted at him to not to touch the horde. It was too late. He stretched out his hand and dropped some iron filings onto the jewels – with no result.

'I knew it!' he exulted. 'The feedback from Vizagriz's spell's blown out the protective enchantment!' and he started filling his pockets with the jewels. As the dug into the mound of coins and jewellery he dislodged the giant diamond. It rolled to my feet. I picked it up and stuck it inside my shirt.

Meanwhile, Nazrat was slowly coming back to full awareness but obviously still couldn't see. She was roaring her head off for the Kuntz to rejoin her and, tentatively, they were. Lunging parries from Rongwei and Egric held them at bay for a few moments while, Egric shouted, 'Mindador! Can you make smoke?'

Mindador looked up from his treasure hunt and nodded. He fished in his robe, drew out a powder vial and, with a muttered chant, threw it between the Kuntz and the two heroes. It billowed into the tunnel entrance, blown there by the back-draught from the chamber mouth.

Before the smoke could clear and while the confusion continued, Egric barked a command at Rongwei who nodded and hoisted the barely-conscious Vizagriz onto his shoulder. For his part, Egric picked up Winolene under one arm and Mindador under the other and before I could make any protest, propelled me before him towards the chamber's mouth, which looked out into thin air.

With a shouted "Hieronymous!" Egric kicked me out into the wild blue yonder, leapt after me with his double burden and looked back only once to see that Rongwei had followed, carrying my master.

As I curved outwards into nothing I remember thinking, 'It's not a bad way to go,' and braced myself for the plummeting fall towards the ground far, far below.

CHAPTER THE TWELTH

In which Slouch and the Questers find the Holy Quail and discover something of its properties, such as they are.

I hit something a lot quicker than I expected to, and not what I expected to hit, either. About twelve feet below the chamber mouth there was a pool of water into which we all plunged. Egric let go of the screaming Winolene and the howling Mindador. I saw Rongwei supporting the almost-unconscious Vizagriz and Sparky sitting on a leaf, trying to keep his feet out of the water and prevent a short. I spluttered to the surface. 'How did you know this water was here?' I shouted over to Egric.

'Don't worry about this water,' he replied. 'Worry about that water!'

I looked in the direction he had nodded towards and saw what looked like the edge of the world and the pool disappearing over it. We were at the top of a waterfall and heading towards it with the steady inevitability of a suspect prawn sandwich aiming for a rapid, watery exit. So this was the sound of running water I had heard from the tunnel. It's amazing how your mind has the ability to contemplate the trivial even when it's about to have itself bashed from your skull any moment. As we spiralled towards the cusp, I had time to wonder how Vizagriz would take the plunge without drowning, in his semi-comatose state. Egric and Rongwei were struggling towards each other and I watched them link arms with Vizagriz between them, supporting him a head higher than either of them. Wonderful what they teach you at hero school, I thought, do they get badges for iiiiiiiiiiittttt...and I was flung headlong down the waterfall.

The fall was longer than the one just passed, and we must have tumbled hundreds of feet by way of a series of small whirlpools, thankfully free of rocks, which broke our fall occasionally. The descent seemed to go on for ever and I was getting more and more waterlogged, inside and out. It occurred to me to wonder if Winolene could swim, but some deeper, more sensible part of my brain slapped the other bit in its face and said:

Don't be an idiot, she probably won't survive the fall.

Finally, the world stopped birling and I was aware of a sense of stillness and calm. Had we reached the bottom? I hardly dared believe so, but I opened my eyes and looked around. Somehow I had got behind everyone else and could see Rongwei and Egric still supporting Vizagriz, who appeared to be coughing. A good sign. Mindador was clutching a piece of driftwood. Winolene was making for the side with strong, firm strokes, which answered that one. No sign of the Amp, however. I looked back up to gauge the full horror of what we had just come through and saw in the far, high distance up the sheer cliff face a number of figures, one with red hair, leaning over the parapet of the cave mouth and shaking weapons.

As I doggy-paddled my way over to where Winolene was shaking herself off I thought what a narrow escape we had had, all thanks to the presence of mind of the two heroes. I banked myself, gave Mindador a helping hand out onto the grass where he lay, gasping and spluttering, and waited for Egric to hoist my master up beside us.

'Good thing you knew that pool was there,' I congratulated Egric.

'I didn't,' he replied grimly, and Winolene fainted again.

We wasted little time in getting away from the waterside and into a nearby wood, just long enough for the heroes to construct a rude stretcher affair out of two stout branches and their jackets, on which they either jointly carried or took turns to drag Vizagriz, now feverish and ranting. The sun was warm and dried our clothes quickly, except Mindador's robe which, being of a heavy material, held the water tenaciously. He had been forced to take it off, wring it out and carry it. He was now hanging it on a tree while we sat and took stock of the situation.

We figured it would take the Kuntz and their dæmonic captain some time to scale the cliff as it looked sheer. On the other hand, perhaps there was some way a dæmon could spirit them all down beside us. We had chosen to enter the woods because of the cover they provided.

Rongwei had found and caught an animal of some description, skinned and butchered it with considerable speed and had managed to strike a light for a small fire from his sword and a flint he carried. This reminded me. 'Where's Sparky?' I wondered.

The answer came with a chirping sound and a small, high-pitched "Hi!" from above my head and I looked up to see the Amp sitting astride a martin.

He stepped off onto a branch and sprang down the tree to perch on my knees. 'That was a bit of luck,' he vouchsafed, 'me seeing that nest in the rock and being able to steer my leaf towards it. Then all I had to do was persuade the bird to fly me about until we spotted you. Good job her old man wasn't there, though!'

At that, the martin chirruped and flew off. I swear she winked at Sparky before she left.

We ate, doused the fire and set off again, in a direction that Egric indicated.

I was deeply concerned about Vizagriz. He alternated between what seemed to be a natural and needed sleep and a sort of semi-coherent rambling that appeared to set Mindador's teeth on edge. I asked him why.

'Because when a wizard starts raving you never know what spell he's going to inadvertently set off. Most wizards die in their sleep, did you know that?'

'No.'

'Because they eat too much cheese one night, have a bad dream and dismiss themselves to some forgotten nether-realm. Or blast the wall out so the roof falls on them. You've heard of "snoring the place down" haven't you?'

I said I had.

'Well, it started with a wizard who did it literally.'

However, there was no alternative but to carry on and try to keep Vizagriz's fever down with cold compresses to the head and occasional sedation with leaves that Mindador found and thought they resembled something that he might have seen used once for such a purpose. This seemed hazardous in the extreme to me and I begged him to stop, which he did, albeit with the appropriate protestations about a mere apprentice calling his professional acumen into question. I apologised humbly and honour was satisfied.

It was starting to get dark when Egric suddenly stopped, sniffed and looked back at Rongwei, who was taking up the rear. He also sniffed and nodded. Men of few words, these heroes, except the ones who want to start conversations about the nature of meaning while you're disentangling twigs from your hair and fighting off thorn bushes.

'I'm tired,' Winolene announced. When she started to whine things were getting bad, I thought. Mostly because it annoyed everyone else.

'Better get a move on then,' Egric told her.

'Why?'

'Because I can smell wood smoke,' Egric explained, nodding towards the deeper forest. 'From over there.' He trudged off at an angle and we followed him. There was nothing else to do.

It was only a few minutes later that we entered a clearing of sorts in which there was a small cottage, smoke gaily pluming from its chimney. Outside, sitting at a small table and scribbling with a quill on parchment was a tall, thin man with a pair of spectacles on the end of a long nose and an extra pen stuck behind his ear. He looked up at our approach, started a bit when he saw Egric first, then calmed down at the sight of Winolene and the rest of us. He stood up as we approached.

'Travellers?' he enquired. 'Itinerants? Way-farers? Globe-trotters?'

'Greetings,' I said as I stepped forward. Chances are Egric will say nothing and Rongwei will say the wrong thing, I thought, so I should take the initiative. 'We are indeed travellers and we would appreciate shelter and perhaps some rest for our companion who is hurt.'

I must say, the man was a trusting soul. If a raggle-taggle admixture of swordsmen, wizards and the like had turned up at my door I'd be wanting some form of identification before I put the broom down. But he seemed to have no such qualms and, gathering up his papers ushered us towards his front step.

'Come in. Enter, cross the threshold, darken my door, obtain ingress. Gain admittance.'

I was first in, and when my eyes accustomed themselves to the gloom I could see a jumbled collection of quills, inkpots, blotting paper, sand shakers and parchment everywhere plus rows and rows of books on shelves. He was making a fuss of Winolene, showing her to a large, stuffed sofa. 'Charming,' he smarmed as she passed him, not without a certain pleasure it must be said. He also indicated some chairs to Mindador and the heroes.

'Be seated, recline, stretch yourselves out, take a pew, pull up a perch.'

'Pardon?'

'Do sit down.'

Winolene sank into the sofa with a sigh and Mindador found an armchair which released a puff of dust when he flopped into it. We laid my master in front of a small but functional fire and he was quiet for the present.

'Something to drink?' our host asked. 'A beverage, thirst-quencher, draught, noggin or bumper?'

I could see the way this was going. 'You're a scribe, aren't you?' I ventured.

'Scribe, penman, scribbler, quill-driver, scrivener, clerk. Yes. I suppose the quills, inkpots, blotting paper, sand shakers and parchment are a bit of a give-away. And the spectacles. Glasses, pince-nez, gig-lamps, lorgnettes...,' he said as he dispensed a sort of sweet wine into ridiculously small glasses that Winolene and Mindador seemed to be able to hold with ease and sip with some satisfaction but which the heroes found almost disappeared in their fists and completely disappeared in half a mouthful.

'Do you always speak like that?' asked Rongwei, perched on a stool near the window.

A dozen words all meaning the same where one's adequate?

'Sorry. Force of habit. When one gets paid by the word and they've all got to be different, one does tend to gild the lily, embellish, adorn, adonize, look, I'm doing it again,' he laughed with an affected sort of braying that would quite possibly get on my nerves if I had to live with it for any time.

'So you scribe. For a living.'

'Yes. A bit of transcribing, some manuscript work, translations, technical documents. That sort of thing. Occasional hack work for the women's market – romances, that sort of thing. Not my real interest, of course, but it pays the rent. That sort of thing. I say, is your friend going to be all right?'

'We hope so. He's had a bit of a shock. But did you say "translating"?' I asked.

'Did you say "romances"?' Winolene asked.

He chose to answer me, possibly out of embarrassment at Winolene's query. 'Yes. That's why I'm spending the summer in this delightful cottage. Got a scholarship to look at the ancient languages of the region, record the scripts used, that sort of thing. Bit of a change. Not may visitors, though. So I'm very pleased to see you. That sort of thing.'

You might be getting more visitors than you can handle, I thought, but kept it to myself. It was the mention of translation that brought me back to the subject in hand.

'Could you look at something for us?'

'Of course. What is it?'

'It's a book.'

'Ah!'

I went over to Vizagriz and drew out of the folds of his robe the book from the chamber of Quaxialcaybl, still wrapped in its oil cloth and mercifully dry. I also found the bag of gold Thalers.

I handed the book to the scribe and said, 'Sorry, I didn't introduce us, did I?'

'No. So let's see this book, then. That sort of thing.'

Not much on the social skills, but dedicated, I thought. He took the tome from me, handling it as if it were a revered, sacred article, which to a scribe it probably was. He carefully withdrew it from the covering, laid it flat and turned open the first page. There was a great of "Hmm," and "Well!" and "Yes, yes, yes," and other expressions of delight and interest. That sort of thing.

While he examined the book I went to see how Vizagriz was faring and the answer was, badly. His brow was damp with sweat and he was shivering. I saw a water jar on a table and poured some from it into my small wine glass, offering it to his lips. He sipped some but gave no other sign of being with us in more than body. I was worried.

Egric and Rongwei had gone outside, possibly to check if we were being followed. Winolene sat upright on the sofa, watching the scribe. Mindador had dropped off from his exertions and was snoring gently.

At last the scribe closed the book, took of his glasses, pinched his eyes and said, 'Fascinating. Quite fascinating. What a find.'

'Do you know what it is?'

'Yes. It's a description of something called a Holy Quail, obviously derived from earlier work in the Gnomion, judging by some of the terms used.'

Bingo! 'Can you tell us what it says?'

'No, sorry.'

'Why not?'

'Well, it's written in Askey, a most recondite language. That's all right, I can make sense of some of it. But there are various passages that seem to be just, well, gibberish.'

'That's what Vizagriz said! Can't you read Gibber?'

'No, I mean it's nonsense. Wrong spellings, poor grammar, appalling punctuation. If I didn't know better I say it had been written by someone who wasn't fluent with the language at all.'

'Like a race of dwarfs from the Islands East of the Sun?'

'That sort of thing, yes.'

'And you can't make any sense of it.' I was crestfallen. So near, yet so far.

'Oh, I didn't say that. It's just so badly written that I can't read it out loud. Anyway, Askey isn't a language for reading. Not prose as such. More a set of instructions.'

'What for?' I pressed.

'Well, for this Quail thing. It seems it has various jewels on it with different functions. The amethysts of its eyes confer on the possessor the ability to see the World as if flying. The pearl beak, where's that bit, oh yes, the beak when touched induces the desire to speak nothing but the truth. The ruby-studded wings allow limited power of flight. The tail feathers offer some ability in camouflage. And something about the feet "standing astride realms" whatever that means.'

This was more like it. 'This is what we are seeking,' I decided to explain. 'We are on a quest to find this Holy Quail and we think we're fairly close to it. We didn't know what it was or what it did, but you seem to have solved that for us. Thanks.'

'That's all right. Did my first degree in oriental technical languages, you know. Useless, but interesting. Anyway, it's a nice story, rather typical of the period – descriptions of fanciful beasts and metal dragons. I thought of writing a comic fantasy once, you know. Wizards and jokes. Swords and Sniggering, that sort of thing. But then I thought, who'd read such nonsense?'

'Oh, the Holy Quail is real and we have to find it as soon as we can. Apparently it's in a volcano. Are there any volcanoes around here?' I asked. Bang on cue there was a low rumble and a mild shaking of the cottage that set the glassware tinkling and the ink shimmering in its pots.

'Well, there's that one. Quite near, I believe. Possibly the reason the rent's low. Nice place, this. Woman who owns it, she's been asleep for over a hundred years, fancy that.'

'Does it, you know, erupt?' I asked, a bit alarmed. I was warm enough, thanks.

'The volcano? Oh, no. All but dormant, I'm told. Bit of underground activity but no spouts of lava, that sort of thing. That only happens every few centuries, apparently.'

I dreaded to ask. 'When did it last erupt?'

And the answer, predictably, was, 'Not for a few centuries. Oh, I see what you mean,' and he giggled.

'Look, I'm sorry, I still don't know your name.'

'Psyclclips K'Nib. Boethian, on my mother's side.'

'Look, Psyclclips, this quest of ours, we are supposed to have a scribe with us. I don't suppose...'

'Oh, couldn't possibly. Too much to do. Translations, researches, you know. Full schedule. That sort of thing.'

I had an inspiration and opened the bag of Thalers, saying, 'Well, let me pay you for your trouble.'

He affected to demur, saying "No, no, no", "No trouble, really", "Well, if it makes you feel better" and the like, never taking his eyes off the bag for an instant. Academics!

I took out a Thaler, pressed it into his open palm and watched as jerked back to avoid the actinic spark that flew up his arm, round his head and out of the window, frightening a third of a cat one-ninth to death, judging by the "Wieaow!" noise from outside.

'Wh-what was that?' the scribe asked, shocked.

Winolene piped up for the first time. 'Tag,' she said. 'You're it!'

It didn't actually take much doing to persuade K'Nib to accompany us on the remainder of our quest. At least, it didn't take Egric much doing. He didn't even break sweat. The same can't really be said for the scribe. It was a shame to have someone along under duress but, as Winolene pointed out, none of us was exactly a volunteer.

He had gathered up what few supplies were in his cottage - he lived mostly off what was growing in a small kitchen garden, he explained, and didn't have much in - plus an assortment of the tools of his trade. He wasn't going anywhere without a couple of pens and some ink and parchment, he said, never know when you'll want something written down, recorded, captured for posterity, that sort of thing.

The volcano was visible from a knoll behind K'Nib's cottage which itself was near the margins of the Wasteland of Sinne. This was a massive plateau rising far above us on which, it was rumoured, lived large, ancient animals unseen since time immemorial. No-one went there or, if they did, they hadn't come back to talk about it. So how did anyone know about the large, ancient animals? Winolene said, reasonably, I thought.

Rongwei replied that it was never a good idea to dismiss myth out of hand since there tended to be nub of truth in every fairy story. Sparky agreed.

Our scribe had been a bit nonplussed to meet Sparky, in fact. As a scholar and tireless seeker after truth he was inclined to dismiss out of hand anything that didn't fit with his pre-conceived notions or hadn't been told about by some older, revered teacher. Sparky reasonably retorted that the proof of the pudding was in the seeing and if that didn't convince then a few volts across the temples ought to do it. The subject was quietly dropped.

K'Nib did, however, spend quite a bit of time chatting to Winolene. He had the right manners, the correct background for her to be impressed. I thought he was a long drink of water with a tendency to bray like an ass and I sulked a fair amount.

Mindador and the scribe found something in common, too. They both had a passing acquaintance with some obscure hieratic language that nobody had spoken for thousands of years, which made it all the more important to keep alive, apparently. The knew schoolboyish rhymes about it and in it and spent a pleasant hour or so throwing quips like "Eheu!" and "O! me miserum" at each other, to some hilarity. I hadn't seen Mindador so animated since we burst in on him that night weeks before, and he actually laughed at one point. There is just no telling.

I filled K'Nib in on our journey so far, bits of which he jotted down in a small notebook. We paused often to check on Vizagriz, give him water and rest ourselves. The wizard passed a fitful night and neither Mindador nor I got very much sleep – me worrying about my master and the old mage keeping an ear cocked for anything that might resemble an injudicious spell uttered in the course of one of the infrequent but disturbing ravings.

The heroes took turns to pass out like a felled ox or slip back the way we came to check for unwelcome visitors. It never ceased to amaze me how heroes, regardless of the circumstances or danger, took every chance to eat or sleep. As Egric had explained to me, there might not be another chance for either for quite a while, you never could tell. I supposed it helped to have a certain lack of imagination, too.

We were closer to Sinne than we had expected, the trip through the tunnel and the water ride having taken a large slice out of an otherwise arduous overland journey. It was the middle of the next day when we found ourselves at the foot of the escarpment that led up to the Sinne plateau, towering over our heads. The next question was - how to scale it?

Egric suggested we scout around a bit as there might be steps or a ladder cut into the rock at some point and this seemed a reasonable proposal. In fact, the plateau was a good fifty thousand paces across and therefore a good two day's march around it. By the time we had walked for half a day there was little point turning back, so we carried on, in the sure and certain knowledge that we would end back where we started if nothing else, and could then think of something better to do. Not much of plan, I'll grant you, but there didn't seem to be any better ideas forthcoming.

Rongwei was all for climbing it single-handed, knotting a rope out of vines or creepers or something and hauling the rest of us up there. Egric told him not to be soft - what guarantee was there that there would be any such things up there? And anyway, impenetrable barriers always had a secret entrance, everyone knew that.

Winolene suggested that Mindador ought to be able to whisk us all up top with Magick and what was the point of having a mage along if you didn't use him? Eh? Apparently he wasn't much of a one for such things. Could levitate a bit in his younger days, got the Top Hat for Most Upwardly Mobile, all that. But mass transit that high? No, that defeated all but the strongest sorcerers even in relays of three or four. Now, he could conjure up a dæmon to help but he didn't think alerting dæmons to our present position wasn't much of a plan since they were all in the same union and word tended to get around.

Vizagriz would know what to do, I couldn't help thinking.

As it was, fate took a hand. Rongwei was gazing at a piece of rocky outcrop when he said 'You know, that looks a bit like a face. Worn away, of course, but if you sort of squint at it, you could just imagine it was the head of a woman on the body of a cat.'

'Body of a cat?' Egric asked peering at it. 'Oh right, that bit underneath it. See what you mean. Have a look at this, mage.'

Mindador looked at the supposed shape from various angles, gave it some thought and declared, 'Head of a woman, yes. Body of a cat, perhaps. If it had pointy ears, I'd say it was a Slynx.'

'Slynx?'

'Oh, yes,' K'Nib butted in. 'Very popular as a cultural icon in certain societies a few millennia ago. carved them all over the place. Usually as a guardian of some kind. That sort of thing.'

'Guarding what, exactly,' Egric asked, guardedly. 'I mean, in my experience, things left guarding things means there's something to guard and some appalling fate awaits those who disturb whatever thing the guardian's, er, guarding. Isn't it?'

'Could be,' Mindador admitted. 'But they were also gateways. In a sense. Three senses, in fact.'

'Five senses,' Rongwei corrected.

'Actually we have twenty-one. But what I meant was, there are three senses in which a Slynx could be a gateway. First, it was a metaphorical gateway – put at the front of tombs to indicate the occupant had passed on to a better life.'

Egric perked up at the idea of tombs. Can't beat a good tomb sacking, he always said, apparently.

'Second, it was a spiritual gateway – some people actually carved their own Slynx to put at the entrance to a house or, indeed, a tomb, oh do stop slavering, Egric, to indicate they had undergone some rite of passage.'

'A passage. That's what we want. A passage into this mountain.'

'You're not getting me into any more tunnels!' Winolene was adamant on that point. She still hadn't forgiven Rongwei for losing our ponies, that was evident.

'Third,' Mindador continued, ignoring all the by-play, 'third, as I say, it could be a physical gateway – the lock or handle or lever that actually opens something. Often, it was all three, for the price of one as it were. I often wonder if that's the origin of the idea that you can only have a third of a cat.'

Egric was all for immediate action. 'If it's a physical gateway, then hitting it might open a door of some kind,' he suggested and proceeded to give it big licks with his broadsword, knocking chunks of both the weapon and the object of its attentions.

'If it's a spiritual or metaphorical gateway, it might have some further significance,' K'Nib opined, complicating things as usual.

'Maybe it was a cat that pined for its master when he died and lay on his grave for years, so they put up a statue to it afterwards,' Rongwei suggested brightly, but that was such a patently absurd concept that it was given the all-round thumbs-down and the hero moped for a bit. I mean, the only reason an animal would pay any attention to its master's grave would be on the off chance a bone might emerge. And cats weren't noted for that sort of loyalty in any case. Go anywhere for a saucer of milk, your average feline.

It was Sparky who noticed a crevice up on the face, or what was left of it, and decided to investigate. He stuck his head into the crack, fired up a bit of light and had a good old butchers, as he put it. When he emerged, he perched on one of the Slynx's worn-away paws and said, 'Now, I'm not an expert, being from the forest and all that, but when you have sort of gear-things and spring-things and wire-things, doesn't that usually mean a mechanism of some sort?'

We all agreed that it did, usually, and that if he didn't mind popping inside again and hauling a few levers about, maybe there would be a result. But he wasn't having any of it. 'No fear!' he said, quite definite. 'Get myself caught up in all them moving parts when it decides to go off? Tchah! Probably rusted to buggery in any case.'

Rongwei, however, had come out of his snit and thought that a good poke with a dagger never goes wrong so he crammed his knife into what had evidently, on closer inspection, been one of the Slynx's nostrils and pulled it about a bit.

'Does he know what he's doing up there?' I asked Egric.

'Ought to. He's had plenty of practice on his own hooter,' he responded and chuckled to himself. Winolene turned slightly green at the thought.

'Just a suggestion, that sort of thing,' K'Nib threw in, 'but isn't it typical to open these things with a magickal utterance?'

'Such as?' Mindador wanted to know. 'Open sesame?'

And wouldn't you know it, the cat-shape suddenly swung out from the rock face and hurled Rongwei onto the turf.

'Well fancy that. You know, that had occurred to me but I thought it was too daft to even mention. Just goes to show, doesn't it?'

'Hmmm,' Egric mused. 'Not too happy about magick words to do with cookery. Baking dæmons and all that. Still...' And he strode forward.

Mindador was a bit put out by all this. It shouldn't be that easy, his professional pride seemed to be saying in body language. No justice, his hunched shoulders said, loud and clear. Regardless, we looked inside. It was a cave, and it had a flat floor. Lacking any other sensible approach, we decided to give it a shot and the heroes hoisted Vizagriz while the rest of us filed in and stood just inside the cave mouth.

Sparky let up a flare and in the brief glare of its light we found we were in a huge cavern. Rocky prominences stuck out everywhere and there were massive protuberances sticking up and hanging down. It was spectacular and in other circumstances I could imagine getting quite a kick out of exploring a place like this. With torches, everyone roped together, wearing sensible footwear of course. And a hard hat of some kind. No, stupid idea, I know.

'Stalactites. Stalagmites. How does anybody remember the difference?' Mindador mused.

'Easy. Stalactites has got a "c" in it, like "ceiling" and stalagmites has a "g" like "ground",' I suggested, courtesy of a rudimentary Geography class back at

SamBernardo's.

'No, stalactites have to hold tight to the roof and stalagmites might reach them one day,' Winolene supplied, with the benefit of a decent education.

'That's not it. When tights come down, mites go up,' was Rongwei's contribution.

K'Nib chipped in too. 'Actually, both are derived from the same root, meaning drippy and it's sort of a linguistic accident that they are slightly different words.'

'You said "drippy"?' Egric queried. Unlike him to be interested in, well, anything.

'Yes.'

'And "linguistic accident"?' he continued.

'That's right.'

'Must have been a scribe involved somewhere, then.'

Ah.

The trip through the cavern was uneventful, but boring and slow. In the absence of any light, we had Sparky throw up a brief glimmer by which Egric might see a bit further forward. He would then walk as far as he felt was safe and call to us so that we could follow his voice, everyone helping to carry Vizagriz's stretcher, largely as an exercise in keeping us all together. When we reached Egric Sparky would light up again, the hero would peer at the floor ahead then move off as far as could. And the whole process was repeated again.

Sparky was getting exhausted after an hour of this. Mindador said he would have helped, honest, but all his phosphor powders had got soggy and useless in the waterfall. Eventually we reached the other side of the cavern and with one last, brave effort the little Amp let off a glare that lasted a few seconds and we all looked frantically for anything that resembled a way out.

'Look,' exclaimed K'Nib, pointing along the cavern a bit. 'That might be a tunnel.'

'I'm not...' Winolene began.

'You are!' Egric finished.

We felt out way along to the place he had indicated and found what did seem to be a hole in the rock. It went down into the floor a way.

Ever the man of action, Rongwei lowered himself into it and announced that is was full of running water. Running water had to exit somewhere, so he would go and have a look.

It was fully twenty minutes before he returned, drenched and gasping. There was a way through, he said, but it involved diving under water and swimming for a good ten paces. Did we all think we could manage it?

'We might, but what about Vizagriz?' I pointed out.

'He's not breathing much as it is,' Egric said with some justification.'Maybe you could, sort of, blow in his lungs then hold his nose and mouth shut while we pulled the pair of you through.'

This didn't seem like it would work, but what was the option? Rongwei got into the hole again and went through. Next, Egric got in and helped me lower Vizagriz on his conveyor carefully onto the water surface and I followed. We manoeuvred the recumbent figure to the start of the water-filled chamber and on Egric's signal I blew a lungful of my air into my prentice-master's mouth, clamped my hand over his jaw and nose, took a breath myself and plunged under the surface, keeping the prone wizard as high as possible. The rubbing of rock on my hand told me that there was a gap of some few inches above us so even if Vizagriz did breathe, he would not take in much water. After what seemed to me like a lung-bursting eternity I was pulled upwards by the hair and, regardless of whether there was air or not, took a deep gasp. When I opened my eyes, I saw that we were in a second cave, but one in which the rocks glowed with a dull, green iridescence. Egric was supporting Vizagriz and I helped the hero get him out of the water and onto solid rock beside us. Rongwei had gone back to pull each of the others through, all except Sparky.

It had been a miracle that he had survived the experience of the waterfall but total immersion was not an option for the Amp. We discussed the possibility of his sitting atop Rongwei's head, but even this would involve a dunking. 'If only he was waterproof,' Winolene said after she emerged, which gave me an idea. Mindador was not through yet and I made my suggestion to Rongwei who nodded and went back for the old thaumaturge. When he returned pulling a drenched mage with him, coughing and spluttering, I asked, 'Did you get him?' and the younger swordsman held aloft the book, wrapped in its oilcloth which he proceeded to unfurl and from which out dropped Sparky.

'Strewth. I feel like a bleeding flower what's been pressed!' he exclaimed, but he was clearly none the worse for his water-free journey.

We rested and wrung out our clothes as best we could, then Egric suggested that as it would by now be as dark outside as it was in the cave, we might as well press on and if we found an exit, stop until daylight.

The floor of the cavern had an incline upwards and as we followed it there seemed to be an irregularity in the surface that increased as the cavern narrowed. This continued until we were in a narrow passage with a steep but irregular slope. 'These are stairs, I think,' I said.

Egric replied, 'I know. And steep.'

'Vertiginous, acute, sloping.'

'You're not helping,' Rongwei point out to K'Nib, who had sufficient energy left to look abashed.

It was a long, arduous climb up the rising treads, made all the more so by a kind of slimy moss that had grown on the ground. Mindador said that this indicated we were near fresh, outside air and I had no reason to doubt him.

We must have paused eight or nine times on our near-vertical trek. I couldn't help thinking that the way the two heroes managed to keep Vizagriz more or less horizontal with the minimum of shaking was a testament to their muscular strength as much as their resolve. In truth, heroes are something else, and well worth the name.

Finally, after our legs had all but given out we reached what was clearly the open air. It was pitch black but for the odd pin-prick of starlight and bitingly cold. Still damp and somewhat hot from our exertions, we all started to shiver. We were standing on a ledge at the mouth of a cave and staring down a steep, icy slope to a flat plain below, devoid of trees or, as far as I could see, any vegetation. Neither moon was up yet, which contributed to the grim blackness.

'So how do we get down there?' K'Nib asked and for his answer, the snow and ice of the ledge we stood on – not capable of taking weight for any time – gave way, and were plunged onto a precipitous glacier, hurling us below.

There was a fairish amount of screaming and the like, not all from Winolene by all means. I contributed my share. I did notice that Egric and Rongwei had not managed to keep hold of Vizagriz's stretcher and it was heading off on its own gravity-driven path. Fortunately, and before anyone's heart gave out with panic, the slope became gentler and our skidding, rolling descent slowed until we all slid to a halt in a deep, powdery snow bank on the shores of a frozen lake. As I came to halt I saw Vizagriz's stretcher glide, sled-like, alongside me. He had had the easiest descent of all – flat on his back with a set of ready-made runners to guide his way.

As we each dug ourselves out and stood upright, beating our arms to keep warm in the chill air, Mindador said, 'Remember? "Empty onto a flat surface, then leave to cool overnight. Next day, put in a high place." He got that right!'

'Who?' K'Nib asked.

'A dæmon I once knew.'

From the middle of the lake there rose a protuberance, conical in shape and about as high as the cave we had fallen from. The top of the cone smoked and thick, yellowish fug dripped down the sides.

'Oh, great,' Egric's voice said from the same direction as a puff of steamy breath.

'What?'

'It's snowing!'

CHAPTER THE THIRTEENTH

In which Slouch at last plays his part in the Quest and a baking daemon comes to a suitable end, not without some troubles beforehand.

Everything Will End. All the ancient books and legends are quite firm on that point. There will come a time when all the rubber bands unravel and crumble away to nothingness and then there will be nothing. Never will have been anything, in fact, since if Eternity is circular it must always exist everywhere at once and if it doesn't exist at one place, then it doesn't exist anywhere or anywhen at all.

Why some dæmons and other entities want to bring this about is a mystery, since it entails their disappearance as well. It may be that some things are just so tetchy that they'll happily go for the cosmic equivalent of cutting off their noses to spite their faces. Or maybe there's some kind of pension plan for them. Perhaps it's just such hell being a dæmon that nothingness would be a relief, which would also explain their tempers.

Where we came into all this was still not clear to me. If there are beings of immense power in Eternity and they want the Holy Quail why can't they just go and get it? What was the point of recruiting a bunch of, let's face it, inadequately-equipped and under-informed grunts like us to go and do the job of dæmons and deities?

I pondered all of this as we trudged our way to the top of the volcano. It was cold, it was still snowing and it was altogether the most miserable time I had ever had. By the standards of the quest so far, that was some going.

Winolene was finding the climb rather hard. Rongwei was helping her most of the way while Egric hauled Vizagriz on his sled-stretcher all the way up. The two heroes had not worn their jackets since the wizard had been incapacitated and they had used them to build his conveyance, but they had never complained, or even shown any signs of discomfort. Stoics, both of them. Mindador was falling further and further behind and K'Nib helped him often, which was good considering he didn't want to be here. Neither did I, but I was determined to get it over with.

Sparky was tucked inside my clothing and did not appear to be moving. I hoped he was all right but it would be foolishness to bring him out into even more cold to check. I left him, rationalising that if he was fine, the worst thing I could do would be to let cold air in about him, and if he wasn't there was nothing I could do in any case.

Once or twice we saw an indistinct looming shape in the snow flurries. A mirage, I though. Can you have mirages in show? Or is that heat? My brain was too cold and numb to be bothered remembering.

The climb became mechanical after a while – hand after hand, foot after foot. The occasional slip or stumble served to keep me and then others awake. It would be all too easy just to lie down and succumb to a freezing death. Occasionally we had to make a sideways detour to avoid a rivulet of dribbling, sulphurous ooze that ran down from the rim. The sun fell and rose again during our climb but it made no difference to the temperature and fortunately both moons were out so there was sufficient light to see by, at least as far as the next handhold.

At one point just after the dim, dank sunrise we found a flattish outcrop with a snow-free hollow out of the wind blast and we collapsed into it to rest up. I put some snow in Vizagriz's mouth in lieu of water. He had not eaten for a long time – was not capable of it – and this must be sapping his strength even more than the coldness.

We ate what we had, the last of the food K'Nib had brought, and a cold and cheerless meal it was. He did, however, suggest that some of his parchment might make a bit of a fire and this plus some scrub growing out of the rock face was enough for Sparky, when I coaxed him out, to ignite and provide us with some minimal warmth. The he shivered and disappeared back inside my clothes with a small piece of fruit.

After a while the fire all but died. There was a low, whistling-mewing sound somewhere off in the distance. More by way of making contact with another human than anything else I said, 'Was that the wind?'

'Probably mice,' Rongwei answered, his gaze fixed on the middle distance.

'Must stop eating them, then,' Egric replied. But neither of them chuckled or even looked at each other and I strongly got the impression they were paying attention to something no-one else had even perceived.

'Shouldn't we be moving on?' I ventured.

'Wait.' Egric said. 'It won't be much longer, I think,' and with this mysterious utterance he and Rongwei got carefully to their feet and unsheathed their swords.

'What is it?' I asked, alarmed, but Rongwei put his fingers to his lips and indicated that we should all get back against the rock wall.

It wasn't long, right enough. After an anxious pause there was a snarling sound and a large, white cat leapt down in front of us, growling and baring long, white tusks. It had pointed ears and eyes that glowed red. The Slynx was real, and this one intended to stay real a bit longer by adding us to his protein intake.

The ensuing battle was a textbook piece of attack and defence by the two heroes. While one lunged and the Slynx raked out with its long, vicious claws to parry, the other dived at its side to thrust a blade into it. When it turned to counter this attack, the strategy reversed. This carried on for quite a while, neither hero getting close enough to do any significant damage but holding it off sufficiently far that neither did it get a good swipe at either of them. Then it looked like the end had come - Egric slipped, lost his footing and fell, dropping his sword.

Winolene gasped and huddled against me. I put her arms around her and held her, both of us shivering and moaning at the same time. K'Nib and Mindador were pressed up close against the back of the hollow as they could manage and had dragged Vizagriz with them.

The cat was on Egric in an instant, thrusting its huge, slavering jaws at his face. Egric held it off with his hands around his throat and shouted, 'Come on, then!' Rongwei took the cue and leapt on the creature's back, taking out his shorter sword and plunging it between the shoulder blades. The cat reared, howled and spun away from Egric, turning its rage on Rongwei who had been thrown clear. This was the chance Egric needed - as its underbelly was exposed he retrieved his broadsword and hurled it at the animal, the weapon disappearing into its ribs and lodging there.

The howling and roaring was terrible and the Slynx writhed about with one blade in its back and one in its side, the movements only serving to drive them deeper. Rongwei and Egric stepped back while the cat lashed out with its paws, knowing that these were its death throes. When it had exhausted itself and the show was red with blood, Rongwei moved cautiously towards the prone figure, staying outside the range of its raking talons and delivered the final blow with his long sword. Winolene shuddered and turned her head away into my shoulder.

The heroes recovered their weapons, cleaned them and put them away. 'Right,' Egric said. 'It's probably got a mate or a sister, so the sooner we leave the better. Rongwei will catch us up.'

Why was Rongwei staying behind? I didn't have time to worry as Egric hustled us all back onto the mountain and upwards, hoisting Vizagriz behind him.

It was only a short while later that I noticed the snow under our feet was getting sparse and there was rock beneath it. A few minutes later the snow flurries stopped and the wind died down and I could see that we had left the snow field behind us and were neat the top of our climb.

'It's warmer, all of a sudden,' Winolene said and crouched down to touch the rock. 'And so is the ground.'

'It's a volcano!' Egric replied. 'Ah. Here comes Rongwei. Did you get them?'

The younger hero joined us and held up something in his left hand, grinning. It was two Slynx ears, still dripping blood. Winolene grimaced at the trophies and Mindador said something about how it was good that they could prove the beast was real and not mythical. K'Nib said he wished he hadn't burnt his parchment as he'd like to have drawn it and taken down a description, might even be the start of a bestiary, that sort of thing. I just wanted to get on with the rest of the climb.

Rongwei took the other end of Vizagriz's stretcher and we aimed for the summit of the volcano, the Wasteland of Sinne stretching out below us as the snow cleared. As we approached the crest of the mountain the air started to stink of sulphur and became uncomfortably warm. At last we scaled the final rise and found ourselves standing at the very peak of the mount. Egric put Vizagriz down. The wizard was mumbling and moving his head from side to side.

The top was not what I had expected. It was another plateau but with two large depressions in it. From one there was the stench of brimstone and other foul gases bubbling up from the very heart of the volcano and probably further. It looked like it went down forever. Rongwei, Egric and I went as close as we dared to have a look..

Peering down into the hole we could see, far below, the glow of molten rock. The heat rising directly towards us was unbearable and we could not breathe for the vapours that swirled just below the lip. The other depression was dark, with what appeared to be a ramp circling all the way around the inside and down into the darkness.

'I hate to say it,' Egric confided, 'but it looks like if we're going anywhere, it's down there.'

'Do you think so?' I asked, hoping against hope there was some other possibility. I had had quite enough of climbing, caves and rock in general for the time being.

'Must be. I don't see anything interesting up here, do you? I wish that Gnome fellah had been a bit more long-winded with the instructions rather than going on about old books and bicycles, whatever they are. Still. He didn't get the chance, really, did he?'

We walked back to our companions, who were all sitting, sweating with the heat and attending to Vizagriz, who seemed to be regaining consciousness. I rushed over to him. 'Master!' I said. 'Master, are you all right?'

Silly question, I know, and in normal circumstances I would have expected him to point this out. But he turned his head towards me and whispered, 'Thirsty.' I put my water skin to his cracked lips and he took the first real swallow for days. After he had had enough he lay back and said, 'Sleep,' which he did.

I wanted to wait longer, until Vizagriz had recovered some more, but Egric vetoed it. 'We might as well get going. We don't know how long he'll be out and if there's nothing down that hole we'll have to get off the mountain in any case. That won't take long and we can look after him then. I don't know what else we'll be doing anyway. This is where the clues run out. Right, Mindador?'

The old mage recited the two divinations again. 'The dæmon said, "Three times three times three nights from tonight, take one wizard. Spin until giddy. Raise to a high dudgeon. And put to one side". That seems so long ago, now. Then it was, "Place all the mixture in a cart lined with straw and set it off at a steady pace, until done". And finally, "Empty onto a flat surface, then leave to cool overnight. Next day, put in a high place". That would seem to be here.'

'It would,' Egric confirmed. 'What else was there?'

Mindador continued, his eyes closed as he remembered. 'The Talking Heads of Dbyrne said, "Seek the place where webs are woven. Find the weaver and ask the question. There is a jewel without equal. A man must read the words. It is far, but near. It is inside, but without. It is high, but deep. Once found, it must once again be lost, or all is lost". That was it.'

'"Far, but near", eh?' Egric repeated. 'I suppose that means the shortcut we took through the tunnel. Or perhaps the cavern. Hard to tell, really. Why couldn't these heads just give you a straight answer?'

'You had to be there,' Mindador sighed, plainly exhausted.

'And "Inside, but without". Without what?'

Rongwei chipped in. 'Could mean outside, could mean lacking something, could mean... something else, perhaps. Maybe.'

'The reference to "High, but deep" sounds like that pit, chasm, abyss or hypogeum you've found,' K'Nib added, helpfully.

'That's what I think. So let's go.' Egric stood up and went to lift Vizagriz on his bed.

'Shouldn't we perhaps leave him here? It might be safer,' Winolene suggested.

'Not unless you think he likes Slynxes,' Egric replied. ''Cause I can assure you, they'll love him.' Rongwei hefted the other end, and we moved towards the pit.

At the rim, we surveyed the helical ramp. It was about a man's height wide, as wide as many pavements I have walked or even run along without fear of falling off. But somehow this didn't reassure me, with a well of darkness plunging down at the side of the path. We all kept as close as possible to the wall, fixed our eyes on the next step ahead and edged our way along, gingerly. It was hardest on the two heroes who had to carry the stretcher flat and level.

We spiralled the inside of the rim twelve times – I counted – before the ramp flattened off to a circular path that ended in a hole the size and shape of a doorway. Above it, incongruously, was a single word, carved into the rock. 'IN' it said. There was a light shining from it.

'I'm not an expert,' Egric admitted and spat into the far depths. 'But I'd say there was a fair chance that's the way in.'

'I think you're right,' added Rongwei, totally unnecessarily. 'Reminds me of the back door to that harem we razed in Embra last term.'

'Does it?'

'No. Not really.'

We edged our way towards the hole and one by one passed through it into a square room with dim, sputtering torches arrayed along the walls. The floor was an inch or more thick with dust and everywhere there were cobwebs. I looked across through the gloom. I don't know how long it was before I noticed that I had stopped breathing, but my eyes had just fallen on the most magnificent sight I had ever seen, or would ever see again.

At the other side of the chamber there was a raised dais and on it rested a golden statue the shape and size of a small bird, covered in jewels. The eyes were a purple gem, possibly amethyst and the beak shone iridescent like pearl. On the wings there were rubies or garnets and the tail was carved of what looked like the finest chrysoprase, reflecting green in the torchlight. So this was it, the object of our quest. We had come to the end, seen off dæmons, survived boiling and freezing, starved, gone thirsty, been attacked, bound and rescued and at the finish of it all, we had made it!

'It's beautiful,' I heard Winolene gasp.

'Beautiful,' K'Nib echoed. 'Exquisite. Sublime. Gorgeous.'

Sparky had been looking at the bird from where he was tucked in my shirt and he let out a low whistle of amazement.

All we had to do now was take the artefact, find the way back and... do whatever we were supposed to do with it. My heart sank slightly as I thought of us retracing our steps then making our way round half a world. But perhaps Vizagriz would know what to do. He seemed to be rallying.

I looked at Egric who said, 'It's your quest. You pick it up, then,' and slapped me on the back. I walked slowly over to the fabulous bird and stretched my hand out. I was half expecting a jolt from a spell of some kind, but there was none. I lifted the Quail from its resting place and looked at it closely. It was even more captivating when seen close up and was vibrating slightly in my hand. Behind the dais I saw another doorway like the one we had entered. Above it was carved "OUT". 'Look, Mindador,' I said.

The thaumaturge shuffled over, peered at the inscription and repeated, '"It is within, but with Out". I see now. May I hold the Holy Quail?'

I handed it over and watched as he turned it this way and that, over and under, careful not to touch any of the jewels, I noticed. 'So it's all been for this,' he sighed as he handed it back. 'Hardly seems worth it now.' And he sank to the floor, crying silently.

I took the artefact over to Winolene and showed it to her. She was as captivated as any of us although she forbore to touch it. Then I knelt down beside Vizagriz and said softly, 'Master. We have the Holy Quail. We have it!' He opened his eyes, turned them towards me then the bird and smiled weakly. He nodded twice, closed his eyes again and appeared to go to sleep.

I showed it again to Rongwei and K'Nib both of whom said nothing for a change. Then Egric pulled us all back from whatever reveries we were each lost in by saying, 'Well, we've got what we came for. Now we have to get it out of here. Let's get on with it.'

'I would suggest the egress,' K'Nib proposed.

'Ooh, I hope we don't meet one of them,' Rongwei said as he and Egric lifted Vizagriz and headed for the OUT doorway. They didn't get far. As they entered the tunnel they were jumped on by at least eight Kuntz who knocked them cold and sat on them. Vizagriz's stretcher fell heavily, the wizard letting out a cry of semi-conscious pain as he hit the rock floor. A pair of high leather boots stepped over him and through the entrance strode Nazrat, red hair glistening and a smile of satisfaction on her lips.

'Well done. You made it. Pity you won't live to enjoy the fruits of your quest.'

We were each grabbed by a tribesman and roughly bundled towards the exit. I expected Nazrat to take the Quail from me but she showed no inclination to do so. She must have seen my surprise because she said, 'Oh, no, no, no. I don't want it. I can't even touch it. I do, however, mean to take it back to the oxterworld and you will be carrying it there for me. Seems only fitting, doesn't it? Now move!'

'I wondered who had lit the torches,' I heard K'Nib say as were manhandled through the doorway.

We were dragged and pushed up a flight of winding stairs that brought out into daylight just under the lip of the lava pit. No-one would ever have seen the exit from above the pit and we each had to scramble to get over the rim. Some of the Kuntz went first to make sure we were grabbed again when we surfaced. Rongwei and Egric had been bound hand and foot and were being carried. Vizagriz's stretcher was roughly thrown over the top after them, causing him to cry out again.

When we were all back on the mountain top Nazrat walked over to me. I was still holding the Holy Quail. 'Now, boy. You are a snivelling little wretch but you have had your uses.'

'Don't you be nasty to him!' Winolene shouted, possibly feeling she couldn't be in much more trouble so what the hell. She was wrong, mind.

'The boy here has one more task to fulfil,' Nazrat continued. 'He will be bringing the bird with him to my realm where we will have such a banquet to celebrate our victory. He will be the main dish and you, girl, have just assured yourself a place as the pudding.'

Egric and Rongwei snarled and spat curses at the dæmon but were subdued by blows from the hill-dwellers.

Nazrat was starting to metamorphose into her dæmonic shape, the winged dragon Patisse, while she spoke. 'Don't think you have been clever. It was only by dint of luck, accident and sheer effrontery that you Questers managed to get this far. Still, it saved me some time although you have caused me much trouble. Not to mention the deaths of my loyal Kuntz. I think they may have the heroes to play with when I am gone. No-one may subvert the plans of the dæmon Patisse. The End of Everything is nigh!'

Full in dragon-dæmon shape now, Patisse was hovering above the lava bowl, bathed in a lambent green fire. It threw back its head and roared with laughter, belching noxious flames into the already sulphur-laden air.

Winolene was being held, none too carefully, by one of the Kuntz, who took the opportunity to rummage about in her shirt a bit. She bit his arm and he pulled it out, snarling, giving her a hefty, back-handed clout on the way. Something glittery flew through the air and landed at my feet. Winolene's mirror! And I could see that Kylie's cobweb was still stretched across its flat surface. I remembered what the Web Mistress had said about calling her if we ever needed to. Nothing ventured, I thought, and picked up the glass. One of the Kuntz started towards me with his shield raised, possibly imagining I had lifted a stone and was about to throw it. I ducked under his upraised arm and bought myself the few seconds I needed to pluck one of the strands of the web. It went "ping" and then all was quiet.

The Kuntz I had wrong-footed lunged at me, clearly intent on murder, but Patisse roared an order and he stopped. 'Do not harm the boy and do not damage the Quail,' the hissing, fiery voice said. 'Take his shiny plaything from him and hold him fast. I must prepare a portal.'

The Kuntz tore the mirror from my grasp and crushed it under foot. Patisse started to shake and quiver as the lava pit roiled ever more furiously and started to swirl with a magickal vortex. Eruptions of molten rock and yellow gases retched upwards and fell back into the caldera.

'Now – bring the stripling to me!'

Just as the Kuntz holding me started forward, another of his compatriots screamed. I looked at toward the source of the sound and saw, not a Kuntz, but something in the shape of a Kuntz, but browny-black and strangely indistinct in shape. Then my brain made sense of what my eyes had seen – he was covered from head to hairy foot with thousands – possibly millions – of spiders. Over and under his screams could be heard a myriad of scrunching, chewing noises, each tiny in itself but the whole adding up to an audible buzz. He was being eaten alive, a condition which didn't last long as he keeled over, probably as much from shock as from the poison being injected into every mote of his skin surface.

The Kuntz holding me was as immobile as the others, then suddenly he lifted his sword-arm, pointed it at the chamber exit hole we had emerged from and uttered a single, strangulated, gutteral sound. It may not even have meant anything in Kuntz but the others followed his gaze and saw, emerging from the hole, what I can only describe as a flood tide of spiders pouring out and towards us. I'm sure Winolene screamed as loud as she could but I doubt she outdid me. Some of the Kuntz tried stamping on the deluge of arachnids but for every few they crushed three times as many climbed over their feet and started to scale their legs. Patisse was still quivering in an ecstasy of conjuration but the noise must have disturbed its concentration. A huge, yellow snake's eye turned towards the disturbance and the snout blew forth a blast of fire, ripping a roasting path through the onrushing spiders and leaving a large, tar-like patch on the crater floor. But even this did little to lessen the flood – there seemed to be a never-ending flow of the creatures, all heading for one or another of the Kuntz and – I noticed for the first time – leaving all of the Questers alone!

The Kuntz holding me had let go in order to flay himself with both hands in a vain attempt to beat off the invasion and I fell to the side, landing beside the mirror. By some miracle, even though the glass was broken, the web had stayed more or less intact. I watched, stunned, as the strands started to resolve themselves into a word I recognised as BEAK.

Something about the beak, was it? Then I realised what Kylie, or possibly some other entity on the Interweb, was trying to tell me. It was a stupid, foolhardy plan, but what had I to lose?

'K'Nib!' I shouted over to where he was standing, as immobile as everyone else, except the Kuntz who were thrashing about trying in vain to shake loose their moving, chewing, poison-fanged topcoats. 'What does the beak do?'

Trust a scribe – they never forget a word. 'It forces whoever touches it to tell nothing but the truth!' he shouted back. I lunged at the dragon's body while its head was turned to spume fire at the well of spiders and pressed the Quail's beak against the breast.

'Your name!' I shouted. 'Give me your true name! Not Nazrat. Not Patisse. Your real, secret name!'

The dragon head spun towards me and the dæmon writhed and flapped its wings ineffectually. It shrieked and howled, 'Zwvarislanz!'

'Say it thrice!'

'Zwvarislanz! Zwvarislanz! ZWVARISLANZ! Aaaarrrhh!'

'Then begone, Zwvarislanz! Never again trouble this realm! Begone!'

There was a red swirl and the sound of whirring in the far distance. The dragon shape dwindled to a shapeless lump of red flesh, throbbing and pulsating, before it disappeared, presumably forever, leaving only a charred remnant, like a brown, mottled starfish or, in a strange way, a gingerbread man baked too near the flame. So that was what dæmons really looked like. No wonder they took on dramatic shapes whenever they appeared.

I noticed that, with the disappearance of the dæmon, the spider-tide was ebbing and those Kuntz who had not been engulfed were free and furious. I side-stepped just in time to avoid one of the Kuntz as he lumbered towards me, screaming, and plummeted over the rim. He hung there for a moment, holding on and scrabbling for a foothold. But the spider-poison must have got the better of him and he fell backwards, limp and silent, into the sworl. His sword had fallen near Rongwei who rolled towards it, turned his back and cut his wrist binding on the blade before grasping the handle and thrusting it upwards into the belly of a Kuntz who was about to sever his head with an axe. Rongwei jumped to his feet, slashed the tongs around his ankles with a single stroke ducked as a second tribesman swung a war hammer at his head. On the way down he picked up the axe belonging to his first assailant in both hands and with an upswing disembowelled his attacker. He swerved another sword thrust and somersaulted over to Egric, cutting his wrist ropes and leaving the axe beside him. In a moment the elder hero had slashed through his remaining bindings and was on his feet and rushing at the remaining Kuntz, screaming bloody murder.

Two of the savages had hold of Vizagriz on his stretcher and, when they saw the battle going on looked at each other, shrugged and flung Vizagriz straight off the stretcher and into the lava pit.

I stood, horrified as I saw the body spin in the air, hang for an instant, then start its descent towards the bubbling fury below.

'NO!' I screamed uselessly, but behind me I heard K'Nib shout. 'The wings! The wings give the power of flight!'

Not knowing what else to do nor caring for my fate, I pressed my hand around the rubied wings and threw myself after Vizagriz.

Miraculously, I soared. I had only to think of a direction and I was speeding towards it. Instinctively I knew how to control my flight, as if the Quail had given me the knowledge along with the power. I went into a swooping dive, caught Vizagriz by the robe with my free hand and hurled us both back to the mountain top.

As We alighted I made sure to lay him down gently and Winolene and K'Nib took him in their arms and rested him on the ground. Mindador rushed over and held him, saying, 'Brother. Oh, brother,' over and over. Touching, I thought, the concern of one mage for another.

Behind me there was the clashing, grunting sound of ongoing battle. There were still four Kuntz left and they were pressing the two heroes very hard indeed. I had a sudden thought. 'K'Nib! What else does this thing do? Quickly!'

'It, it, it's tail grants the holder invisibility or camouflage!' he shouted. I needed no further encouragement. Picking up a fallen sword I rushed towards the battle, grabbing the bird's chrysoprase tail feathers as I did so. Everything went slightly blurred, as if I, too, could not see the world exactly as it was and I felt that I was not only disappearing from sight but becoming incorporeal. I had time, however, to push the sword through the back of one Kuntz and jump back as he fell, looking around wildly for his killer. I also slashed behind the knees of another, making him fall to the ground so that Rongwei could dispatch him with a backhand swipe that took his head off, before giving his undivided attention to the remaining savages. The odds equalised, Rongwei and Egric had no trouble finishing off the others, one being cleaved in half by the huge axe and the other having a sword flung with pin-point accuracy at the back of his neck as he tried to flee. I let go of the tail, dropping the Quail, and felt myself slowly swim back into the real world.

When all the bloodletting was done Winolene rushed over to me and collapsed on my neck. 'Oh, Slouch. That was so brave. I truly thought we were doomed! And poor Vizagriz. When I saw him falling...' Then she collapsed in sobs.

Egric and Rongwei were sitting on the ground, breathing heavily but grinning. Mindador was still holding Vizagriz and keening softly, with Sparky perched on his shoulder, stroking his hair. I joined them. The old wizard's eyes were open and he smiled weakly at me, speaking in a thin, cracked voice. 'Well done, lad. You got us here, you found the quested bird and you dispatched a dæmon, possibly for ever. How did you know to do that?'

'It was what you said knowing something's true name giving you power over it. The dæmon had to obey my command.'

'You did well.'

'I was taught well,' I replied, tears in my eyes. 'But we must get you to safety and let you recover before we take the Quail to whoever wants it.'

Vizagriz shook his head slowly. 'No, I don't think I will be going. I cannot walk. That backlash in the cavern nearly killed me. It would be best if I made my peace and slipped away.'

'No!' I exclaimed but he lifted his hand to stop me and said in his faltering voice. 'Do as I say. But do one last thing for me first. Find the bag of gold.'

I felt inside his robe and pulled out the pouch of Thalers. 'Now take one,' he ordered.

I opened the string, pried the neck open, reached in and lifted out a coin. Immediately there was a blue flash which spiralled up my arm and then shot away over the mountain into the far distance.

'Ah,' said Vizagriz, ever weakening. 'I thought as much. Our Questers band is now complete.'

Indeed it is said a voice from nowhere and before our eyes, there on the mountain top, an apparition started to coalesce, the like of which I could never have imagined and cannot, even now, truly believe I saw.

CHAPTER THE FOURTEENTH

In which there is much explanation, many surprises, a homecoming – but not for all of the Questers – and an End to All Magick.

We probably all imagine what supreme beings look like. Some have a concept of an old man with a flowing beard, throned in glory. Others prefer human bodies with the heads of animals. To others again, their deities are trees or crocodilians or blue-skinned oliphaunts. It is said that each culture pictures the object of its worship in its own image.

What kind of people, then, would worship two figures sitting in gigantic comfy armchairs, wearing knitted garments and carpet slippers and each holding a cup of thea?

'The Two!' Mindador exclaimed.

As the vision solidified in midair before us the Deities sat, immobile, on their vast chairs, each carpet slipper the size of a decent house. When they spoke it was direct to our minds and without any bodily movement whatsoever.

Ooooh, look Rhon! They've got the Quail.

Yes, Aeth. That's nice. Another bikky?

Ta. Cooeee, everybody. Had a nice quest?

Awe-struck is not the word. Awe-struck is definitely not the word. I don't know what the word is and if I ever get it, I'll let you know. Suffice it to say, I had no idea what to do, say, think or gibber. How does one greet the appearance of the *primum mobile*, the *fons et origo*, the ancient of days? Especially when it likes a nice bikky and wears a cardigan?

'All hail!' Mindador uttered. That seemed to cover it.

That's nice. All hail yourself. Good manners, Rhon.

Yes, Aeth.

That must be Mindador. The sneaky one. Which one's the apprentice wizard?

I burbled something that seemed to fit the bill.

There you are. All right? Good. Can we have our Quail back, then? And we'll be off.

Shan't trouble you any more. Will we, Rhon?

No, Aeth.

I was not holding the bird. Mindador had picked it up. But I finally found my voice. 'Please,' I said. 'Just tell me what it really is.'

The Quail? It's something the Gnomes cobbled up after they got hold of a Gnomion. Isn't it Rhon?

Yes, Aeth.

The Gnomion is really a portion of the original pattern for Eternity. Rhon can explain it better. He's good at do-it-yourself.

When me and Aeth created Existence we divided up the maintenance among the various races. Nice for everybody to have something do, we thought, didn't we Aeth?

We did, Rhon. Gnomes were supposed to look after the hardware, but over the aeons the instructions got a bit garbled and fragmented and all that remained after while was the Gnomion. When the Gnomes made the Quail they were inadvertently recreating the original warp core that drives the whole thing and they got it a bit wrong. Dwarfs were supposed to know how the software worked but the knowledge got corrupted through time.

'Does every race of being have a purpose?' I had the temerity to ask.

Oh, yes. Faeries were Aeth's idea. They're inextricably linked to nature and all things that green and grow. Elementals for every purpose. Your friend Sparky is a lectrix elemental. There are others.

'You mean, there are faeries who look after aspects of everything?'

More or less. "Look after" is putting it a bit strong. "Keep at the forefront of reality" would be a better description. You should meet the Quarks some time, shouldn't they, Aeth?

Yes, Rhon. Lovely colours, some of them, if a bit strange.

'Do dæmons have a point, then?'

Hmmm. They're sort of the swarf that was left when the other races were formed. They've never had a purpose except to bear a grudge. They sot of feel that if the whole thing could start again they might get a better shake, nicer house, chance at a decent job, all that. Pity really, they could have been very useful but they're just so awkward to deal with.

That's right, Rhon. We call them the Underclass, don't we? Between ourselves that is.

'And humans?'

Comic relief, really. Aeth had some spare material and thought, 'What would be fun to watch on a slow Era?' I thought curtains, but Aeth said, 'Let's make a race that rushes about trying to do things but never gets it quite right.' Humans is your word for yourselves. We call you SitComs.

The massive armchairs rotated imperceptibly to face Mindador.

And now, if you don't mind, you might just hand over the Quail. It's far too dangerous to leave lying about where anyone can find it, you know. We've ignored it long enough. Time to put it in a nice china cabinet or something.

Mindador stood up, still holding the Quail and asked, 'Why is it dangerous'

Haven't you been listening? You tell them, Rhon.

The Quail, as I think I said already, but never mind, is a badly-made warp drive. In fact, it's an Extropy generator. That's where all your Magick comes from, didn't you realise? Extropy is not a normal property of Existence – everything is supposed to wind down eventually, just after our supper time, in fact, when we switch the lights off and tuck ourselves up. Extropy keeps everything cycling round a bit longer. It also stops us having any direct effect in your Realm.

'That's why you needed us to find it for you?'

Sort of. We can nudge and push a bit but we can't just reach down and do anything. We can't even see into your Realm very clearly. The interference from Extropy stops us. Snow on the picture, scratchy record, corrupted diskette, that kind of effect. Not that we like to interfere in any case. Bit distracting. So we had to persuade you to get it and bring it to us.

I didn't make much of this picture, record, diskette business, but then I was talking to a couple of unknowable, all-wise beings. 'Why do the dæmons want it, though?'

So they can turn it up a bit and bring about the End more quickly, I heard somewhere. They don't really like the way things are set up.

'So why is Vesta helping them?'

For the first time the two gigantic heads turned and looked at each other, then back at us. It seemed to take an age to achieve, which it might well have done.

Oh is she just?

'Yes. I was supposed to find it and give to the Order and the Priestesses, and they would offer it up to Vesta!'

Well, there's a thing. She only comes in to do the dusting, arrange the flowers, you know. Thought we could trust her. Well, she's out. And she can forget all those temples that have sprung up everywhere. As of now they are closed

You can't get the staff, can you, Aeth?

'Will you destroy her temples??'

No, we can't interfere directly. Can't usually materialise in your realm at all, except here at the centre of the Quail's presence. Eye of the hurricane, sort of thing. But we'll see to Vesta, don't you worry, won't we. Aeth?

She'll just go away and so will her silly priestesshood. When there's no music everybody stops dancing, don't they Rhon?

Yes, Aeth.

'What would happen if there was no Quail?' Mindador said.

Eternity would proceed much as it does now, but you wouldn't get much trouble from dæmons. And there wouldn't be any Extropy except a bit of residual backwash. We could have a bit of a rest, too. All this quest organising, it sort of palls after a while, doesn't it, Aeth.

It does, Rhon. It does.

Mindador stepped forward, still holding the jewelled bird, and said, 'I don't think that would be a bad thing, you know. The world really isn't a place for dæmons and apparitions and the dead walking and all that. Life would be much simpler, wouldn't it?'

It's not up to you. There is a grander plan. Now, hand us the Quail and we'll be off. Nearly time for our cocoa.

'I don't think I can do that,' Mindador said as he backed away. 'You want it. dæmons want it. Brer Dryberg and the priestesses of Vesta want it. And the more I find out about it the more I think no-one should have it at all.' He started banging the side of his head again. All this Magick and extropy about the place had obviously started his head dæmon fragment itching. 'I don't know what to do. It's all very confusing. I need time. I need space, I need...'

'MINDADOR!' Egric shouted as the old sage backed away, but he was too late with his warning. Mindador had strayed too close to the edge of the lava pit and the rock crumbled beneath his feet. Both Egric and Rongwei flung themselves towards him and Winolene and K'Nib let out identical screeches as the thaumaturge fell backwards into the sulphurous, bubbling cauldron of molten stone, taking the Holy Quail with him. We all watched as he plummeted towards the incandescent surface until we could see him no more. Then there was a flash in which Mindador must have been vaporised instantaneously. From the depths of the pit a strange, ghastly bubble arose, bearing within it the Holy Quail, which was now white-hot and thrumming. The bird seemed to float for a second or two in front of us then glow even more and hum. There was a loud pop and it just winked out of existence.

We all stood, stunned, and Winolene burst into tears. The only one who spoke was Rongwei. 'He still had the treasure on him. Did you notice?'

The Two looked on impassively.

Oh, well. Can't win them all. Probably for the best. Now. What's on next, Rhon?

There's a new universe materialising over in the next reality, Aeth.

Oooh. Lovely. I like a good nature programme! Bikky? Choccy one?

Ta. Pity about this plane of existence. I was just getting to enjoy it.

Never mind, Rhon. I've got a pattern for a better one here.

The Deity called Aeth held up two knitting pins from which dangled what seemed to be a scarf, except that within it I could see stars, twinkling dust and strange, swirly, cyclone-like shapes that glistered.

I don't think I've got that last cable stitch right, Never could read Askey very well. Expect I'll need a few of your rubber bands again, Rhon.

Plenty more where they came from, Aeth.

They slowly dematerialised, slippers last. We are like gnats in the eyes of Deities, I thought. They don't really care about us, so from now on I don't give a stuff for them. But I was drawn from my musings by the sound of Vizagriz, crying.

I looked at him where he was lying on the ground. There were tears streaming down his cheeks. Sparky was wiping his forehead with a sprig of moss. 'Poor old Mindador,' Vizagriz croaked. 'At least he'll be at peace, now.'

'I thought you didn't like him?'

'I didn't. But he was my half-brother, after all.'

This news hit me like a sledge hammer. That would explain why Vizagriz had put up with some much of Mindador's appalling behaviour, moods and refusal to give us information. It also explained why he hadn't throttled Mindador on at least ten occasions, right from the start. I was still confused, though.

'But he's a Hebryd. Are you?'

'No. Same father, different mothers. We were brought up separately. His mother was a Hebryd and it carries on from the maternal side. Our old dad was a wizard too, so he never married either of them. I was his apprentice, though, which gave Mindador a bit of a chip on his shoulder. I've always felt responsible in a funny sort of way.'

I wanted to comfort the old man – which is all he looked – in his final, dying minutes. But then there was a shimmering in the air over the lava pit and the sound of a roller-blind being pulled down. There appeared before us a Dark and Stormy Knight whose great, visored helm swept the plateau with its gaze before alighting on me. 'Be you... Slouch?' it intoned.

'Of course,' I said, getting to my feet. 'You've seen me twice before, remember.'

'Right. "Before" is your word, though. It's a bit more complicated for me. I have come with a message. Prepare yourself – you are to meet... The Two!'

'We've met them.'

'What? When?'

'Just now. They've been and gone.'

'Sod. I was supposed to herald their manifestation,' he said, tapping his wrist, shaking it and putting it to the side of his helmet. 'Ziggy's got it wrong again. D'you think they'll be back?'

'I shouldn't imagine so. Not in this existence.'

'Never mind, then. Just give me the Holy Quail and I'll be away. Night off tonight and last one down the club gets the Ambrosia in.'

'The Quail is destroyed,' I told him.

This seemed to have a disorienting effect as he struggled for something to say or do. His limbs jerked slightly and there was a noise like a hacksaw skidding across metal once or twice. Then he visibly slumped, with a shallow, creaking noise that a small can of oil could probably have done wonders for.

'That's it then,' the Herald said, with a note of resignation. 'Job done. I'll be getting a bollocking for this one, mind. Might even get my jotters. Don't suppose you could write me a note saying it wasn't my fault, or anything?'

'Would it work?'

'Probably not. Got long memories those Two. Well, they would have, wouldn't they. Okay. I'll go and face the music. Sign this.'

He presented me with a sheet of paper with a large X at the bottom.

'What is it?'

'Expenses indent. Those gold Thalers, you know. Got to account for them or it comes out my pocket.'

I took a pen and inkpot proffered by K'Nib and scrawled Slouch, Apprentice Wizard beside the mark. The paper disappeared.

'That's it then. I won't see you again, I don't suppose.'

'That's a relief. No offence, but it's all been a bit hectic since we first met.'

'None taken. Now, I'm late for a piss-up. Probably missed happy hour,' the Herald announced and promptly disappeared from the feet up.

Then he suddenly reappeared again, from the head down. 'Sorry. Nearly forgot. Memory like a sieve. Everybody gets a wish, okay? That's the reward for questing. Who's first? The lady? That's traditional.'

Winolene, still sobbing, stepped forward and said, 'I'd just like to go back.'

'Easy. Click the heels and say "There's no place like home". Got it?'

She had, and she did, and she went. K'Nib was next.

'What I've always wanted was a tenured lectureship somewhere. Oxenford would be nice.'

'You start on Monday, ten o'clock lecture, last week's essays on Rhyming Slang in Marmorian Bingo Calling already in your study,' the Herald said and the scribe was no longer with us.

'Rongwei and Egric. What do you want? Riches? Palaces? Slave-girls?'

The two warriors looked at each other, nodded and stepped forward. Egric spoke for them both. 'There's no point giving us untold wealth or anything. Just fritter it away, us. What we would like, though, is another quest. But after a nice holiday. With quaffing, of course.'

'There's a revolution due in the Desert Kingdoms in about a week. Something about whoever finds a Magick lamp can become the Sultan. What say I drop you off there, you have a bit of a rest by a verdant oasis, sink a few, then get stuck in?'

'Perfect,' they both grinned, and they were off.

'I'll be seeing that Egric again, I think. Seems to be about a lot where I go. Now. What about the Amp?' the Herald said, looking about for the tiny form.

Sparky jumped down from Vizagriz's shoulder and scuttled towards the Herald. 'Is there anywhere you know that has lots of animals in cages or tied down or immobilised or anything?'

'There's the Natural Historical Museum,' the Herald said. 'That do you?'

'Probably,' Sparky said with a leer and he disappeared.

'Was that wise?' I asked.

'Oh, yes. He's in for a shock, mind. They're already stuffed. Right. Wizard?'

Vizagriz had pulled himself together enough to say, 'There doesn't seem to be much need for anything. I'm paralysed and I'm dying.'

'Like to be not paralysed and not dying?'

'Is that possible?'

'Certainly. Funny, wizards usually want power and wealth beyond imagining. But then, you've got the Thalers. And Slouch has the diamond. Well get up, then!'

Vizagriz struggled onto his elbows, rolled from the stretcher and tried a few tentative steps. 'I can walk!' he announced. 'And I feel fine!' He even did a little jig and gave me a hug. First and last time.

Then it was my turn. I had been thinking about this quite carefully while everyone else was getting their deepest desires fulfilled. What was mine? I knew, without much effort. 'I want Winolene to love me and marry me and settle down with me.'

'Ah. Affairs of the heart. Can't guarantee this one, but I'll give it a push. Just the love bit, mind. The rest is up to you. Off you go, then!'

There was a blur and a whrooshing feeling in my stomach and I suddenly found myself standing in Vizagriz's cottage. So was the wizard, who was peering out of the open door which wasn't, for once, moaning about the draught. The brooms, coal scuttle and smaller footstools weren't shuffling round his ankles as they usually did when they were pleased to see him. The sofa didn't roll over and put its feet in the air.

'That's it then,' he said. 'We're home. And home is here. A permanent door in a permanent place in Hanging Basket Street.'

The full import of this hadn't really hit me until now. 'You mean...'

'That's it, Slouch. We've just seen the End of All Magick. Stick the kettle on, there's a good chap.'

We had some thea and sat gazing at the fire which I had lit, not without some difficulty as I had to do it myself with no help from the sticks or the coal. Vizagriz was turning the diamond back and forth, watching the prismatic effect of its light dance off the cottage walls. I had been musing and wanted to talk about it all. Just a bit.

'I don't suppose I'll ever be a wizard, now. What with all the Magick gone.'

Vizagriz put his cup down, leaned back and put his fingers together. 'You are a wizard. Didn't you know that?'

'No! How?'

'What about all that flying and invisibility? And you blasted Nazrat, Patisse, Zwang-thingy with the Quail. That was quite a bit of Magick, dismissing a dæmon. It was also your purpose on the quest. Remember, "wizard, wizard, girl, hero, player, imp, scribe". You and I were the wizards.'

I was astonished. 'Then what was Mindador?'

'Don't you think his refusal to hand over the Holy Quail was heroic? Mindador was the hero in all this, bless him.' A tear trickled down the old man's face and he sniffed.

'But, there's Egric and Rongwei. They were the heroes, surely.'

'We were only supposed to have one hero. Did it never occur to you to ask what was meant by "player"? That's a term for the eternal pieces in whatever vast game The Two imagine they've got going. They are the King and Queen. The Herald is another player. So is the Stooge Eternal. I told you that at the very start.'

'I thought that was me!'

'You didn't even get the Recognition until you zapped the dæmon. That's when you were recognised by The Two as a wizard.'

'So who was the player?'

'Either Rongwei or Egric. The Herald said he see one of them again. I'd go for Egric.

He has more staying power and he's the sort that'll hang about in different incarnations for a long time, helping things happen and being there to observe them. He thinks he's a hero – in this existence, he is, right enough – but in others he might be a carter, or a palace guard. Or even a bird on a tree for all I know. The Stooge Eternal just has to be there as a sort of witness. Not much of a job at the time, but quite important in the grand scheme.'

'Rongwei?'

'Just along for the ride since he happened to be with Egric. That's how come we ended up with eight of us. Alternatively, maybe they're some kind of everlasting double act, like that masked chap and his noble savage side-kick.'

'But Winolene? What part did she have?'

'No idea. Probably to stop us getting all blokeish, or something. On the other hand, having a female on a quest tends to slow the pace a bit. There's also a theory that says they put a damper on the effing and blinding, which can take the holy edge of a quest.'

'Didn't seem to take the edge of your effing and blinding.'

'No. Well. Been at it a while, haven't I?'

We sat silent for a while as I mulled some of this, Vizagriz stared into the wholly natural fire, as if seeing it for the first time and quite enjoying the experience.

'And what will happen to The Two now the Quail's gone?'

'Rhon and Aeth? Well. It's not for us to peer into the minds of Deities. Not that we'd make much sense of it all if we did. They just seem to be watching it all unfold, then they'll wind it up and maybe start it again. Or not. Precious little we can do about it, whichever way it falls. One thing's for sure: they'll be around for ever. By definition.'

'I still don't understand what the baking dæmons wanted the Quail for,' I said, confused as ever.

'I imagine they wanted the End Of Existence And Everything because the heat created by the final explosion would be enough to bake the largest pie they ever contemplated, and all the living creatures would become the filling. Quite what they were going to do for flour I don't know.'

'And what about Vesta and the Order?'

'Goodness only knows what foul purpose Brer Dryberg had for the Quail. Probably thought he could wield immense power and become second only to The Two or something like that. Or maybe he was helping Vesta do something similar. I mean to go and have a word with him in a day or so and tell him whatever he had planned, it's off. I'm looking forward to that. But there's other things to attend to first.' He stood up and arched his back.

'What's that?'

'Going to bed for one. And first thing in the morning, I'll be getting this diamond down the appraisers and cashing it in for something a bit more liquid. Or do I mean drinkable?'

Vizagriz rose to his feet, still unsteady after his ordeal. 'As for you, you're still an apprentice, albeit a rich one.'

'Rich? Me?'

'Of course. Half of the Thalers and the cash from the diamond will be yours. If I kept it, who would I leave it to except you? You might as well have the benefit of it now. But for the moment you are still an apprentice, which means...'

'I know. Get up early, light a fire and make the breakfast.'

'That's it. Try to do the first two quietly and the last not much before lunchtime. Goodnight.'

CHAPTER THE FIFTEENTH

In which much has changed but everything is the same. For some people, anyway.

The sun was down but the last, refracted glow flickered greenly along the flat horizon. The moons continued their slow minuet to the music of gravity in the great ballroom of eternal night. As the desert winds soughed across the sands, causing the dunes to ripple like waves on a shallow sea, the palm trees shifted slightly in the breeze, wafting their subtle fragrance into the twilight. Camels shuffled and chewed cud, gazing into the middle distance and each dreaming of its particular nirvana – making it big in advertising, tobacco probably, or getting a walk-on part in an epic drama. Camels have a rich inner life and a complex theology. A tent flap flapped. A tumbleweed tumbled. And a hero-in-training got on his supervisor's nerves.

'But they can't be. If the stars were suns, they'd be big. They're not, so they ain't.'

'Once again, Rongwei, for the benefit of the hard of thinking: they're big, but they're far away. Probably.'

'Is our sun far away?'

'Not as far as the stars.'

'But it's a star.'

'Yes.'

'But close up.'

'Yes.'

'So why aren't there more of them close up? If there are lots of them, like you say, chances are more of them would be closer.'

'They're not.'

'They all look the same size. Maybe they're all the same distance away.'

'Maybe.'

'Except the sun.'

'Probably.'

'So it's different from stars.'

'Yup.'

'And they're not the same as the sun.'

'Whatever.'

There was a pause. A camel farted and blew, as it were, its chance of making it in a more sophisticated afterlife. Camel deities are a bit sensitive to that sort of thing.

Egric settled back a bit deeper into his blanket and wriggled his shoulders until he was comfy.

'Egric?'

'What.'

'Want to talk about why grass is green?'

'Not in the slightest.'

'Well, I think it's because water is yellowish and air is sort of bluey and in grass they get sort of mixed up to make green.'

'Water isn't yellowish.'

'The water here is.'

'Yes. I'll give you that one.'

Another pause.

'Egric?'

'What!'

'Enjoying your holiday?'

'Not in the slightest.'

'Me neither.'

At that moment the desert calm was cut to ribbons by a horde of screaming warriors on horseback bursting over the top of a sand dune, their long robes billowing behind, their curved swords glinting in the moonslight and their throats screaming blue murder.

Egric sprang to his feet just as one of the horsemen screamed and tried a downward sweep with his scimitar then screamed even louder as the hero's blade took his arm off neatly at the perigee of his stroke. Rongwei had been slightly quicker off the mark and managed to uproot a tent pole, ramming one end into the ground and the other through a horse and rider both, making good use of their momentum.

Egric dispatched two at one time by feinting them into making opposite-direction side thrusts then not being there when their swords met in the middle and carried on into each other. Rongwei had found a bow and arrow and was giving it rice from a lying-down position where nobody could reach him with a blade. Two who tried to ride over him found themselves on horses that suddenly weren't as full of internal organs as they had lately been and shortly afterwards flat on the ground with their throats cut

There was a fair amount of the standard thrust-and-parry stuff enlivened by a particularly interesting moment when Egric vaulted onto a riderless horse, reared it up and brought its front hooves down on the skulls of two of the attackers.

When the odds were down to a more or less usual five-to-one and there was only a bit of routine tidying up to do (remembering to leave two alive, one without a tongue to guide the one without eyes back to where they came from to tell the tale) Rongwei shouted over to the elder hero.

'Egric?'

'What?'

'Enjoying your holiday?'

'I am definitely coming back here! Tremendous hospitality.'

Then they finished off the last but two, did the necessary on the survivors and settled back down to a last quaffing session with a much lighter heart.

Egric drained a wineskin and wiped most of his face with most of his arm. 'I enjoyed that. Mind you, if I was taking notes I'd have knocked points off of you for that daft double-dagger throw.'

'What? I got him in both eyes!'

'What I mean. Waste of effort. And showing off.'

'Aw, you're not marking me, are you?'

'Nah. It's the holidays. Back to work tomorrow, mind.'

'Oh, yeh. That lamp and cave business. What was the name of the lass we were to look out for?'

'Jeannie, the Grand Vizier said.'

'Sounds a bit of a doddle, this one.'

'Never mind. Might lead to something more tasty. I hear there's forty thieves keep their stash hereabouts.'

'Have a go at that, then!'

'Sure. G'night.'

'G'night, Egric.'

And the rest was silence.

Somewhere, not far from where two happy heroes are snoring loudly, there is a cavern. Inside the cavern is a raised stone plinth amidst a veritable sea of jewels, gold and precious objects. On the plinth is a lamp. Inside the lamp is a muttering sound which might just sound something like: "OK. Eggs, flour, baking soda, sugar, salt. Salt? Bugger, no salt, hold on, here it is. Right. Now, pie filling. Human flesh would do nicely. Wait and see what turns up, I think...'

CHAPTER THE SIXTEENTH

In which Slouch gets a bit maudlin towards the end, but you can skip that bit.

Winolene and I have been quite happy, really. When we got back to Al Faq'Ahl she had had to rethink her plans, what with the bottom falling out of the Vesta game. She eventually signed up at Gordon Blue's Academy and learned how to cook nicely, various things about Relating to the Public and other useful life skills. Got a VQ, whatever that is. She's been quite a help to me in the business.

After a year or so I decided the mage business wasn't really for me, what with there being no real Magick left. Wizards were still about and still got consulted. They managed to do minor bits of divination and were happy to go through the hex-lifting and spell-casting motions, of course. I don't think the ordinary people noticed much difference, really. But I did discover I had green fingers with the mystical plant life. I offered to have a go at the Abraculture idea on Vizagriz's behalf and I used my share of the treasure to buy out a struggling market garden on the outskirts of the city plus a shop in the Head Quarter, which Winolene ran. We concentrate on the health and aroma qualities rather than the magickal side and it's very popular. The wizard is our consultant and we see quite a lot of him.

We had a son, called Egric, largely because the old hero had turned up about the time he was born and offered to stand as Deityfather to him. Conan Poly had made him a professor, bit of a desk job he said so he liked to keep his hand in during the long vac. He was round our way with a week to spare between crypt sackings. Winolene took a bit of persuading but she gave in and said that she hoped none of it would rub off on the boy, being as how he was going to grow up and be a tortiflexer with a nice, pensionable job in the Palace. Or a dentist. I'm not so sure, mind – I caught him strangling two toy serpents in his cot one day.

Egric also told us that Rongwei had graduated, albeit with a disappointing third on account of not handing in his pillaging reports on time, but he had landed the job he wanted – as a temple guard with alternate Wodin's Days off so he could go cart spotting – and had married his beloved Sharon who trained temple-dancers up the Adult Edification Centre. He spent the evenings reading philosophy and could even manage the longer words without moving his lips.

Our daughter was born a year or so later and she was already turning into the image of her mother. She has a whim of iron and a temper to match. A right little madam, she'll go far. We also bought a foundling from SamBernardo's. Not from Brer Dryberg, who disappeared a couple of days after we got back, some said in a puff of smoke, some said in a carriage and pair, but, everyone agreed, in a hurry. We called the boy Bamber and he's certainly going to have a better start in life than I did.

Winolene's father is not well and hasn't got long to go. There is talk of us taking over the farm and I don't think I'd mind that. The wife says she wouldn't be averse provided we kept an apartment in the city and she and her mother could come shopping occasionally, see a bit of mummery, that kind of thing. They're welcome.

We even went on a round-the-globe cruise holiday before the kids came along and took a side-trip to Swilbury. Mukk was pleased to see us. He had extended the Frog and did coaching parties. Abigal ran it, now Mukk was older, and she had turned into a fat, jolly woman who laughed constantly. Same rosy cheeks and green, flashing eyes, though. She has seven children, imagine that. After a couple of hours we all ran out of things to talk about and Winolene and I left early the next morning.

It's nearly Watching Hour on Wodin's Day, in the third week of the constellation of Rumpot and I'm tired. Got to be up first thing as there's a new line in gecko-eating Frummage to replant. I don't think it'll take off, unless we market it as a novelty item. I must find a reliable gecko supplier. Nothing worse than a hungry carnivorous plant and I don't need all the complaints about disappearing budgies like the last time. Winolene will sort it out, though. She's good at dealing with that sort of thing. Nobody complains twice, that's for sure.

I do the odd bit of parlour Magick for the kids but I can't say I've kept in practice. Uncle Vizagriz always comes to the parties and I'm not a patch on him.

They say there's going to be a new Dikkeadh soon, although the present one hasn't twigged yet. I don't suppose he'll be much different. They never are.

The fire's going out. My wine is finished. And Winolene is calling, wondering if I'm going to be up much longer.

I don't think so.
It's a dark and stormy night.

THE MAGICK IS OVER BUT THE MUMMERY LINGERS ON...

The next two volumes in the End of All Magick saga

THE KING OF ELFLAND'S DAFTER

A funny thing happened on the way to the forest. The Magick is gone. Suddenly, grown to full size without the existence of extropy to keep them thumb-height, the Faerie Folk have to find a new way and a new place to live. But there is hope – the Crystal Dwarves are dying out and they want an infusion of new blood, preferably female and a bit dim. The King of Elfland leads his motley tribe of Imps, Emps, Amps and Umps to the Hole of the Mountain King where the Diamond Duke and five guys named Mho take a shine to Princess Titania and her gels. Little does anyone know that some vestige of Magick still resides in certain crystals. Anyone, that is, except Lobster Rampant of the Third Ear and his band of New Age Dippies.

Will the crystal elementals manage to tap the Magick before it gets perverted by Plunk Rock musicians? Will Titania get married in white shoes and a mini-dress? Will Prince Vince stage a take-over? And who is Idaho Smith?

Read this, and you'll be none the wiser.

This book is mything something important – New York Review of Gooks

Time will tell if this series is the product of madness or genius – A Lawyer

THE NATIONAL ELF

Magick is truly finished. No, honest this time. The Cunning Crystals are no more. The Globe must now rely on Ticknologgy. Unfortunately, the only ones who understand how to make anything work are the Faeries who used to be representatives of physical principles. Setting up a Collage of Ticknologgy seems a natural step for King Pearly. He's short, he's mean and he understands about cart parking – all the requisite features for a Collage Cancellor, you would have thought.

Ineptly assisted by his Dene, Bursa, Secretor, Pro-Under-Deputy-Vice-Cancellor and Head Inspector, The King of Elfland tries to maintain family values, make education vouchers work and prove that the National Elf Service is safe in his hands.

So why are the students revolting?

Cutting-edge socio-political satire with 60s mystical undertones – Family Circle.

What a waste of trees – Practical Woodworker.